SHE MOVED
THROUGH THE
FAIR

Susanna M. Newstead

A LOCKED TOWER ROOM.
TWO YOUNG PEOPLE.
MURDER HAS CLAIMED
THEM BOTH.

She Moved through the Fair

A Savernake Novel

Copyright © 2025 Susanna M. Newstead
ISBN-13: 978-84-129716-0-6

M
MadeGlobal Publishing

For more information on
MadeGlobal Publishing, visit our website
www.madeglobal.com

Cover Design: Tai Lago & MadeGlobal Publishing

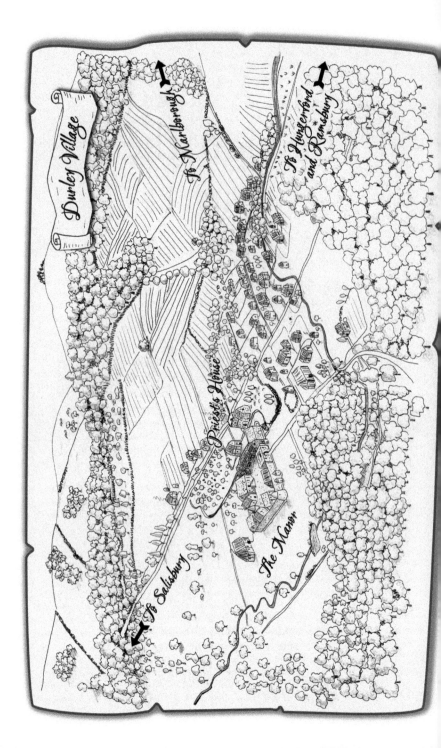

Durley Village

To Marlborough

To Hungerford and Ramsbury

Priest's House

The Manor

To Salisbury

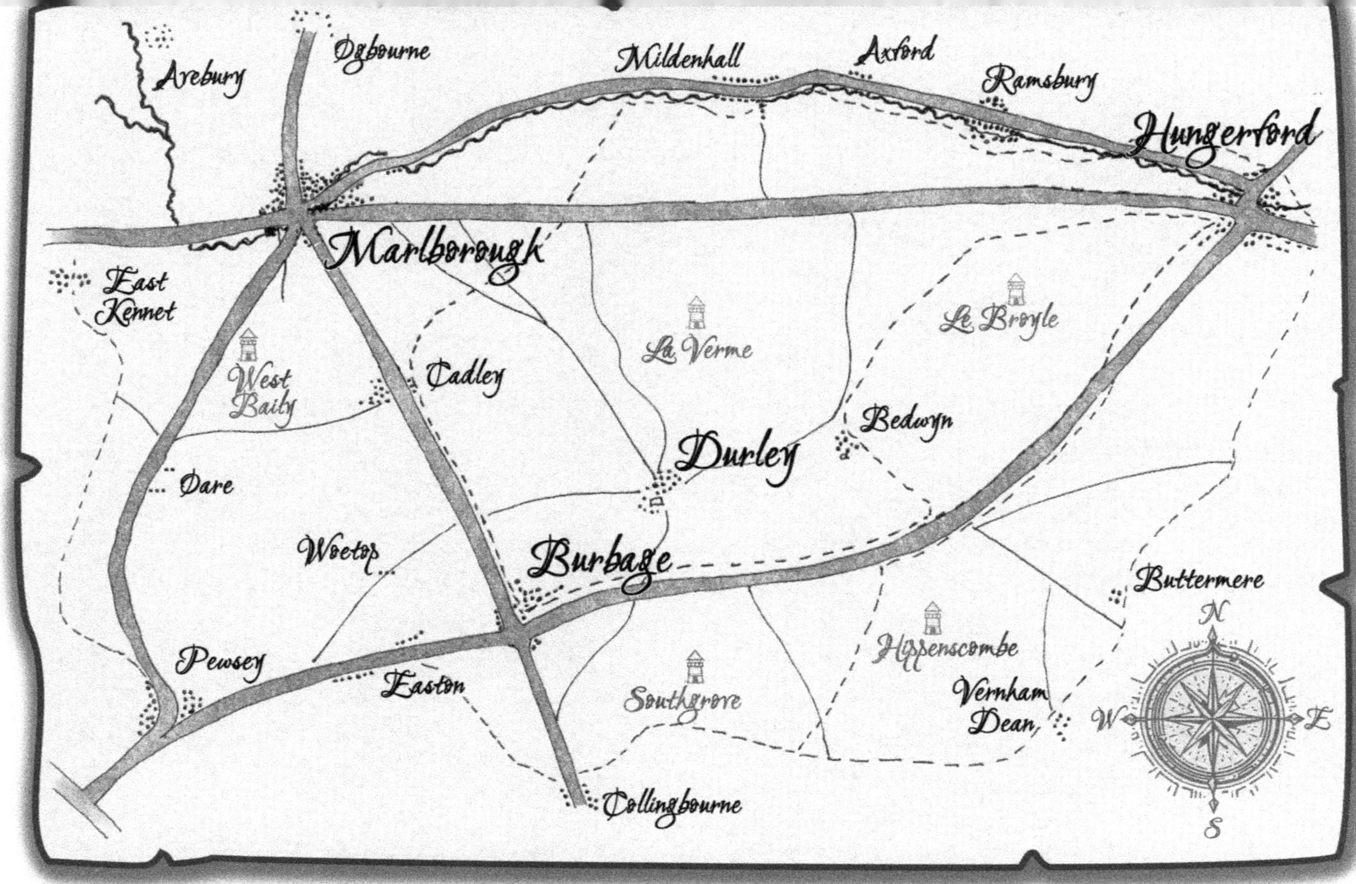

Ogbourne
Avebury
Mildenhall
Axford
Ramsbury
Hungerford
Marlborough
East
Kennet
West
Baily
La Verme
Le Broyle
Cadley
Bedwyn
Durley
Dare
Wootop
Burbage
Buttermere
Pewsey
Easton
Southgrove
Hippenscombe
Vernham
Dean
Collingbourne
N
W
E
S

Marlborough c. 1200

Aldous' House

St Martin's Chapel

St Martin's Church

Johannes' House

St Mary's Church

River Kennet

Salisbury Road

Savernake Forest

St Peter's Church

High Street

Conjuanor's House

The Priory

The Mill

The Castle

N
E
S
W

She Moved Through the Fair

My young love said to me, my mother won't mind,
And my father won't slight you, for your lack of kine,
And she laid her hand upon me and this she did say,
It will not be long till our wedding day.

She stepped away from me and she moved through
     the fair,
And fondly I watched her, move here and move
     there,
And then she went homeward with one star awake,
Like the swan in the evening moves over the lake.

The people were saying, no two were ever wed,
That one had a sorrow, that never was said,
And I smiled as she passed me with her goods and
     her gear,
And that was the last I saw of my dear.

SUSANNA M. NEWSTEAD

Last night she came to me, my dead love came in,
So softly she came, that her feet made no din,
And she laid her hand upon me and this she did say,
It will not be long, till our wedding day.

Irish Folk Song - Padraic Colum

1204
Chapter One

*W*hat do you see, Henry?"

"Nothing yet, sir."

There was much rustling about and swearing. The holly bush shook, and a tousled, silver head appeared, face scratched and hair bedraggled. I shifted my behind in the saddle.

"Well, if there really is nothing to see...come out. We'll try a bit further down. Maybe this isn't exactly the right bush."

The head disappeared.

The undergrowth shook again and then, "Oh...

"Yes, Henry?"

Silence.

"Henry, what is it?"

Silence.

"Henry, answer me."

"It's a man, sir. A corpse."

"AH...so this is the right bush."

"It seems to be dead, sir."

I raised my eyes to heaven in sarcastic amazement.

"Yes, Henry, most corpses are dead...yes, they usually are."

I dismounted.

"Do you recognise the body?"

"No, sir, it's lying on its face."

"Well, turn it over, man."

"What...touch it, sir?"

"You usually have to do that to move something, Henry."

There was a slight squelching sound.

"UGH! It's all soft and ergh..."

I sighed and took pity on the lad. "Henry just grab it by his boots and pull it out. I'll take a look and see if I recognise him."

There was a general uncomfortable milling about of people: the woodwards and foresters who had accompanied me on this little trip.

"He doesn't have any boots, sir," said Henry queasily. "His feet are bare and..." I heard him retch. "Eaten away a bit, sir."

I nodded to John Brenthall my chief woodward. "Go and help him, John, please."

With no more ado, John burrowed into the prickly bush. A moment later, he reappeared, rear first, dragging the corpse out by its ankles.

Henry followed and, running to the side of the path, was sick in the May hedge. There were a few sniggers. I turned and stared at the offenders. They were instantly quelled.

John rose and turned the body over with his boot.

A putrid smell rose up and assailed ten noses. Clouds of flies billowed up and buzzed around ten heads, ruining the otherwise perfect late May day.

Another man joined Henry at the path's edge.

The face was gone. Eaten by animals and insects, it was just a mass of mushy flesh, black and shining with the dew and the moisture of many weeks.

I sighed again. "Does anyone recognise the clothes... what's left?"

Nine heads shook.

"Well, fetch the blanket, and we'll lift him onto it and take him back to Durley."

It was not an enviable task.

The body was so far decayed that it was almost falling apart. All that kept it from doing so were the clothes it wore and the grey hair clinging to the scalp.

And so began the mystery of which I should like to tell you, in the year of Our Lord 1204, in the fifth year of the reign of King John, and in my forest, the king's forest of Savernake, in Wiltshire for I was then, the hereditary warden of that place and the Lord of Durley Manor and this body, as far as it went, was my business.

Unfortunately.

Now then, Paul, my lad, my scribe, my amanuensis. How do you think this account begins? I know how you like a gory story. You did a sterling job of helping me last month with the history of how I became Lord of Durley nigh on fifty years ago. Let's see if we can make this tale as exciting as the last one.

What's that? Why yes, of course, it's a real story. I have a fund of them, you know. You can't be warden of Savernake Forest and not have a tale or two to tell, especially when it concerns the reign of John Plantagenet, God assoil him. A great deal happened, you know, in those years.

Well, then, tuck the rug a bit tighter around my knees, take up your pen, and you shall write as I dictate.

My forest that summer was parched and dry, for we'd had little rain that spring. The trees were wilting at their tops for lack of moisture, and the soil underfoot was baked in the open glades and dusty under the trees. I looked up at the birches along the Ramsbury Road.

"Anyone of the forest reported missing, John?" I asked when we had got our body home and eased him onto a trestle board in the little mortuary at Durley village.

"No, sir. No one."

I scratched my head. "I shall go up to the castle tomorrow and see if anyone from the town has reported a missing loved one or maybe a missing worker. The man is too old, by his greying hair, to be a runaway apprentice."

John followed me up the manor stairs and into the screens passage. "Would you have me put it about in town, m'lord, that we have found him? I can send Peter this afternoon to Master Barbflet. He is elected this year to be town reeve. He will know and can ask around. You would not know that, sir, you being away for so long."

"Aye, do that."

Yes, I had been away—November 1203 to late May 1204—in Normandy with my king on private business.

I turned to unlock my office door.

I turned back and, waving the key at John, added, "And can you see if Doctor Johannes will come and look at our mystery man?"

The key was turning in the lock as I said, "Of course, he may be a masterless man, living rough in the forest and the weather just caught him out."

However, I thought to myself that our corpse did not look as if he had been living rough for a while, as far as it was possible to tell. It was more of a feeling than a fact. Besides, I didn't allow masterless men in my forest and our winters had been relatively mild.

John nodded and was off down the steps.

I would wait to see what Johannes of Salerno, my friend and Marlborough town doctor, would say before I called for the coroner to chivvy up his jury of twelve men over 14 years of age for a verdict on how the man met his end. If our man had died a natural death from illness, cold or starvation, then we need not bother the coroner. If it was foul play, however, he must be informed.

I had good cause to know how this system worked, for in the past few years, we had had many unexplained deaths in the forest. Each one had eventually been firmly laid at the doorstep of a cunning murderer who was at present mouldering in a churchyard in Rouen.

That man had been in Normandy since November and dead since April 1204. It was now approaching the beginning of June. This death was not of his making.

I sat at my table and pulled my books and parchments towards me. I would also need to inform our new priest.

Father Benedict had been the priest at Durley for as long as I could remember. He had died of liver disease in the Autumn of 1203 and I had appealed to the Bishop of Salisbury for a replacement, for there was no one in the village I could appoint, who could fulfil the role. Many lords appointed their own priests, but our little village had for many years now relied on the Bishop of Salisbury and his diocese to find us our clergy.

The man chosen had arrived in late October when I was travelling to Normandy.

He had been ordained a priest in the summer of 1203 and had come directly from Salisbury. Durley was his first parish. John Brenthall had reluctantly told me that Father Swithun seemed to resent being pushed out to our little enclave in the forest, for his manner was surly and detached; there was a hint of arrogance in his step, a smidgeon of bitterness in his look, a pinch of superiority in the set of his head.

He took over the priest's fine house and banished poor Old Joan, who had been twenty years the housekeeper to Benedict of Cadley, to her bothy by the manor wall.

He needed no woman to look to him. He was perfectly capable of seeing to himself, he said.

So far, he had buried but one person, Benedict himself, in our little churchyard and it was there I found him, some few hours after our mystery body had been brought in.

"How goes it, Father Swithun?" I asked, "Are you settled into the house now? Do you find it to your liking? I have been much busied with manor and castle work these past few weeks, and I'm sorry I haven't been able to..."

The man swivelled round slowly to face me. He was slight, with more than a touch of asceticism. Pale brown hair grew thinly around his tonsure. He wore a black cloak over a dark brown robe, a faded version of the black of the Benedictine and with no adornment, not even a cross. His manner was serious and cold and his face wore a permanent scowl.

"Well enough, lord," he answered, and no more.

"You must let me know if there is anything I can do to make your role easier. I'm very sorry I was not here when you arrived. It must have been a poor welcome."

Swithun sniffed."The house is adequate and well-kept. The village is a poor sort, not above one hundred souls and a number of them not brought fully to God as they should be."

"I'm sorry you think that. I have always found my folk God-fearing and good church supporters. Perhaps it will take time. Benedict was a long time their priest. The simple sort often take to such changes slowly."

Swithun scoffed. "Too soft on them, too easy on their

pagan ways, he was. Such back-sliding into the path to the devil. But I will root it out, never fear. Such silly superstitions will be ousted, and they will be brought to the way of the Lord once more."

"To what do you object then, Father?" I asked, puzzled. "What superstitions have aroused your dislike?"

"You were not here…you did not see. Dancing at Mayday, lewdly around the pole that is nothing but a phallus disguised with ribbon." He made a moue, "Encouraging ungodly behaviour…girls prinking themselves up with flowers, making themselves available to the lusts of the village lads. Disgusting."

Oh dear. I foresaw trouble ahead. I quickly changed the subject.

"I have come to talk to you about a body we have found in the forest. We know not who it is as yet, and if we cannot find his kith or kin locally soon, I fear we must bury the poor soul with all due rites in our churchyard. I will let you know…"

The look on Swithun's face stopped me in my tracks. "Bury him here? Certainly not."

"Why ever not?"

"If he is not one of my flock, he may be an unbeliever. He may be a man without the law. I cannot give burial to an unknown soul. He may be unclean and may pollute the souls of others laid here. No…it cannot be."

I rubbed my forehead. I hadn't the energy that day to argue with him. "Nevertheless," I said, "It would be a kindness to allow him to lie here."

"No. I will not bury him here."

"Then let us hope that we can find someone in the town who knows him and can vouch for his soul. The priest of St Mary will take him then, willingly." I turned my back on him and stomped off.

Henry Pierson was the son of my old manor steward, Piers of Manton, who had been foully slain in the summer of 1191. I had been but 17 years of age when I came into the manor after the death of my father, Geoffrey Belvoir. Shortly afterwards, I had been confirmed as warden of the forest, after him, by the king. I had relied heavily on Piers until his death when, suddenly I was thrown into the job myself. However, I was not completely alone. My Uncle William, my mother's brother and a wool merchant in Marlborough town, had been a strong rod on which to lean, until his untimely demise in the winter of 1194. John Brenthall, my chief woodward and Walter Reeve, now an old man, had also been reassuring presences at my back and Father Benedict, too,had leant his arm. I was not lacking in help.

Henry had been a young boy when his father was killed, but I felt that grooming him from a young age to take over the running of the manor was not such an impossible task, and so for the last few months, whilst I had been away in Normandy, he had been in charge of the house and outbuildings, the daily business of running the manor and keeping it afloat.

He was as exacting as his father had been and I was well pleased. He was now twenty-three and a good-looking lad with silver blond hair, blue eyes, an open face, and a complexion which would not disgrace a girl.

So what had he been doing with me out in the forest when this was not his area of expertise, his metier?

Henry had a younger brother, a lad of fourteen who was apprenticed to a thatcher in the town of Marlborough, a few miles from my manor at Durley. I had given his master, Giles Thatcher, permission to collect hazel withies—the fallen and cut wood of the forest was my own property—for splitting to make pegs to secure the thatch, the best kind of wood for this purpose. Whilst the lad was out with the other apprentice in the forest, they had stumbled over the body we had collected today. Henry had volunteered to come out and help recover it. It would do him no harm to toughen up a little, I thought.

Now, he was sprawled on a stool in front of my work table, breathing a little hard from his run across the yard and up the stairs and his supervising of our dead man's deposition in the mortuary, which lay on the western wall of the manor.

He straightened up, raised his fair, almost invisible eyebrows and wiped his brow. "All done, sir. The doctor is there now having a look at him...what there is of him, I mean. He rather fell apart a bit more as we carried him, but we managed to save the bits which fell off."

He looked a little green around the gills. "Well done, Henry. It cannot have been a pleasant job to have to do."

"I would save Young Piers the job of seeing it again, sir," he said. "It fair gave him nightmares, and brought on his asthma, Ma said, stumbling over him like that."

I smiled. "It would any man, but the most seasoned to the presence of death, Henry." I smiled again. "But he is the first-finder and will have to be present when and if the coroner gets here."

I heard the measured tread of my friend Johannes crossing the screens passage floor.

"Wait while we find what Johannes has to say, then, we shall see if we need to call the coroner. Can you organise that if needs be?"

"Aye, sir. Young Peter Brenthall will go. He's standing by. It's early enough yet for him to go and be back before dark."

Johannes of Salerno scratched at the open door. He was

a big man, tall, over six foot, near to forty years of age. He had shoulder-length brown hair—scrupulously clean and shining, with just a hint of grey at the temples— was tied back in a queue, and he was clean-shaven, contrary to current fashion, which dictated that men wore short beards, as I did myself. His eyes were an amber brown, clear and direct of gaze and they fixed themselves on me now.

"What do we have, Johannes?"

He was wiping his hands on a square of thin rag as he walked and when he had finished, he dropped it into my lit charcoal brazier; the weather was not so warm for the last day of May. I had never known such a man for cleanliness, but that exactness paid off, for he lost fewer patients than any doctor I had known. The linen sizzled and fizzled and was gone to ashes.

"A knife wound to the ribs, up into the heart, I think, and the face was erased after death—smashed to a pulp, in addition to the wreckage done by the creatures of the forest. Not a chance that even his mother would recognise him. We must get him into the ground soon, Aumary, or we shall have a danger to health."

Poor Henry looked sick again.

"Off you go, Henry. Send Peter to the coroner and town reeve's house, please. We have a murder to report."

That afternoon, young Peter Brenthall came back, weary and hungry. The coroner would be on his way on the morrow and the town reeve, Master Nicholas Barbflet, had been informed of our dead man. He would inform the sheriff's office. The man's clothes had been described; the small mole on his right shoulder might help to identify him, and the salt-and-pepper greyness of his hair might jog a memory. We had brought the body to Durley even though we should, by rights, have left it where it was for the coroner to look at. The man would not fine us for that, though strictly he should.

Now, we simply waited. Whilst we waited, I wondered how I was going to persuade Father Swithun to bury our poor soul should we not be able to find out who he was. Must we cart him from Durley to Marlborough town to inter him? Was he a stranger, a passing forest traveller who fell foul of a desperate murderer? Why, then, destroy his face? He was not, in life, a man who went barefoot, that much we could tell, for there were no calluses on his feet, so where were his boots or shoes?

Johannes stayed for a while and drank a pint of wine with me.

We discussed the murdered man and tried to build up a picture of him in life.

"Not a clerk, for his fingers, what was left of them, were not ingrained with ink. Neither is he a hard worker, for he has no calluses on his hands as would a woodworker or a mason, for example," said Johannes. "No nicks and scars as masons have. I wondered if he was one of the new lot of masons we have at the castle, but he isn't a hard worker, for he has no well-developed muscles."

"I wondered that, too," I said. "The masons are all strangers to the area, bar one or two from the last building works. This man's clothes looked as if he had had contact with mortar, here and there a little. Splashed a mite."

"Odd thing...his hands are a bit discoloured. It's hard to tell, really, for he has lost most of his fingers, and those that remain are damaged beyond recognition, but I thought I saw a bit of red and a touch of green on them in the lines of the palms and the remaining fingernails and on the finger-ends. And the hands are a little roughened, but not as much as a manual worker who works with stone."

"A limner? Are there any in the town?"

"I'm not sure. Perhaps at the castle. Maybe the church. St Mary's? Is there any work being done there at the moment? Might someone be painting a scene on a wall?"

"I don't think the other church at the castle end is sufficiently finished for work of the sort a limner might do," I said. "Not quite yet, though I haven't been in to look."

I thought quickly of my own little church in the village of Durley, so close outside my walls and the doom on the western interior face, which my father had had painted by some itinerant dauber when I was young: the painting of Christ judging the sinners and sending them down to be tormented in hell.

"A line of inquiry, should we draw a blank in the town, then," I said. "Let's hope we can get an answer soon."

Later that day, I went to see for myself the hands of our corpse. Henry had been right, he had not fared well on that last journey. The womenfolk had done their best with him. We dared not put him in our church, for he stank to high heaven and was best left where he was, under a cloth. If this had been one of our own, we might have had several pots of herbs smouldering over a burner and a few candles onto which we had dropped some scented oils, but this was an extravagance for a man we did not know. I had to lift my cloak to my nose when I entered the mortuary, which was tucked away at the back of the stables, for the smell was fearsome.

A man of some possible forty-something years with greying hair. His clothes, now washed and drying on a rack in the corner, were a uniform grey. Hose, a little patched but serviceable, a long tunic of green grey wool, no shirt, And a cotte of blue-grey, plucked and in holes, much of it, some darned. Was there a woman somewhere in this man's life missing darning and patching his clothes?

With great distaste, I pulled back the linen covering the body. There was the knife wound. The arms were to the side of the body; the weightlessness of the missing flesh and missing digits would drag them off the chest if crossed and placed there. I swallowed. Well, here goes. I picked up a hand. Yes...there was paint on the palm, the finger-ends and under the remaining nails—bright green.

Find that colour somewhere in the town, and we would know our man.

On my way back to the hall, I washed my hands thoroughly in a water butt, as Johannes had instructed. He was a doctor who had studied at the famous school at Salerno in Sicily and had some strange ideas about doctoring. I had learned to trust him completely. Much of what he advocated made complete sense.

I had been appointed under-constable of the castle at Marlborough by the king. John and I were childhood friends. When he was old enough and had completed his education at the Abbey of Fontevrault in Anjou, France, he spent much time in Marlborough with or without his father, Henry II, and naturally, he hunted in the Forest of Savernake. The constable and chief forester, Hugh de Neville, was often away, and so John had needed someone he could trust to oversee the castle for him. I was close by. I was trustworthy. I would do. John liked to get his money's worth from his able officers.

I had duties at the castle the next day, for the constable was laid up with gout, and as his underling, there were matters needing my attention. So early after dawn, I saddled up Bayard, my beautiful roan gelding, and trotted into town.

I was passing St Mary's churchyard at the top of Oxford Street where it met the High Street, idling along taking in the bird song and the warmth of the sunshine, when a shout made Bayard sidle and miss his step. Recovering quickly, I cantered him to the edge of the eight-foot wall behind the High Cross and peered round it.

Coming from the north, down Kingsbury Street, a steep hill which bent around the churchyard and disgorged into the Market Square, was a cart full of stone.

The mules pulling it were out of control, and the driver was running for his life behind it, shouting.

Suddenly, the left-hand mule missed his footing and went over. The cart slewed. It passed over the animal, snapping the traces and leaving the remaining mule floundering. It, too, went over.

The whole thing came to an abrupt stop almost outside Johannes' house, and the cart bed tipped over and expelled the stone blocks, spilling them onto the roadway and the small space before Johannes' house which served as a path. Folk began arriving at the scene almost immediately.

One mule was obviously dead with a broken neck. The other kicked and kicked to be free, bellowing and braying in pain. I sighed. The stone had fallen away from the animals. In my mind's eye, I saw my son, Geoffrey, crushed by a great stone which had been dropped onto him from the gateway of our manor some years before. I looked again.

Was this just my mind playing me false, or did I see blood trickling from underneath a stone?

It was blood. I threw myself from my horse, ran up and scrabbled at the blocks, many of which had broken and fragmented into pieces.

There, under the largest stone, was Enid, her staring blue eyes gazing from beneath a blood-stained wimple. Enid, Johannes' housekeeper, had been out for her early morning marketing. Her basket was still on her arm, crushed beyond saving, as was she.

The cart driver arrived then, puffing and panting. He

took in the scene and sat abruptly on a fallen stone and began to weep.

Someone, one of the slaughterhouse men I noticed, had put the injured mule out of its misery, and others were gathering to help move the blocks and right the stricken cart. The thing completely blocked the road and was in a sorry state, no longer drivable.

I heard someone say, "Stone for the castle." Someone else said Enid's name.

Then came Johannes, disturbed by the noise, pushing through the throng, wiping his face with a cloth; he had obviously been shaving. He threw down the towel, came quickly onto the road and knelt to minister to his housekeeper, but there was nothing he could do. Not even he, the best doctor I had ever known—would ever know— could bring Enid Fairdotter to life again.

"The brake…just gone…the brake, I couldn't hold it. So steep. It just went…" The cart driver was babbling.

I looked back.

"And overloaded…" I muttered to myself quietly.

Some were tutting and casting furious glances at the driver. Others were patting his back and offering him platitudes.

Simon Smith, whose forge was across the road at the far side of the marketplace, beyond the cross, nodded to both Johannes and myself.

"I'll get the road cleared, fetch a cart for the stone and take it up to the castle." Then he was off at a run.

Someone else had sprinted to the church porch and battered on the door, yelling for the priest.

It was all too much for me and my sad memories. I commiserated quickly with Johannes, told him what I had seen—how the cart had been out of control—then mounted Bayard again and rode with a steady step along the wide marketplace to the other end of the town, to the castle and safety; away from that awful scene, which had opened a wound I thought healed for years now. No, it was not Enid under that block but my much beloved Geoffrey, my son and heir, five years old, cold and dead. Dead and buried in the churchyard at Durley.

It was no surprise I could not concentrate that morning.

I suppose the fallen stone must eventually have been delivered and the clerks saw to it that it was counted and a note was made that some of it was broken. I suppose I saw the chit for its delivery, but I cannot recall it.

I remember a dispute about a garden wall that had to be demolished because the castle was being extended and more land on the southern side was needed for the outer bailey. I remember signing for some timber from my own forest, but where it was destined to go, I cannot recall.

Then suddenly, before me, coif in hand, was the master mason. I looked up.

"Have we a problem, Gervase?" I asked.

"Begging your pardon, my lord," he began.

I threw down my pen, sending inky spots all over the table top, and scrubbed my tired eyes.

"Oh dear, we do have a problem. Give it to me gently, Gervase, I haven't had a good day."

I leaned back in my chair, stretched my shoulders and smiled. I did not feel like smiling.

"It's put about town that there's been a body found."

I sat up quickly.

"Yes, in the forest. What do you know?"

"It may be nothing, m'lord. One of my gang of men, one who comes and goes. He went off to do a job in Hungerford. Went off really quickly, as if he was trying to run away or something. At the church there a while ago. Just a small job. He should have been back soonest, only he hasn't showed up. Well, we wondered if he's got a bit lost, you see, because, well, Alan is a bit of a toper, and he can go on sprees when he's been paid."

"What was his job?"

"He's a fine limner when he's sober and even when he isn't. Works in wet plaster sometimes, so it's a fast job. Has to be. Can't hang about. Only, he does hang about a bit... with the drink and that."

"Can you come out to Durley and see if you think it's your man, Gervase?"

"Well, sir, I haven't really got the time...I've one man down with the..."

"I'll make it worth your while. I need a positive identification."

He thought about it.

"I'll come, sir," he said. "I'll come out to the forest on my pony tomorrow."

It was our man.

Alan of Didcot. Limner. Painter of scenes from the Bible, patterns for the walls of the wealthy and painted cloths depicting legends and stories.

What was he doing murdered in my forest? And still, where were his boots?

"Oh yes," said Gervase, "He was proud of those boots. They were new and made for his feet and his feet alone."

Imagine that. Such a tradesman with enough money to have a pair of boots made especially for his own two feet. Made by the Master Cordwainer in Marlborough. Imagine that. I knew where I must next make inquiries.

Chapter Two.

*M*aster Cordwainer was an avuncular man with a large, round, red face, thick brown hair and a permanent grin.

I knew him well, for he had made my boots and shoes since I was a lad and could first walk in them, firstly as a journeyman, then as his own master. His house, workplace and shop were next to the entrance of the Priory of St Margaret of Antioch, and there is no doubt he benefited from being in such a spot. No pilgrim, visitor, secular or clerical, could pass by into the priory without first casting their eyes over his wares.

"My lord!" He beamed. "It's good to see you. I see my latest creations are still good on yer feet!"

I was wearing my best riding boots, those he had made for me over a year ago and yes, they were still good on my feet, as he liked to say, despite a great deal of wear.

Even though I was not there to buy, Gilbert Cordwainer was still happy to see me. Out came the leather cups—made, of course, by himself—out came the leather flask of good ale, and we sat to chat a little before I said, "Gilbert, I came to ask you something."

"Ask away, my Lord Belvoir. I always have time for you."

I smiled to myself, it was true, he did. Whenever we met on the street, at the castle or perhaps at the church, he was always the same charming and jovial man. Today, he wore a black tunic with bands of embroidery at the hems. His wife Grace had been busy, I thought. Over this, he wore the habitual leather apron of the cordwainer.

"Boots…a pair made especially for a man called Alan of Didcot, a mason's man, up at the castle, one who painted the plastered walls with pictures. Do you remember him?"

Gilbert Cordwainer chuckled to himself. "Aye, I remember." He shook his mop of curly brown hair, "I asked him where he had got the money from. He didn't buy the cheapest leather, ho no! Only the best would do for him."

"And he answered you?"

"Won it in a wager, he said. Up at the castle, something to do with horses up on the downs…racing, I 'spect. There's a whole crowd o' folks at the castle now who like their horse racing."

"Yes, it's the influence of young Guy de Saye. He has a real eye for horse flesh. He has a whole string of horses devoted to racing with him in the town."

"That's the lad who is to marry Matilda de Neville, Sir Hugh, the constable's girl?"

As I have said, Hugh was the chief forester and my immediate senior and resided for some of the time at the castle.

"Aye, the same. So you made the boots. Can you tell me what they looked like?"

Gilbert closed his eyes. "Tan leather, best Cordovan, black band at the top turned over. High polish. Can't see how a man like that is going to keep them in top condition, not like you, my lord." He opened his eyes. "Lovely shine you have on those."

"Thank my squire for that, Gilbert."

Truthfully, Peter Brenthall acted as my squire even though he was not really training to be a knight. He was to be my next head forester.

"So why would a man of his station spend so much on boots? It's usual for his sort to buy second-hand or, at best, ready-made and of lesser quality?"

"I did ask him. Said he did so much walking from this place to that with his job that boots were important. Had to be comfortable. And as you know, I make the best boots in Marlborough, my lord."

"You do indeed, Gilbert." I downed the last of my ale. He made the *only* boots in Marlborough.

"Your journeyman...what was his name? He still with you, or has he gone off to be his own master?"

Gilbert scoffed. "Oh, Bertold Taske, you mean? In the town, up the top end. Serving the hill and up to the Common. Does more cobbling than making, I'm told. Well, he would up there. Lesser folk up there would use him. I let him go, though really his work was not of master quality. Just couldn't stand his miserable face about the place any longer."

"You have a new apprentice then?"

"Two of 'em," said Gilbert proudly "Felix Castleman, son of one of the men-at-arms at the castle. He's the new'un, then Harry Glazer coming into his fourth year now. Fine man. You remember him. Young son of Perkin Glazer, eighteen now. Son of the chap as you have engaged to do yer windows at Durley."

I had indeed, as I had promised my deceased wife, Cecily, all that time ago, engaged a man to put glass in the windows of the solar at the manor.

"He didn't want to be a glazier then?"

"Nah, wanted out the house. Step-mother not too kind, I hear."

I rose to leave, "Well, Mother Cordwainer will look after him, I know, as if he were her own chick."

"Aye," chuckled the shoemaker. "She does that. Us only having girls an' all."

"Could you keep an eye about town for those boots, Gilbert? They have gone missing from Alan's dead feet. Must be somewhere. It would be good to find them."

"Aye, I heard his was the body you found. Didn't know him well meself. Only a little business between us, you understand." Gilbert scratched his curly head, "But why anyone would take boots in that way, off a murdered man's feet, beats me."

"Lawless men, maybe?" Though I had said it, somehow, I didn't believe it. "Perhaps one man killed him, another stole the boots. Who knows?"

"Aye, they'd steal a dew drop from a man's nose them kind would."

I laughed. Gilbert Cordwainer always made me smile.

He was also an excellent source of town gossip, and that was always to the good.

Once the coroner had dealt with the remains of Alan of Didcot and pronounced him dead by a felon's hand, the masons came with a cart to fetch the body. They had a funeral fund to which they all contributed, and they would see him buried in the churchyard in Marlborough. I was glad I would not, after all, need to beard the beast Father Swithun in his den about the disposing of the corpse in his churchyard, though I had been all ready to argue with him.

There was no woman, I was told, to whom we might send the clothes from Alan's back, so they were given to the priory to distribute to the needy as they saw fit. No beggar without warm clothes for the winter was going to be so squeamish as to pass up a dead man's cast-offs.

One more thing puzzled me. In addition to Alan's boots, where were the tools of his trade? His paint pots and brushes, his drawings, his travelling gear?

I asked the masons at the castle. No, they were not there. Still in Hungerford, then? I sent a message to my outlying bailiwick of Le Broyle, to the Forester of the Fee, Nathan Kennet. Could he make inquiries of the church? Were Alan's tools still languishing somewhere in Hungerford?

No, apparently, they were not. He had packed up and left, and Hungerford folk had waved him off, glad that his local drinking and brawling were over.

On my way home that evening, I called into Johannes' house located off a small alleyway close by the church door, to pay my respects and to see how my friend was faring. The outer door of his house was wreathed in dark yew branches, in lieu of cypress, in the manner of the Roman way with death. Naturally, Johannes had spent a very long time in Sicily learning his doctoring and had picked up the traditions of his adopted country.

He was sitting in his workroom, a little room close by the outer door, cutting up small squares of linen for dressings and placing them carefully in a clean wooden box.

He smiled up at me, sadly, "No one to do this for me now."

I sat beside him on the bench and placed my hand on his shoulder for a second. He acknowledged the touch.

"She was a good woman. Hard-working. Kind. Careful. Good with people. It will be hard to find her like."

I acquiesced with a shake of my head, "You must have help, though. You cannot carry it all yourself. The house. Your work. The preparations. Yes, I know that Master Gallipot in Chute Alley can help you, but he, too, is a busy man with his apothecary shop."

Johannes sighed and threw down his shears and strip of linen. "So quickly! It happened so quickly. One moment, she was shouting her goodbyes from the door, asking me what I would like for my supper, and the next..." He shrugged. "I deal with death every day, Aumary, but this..."

"I know."

We sat in silence for a moment, staring out of the door at the dust motes dancing in the sunlight of the passage.

"Shall I send Agnes Brenthall to you a couple of days a week? She's a good, sensible, practical woman."

"You can't spare her."

"I can and I will, and you know she has a soft spot for you. She would love to help you."

Johannes turned and scrutinised my face. "Aye, that would be kind."

"John can bring her in a cart or riding pillion."

We settled it with a handshake and fell to silence again.

Then I brought Johannes up to date with the body in the forest.

"So that is the end of it then?" Johannes said after a few moment's explanation.

"No, I should like to find the boots and his pack."

"Perhaps they are buried somewhere in the forest."

"Why does someone kill and leave a body hidden in the forest and then take just the boots? I suspect those boots are important to the killer.

The body was supposed to decay into the forest floor, and no one be any the wiser. The face was smashed so that he would not be recognised. New boots, well, they wouldn't decay so easily. They would be recognisable."

Johannes stood. "Good luck with that. If I can help, you know I will. Now I must away to work. Ulcers to dress in Blind Lane and a boil to lance in The Marsh."

"Lovely," I said.

Oh Paul, my lad…you'd never make a doctor,
would you? You have gone very green again.

The castle claimed my attention once more later in the month. We were to have a wedding:

The bride was Matilda, the younger daughter of the constable of the castle, Sir Hugh de Neville, one of King John's gaming partners and hunting companions, and, as I have said, the chief forester. She was to marry Sir Guy De Saye from the county of Oxfordshire. She was a quiet girl of middle height, with no bosom and gap teeth. He was a tall eighteen-year-old with a shock of dark blond hair, vainly combed back from his forehead in a lion's mane and a forehead full of spots. He was proud and haughty with chiselled features, brown eyes and the beak of a nose under them, handed down to all de Saye men. He cared about his horses and very little else.

She cared about her devotions; it was rumoured she had wanted to remain at Amesbury Abbey, where she had been residing since she was six years old. Now, at sixteen, she had been recalled by her father to make a good marriage. King John naturally had suggested it, and what John suggested became a fact.

Joining two large estates in different counties seemed to our monarch a good idea. Both were his staunch supporters. Each would pay him grandly for the privilege of marrying their offspring to each other. Everyone was happy.

But were they?

One day, I was ensconced in my little cubby hole in the keep, working out the logistics of storing the wood somewhere in the castle grounds for the fabrication of a raised stand for the gentry to watch the festivities and the accompanying jousting.

Why was I doing this?

No, you're right, Paul, it shouldn't be my job. One of the clerks was perfectly able to do it. So much was going on at the castle; I had taken on this job for I had a good head for figures, and there was no one else spare to take it on. To be frank, I enjoyed this sort of thing.

All was quiet save the occasional shouts of the men in the yard, the rhythmic hammering of the carpenters fixing timbers together with their wooden pegs, and the cooing of the pigeons on the roof. I had no windows here. It was quite stuffy, and I began to nod.

Suddenly, I jerked awake. Above my head, a fierce screeching had begun. The words were not distinguishable, but I could make out the voices of a man and woman. Above me, on the wooden floor, feet were stomping in boots, and another was pattering after it in lighter shoes.

Then silence.

Then, a hubbub of voices, more genial. A door slammed. Feet stomped down the stairs behind me.

Then began the screeching again, interspersed with sobbing and what sounded like things being thrown at the wall—breakable things.

I downed my pen and left my little office, and walking round the internal circular corridor of the keep, I ascended the stairs to the floor above.

I scratched on the door of the chamber where the noises had originated, opened the small portal and peered round carefully. Things were still being thrown. A red pottery bowl came crashing into the door, followed by an indoor slipper and a breviary. I ducked and then I stooped to pick up the small book.

"My lady," I said, "I think you have dropped this."

Matilda de Neville, red-faced and breathing hard, was staring at me as if I was a beast with several heads.

Her nose was running, for she had been crying piteously, and her face was blotchy and bloated. She ran the sleeve of her deep blue gown over her nose and took a profound but struggling breath.

She then sat down heavily on a cushioned stool.

A tiny creature, the height of a child but fully a woman, no higher than my elbow, came running from the window and began to pick up the shattered and dispersed items— Matilda's maid. I remember folk called her the Pixie, for she was indeed a very tiny woman.

Matilda de Neville was a tubby-bodied girl with a face which was not pretty but might be simply handsome as she aged. She had mouse-brown hair and dark eyebrows, which arched perfectly above her full brown eyes, now red with crying. Her skin was normally pasty, but with a little application of cosmetics, I suspected she could be made quite pretty. I doubt this was something that had been available at Amesbury Abbey.

I opened the door more fully and bowed to Matilda de Neville. We had seen each other from afar but had never been in the same room. The maid glared at me, and I handed her the book.

"I am Aumary Bel…"

"I know who you are."

"Then you must know that I have a room underneath this chamber, and I could not help but hear…"

"You heard my father and myself arguing. Yes. It's true." She sniffed and reached for a square of cambric, stuck through her belt, upon which to blow her nose.

"We do it every day and will until he comes to his senses or…or until…I am…". She began to weep again, silently this time.

I looked around the room. This was not especially a lady's chamber, merely a relatively comfortable space high in the tower where perhaps a few people might meet to play games, look out at the surrounding countryside or talk. It belonged to no man or woman but to any who wished to use it. Many did of an evening, for it was a welcoming, almost feminine space amongst the masculine places of the castle at large.

The two windows looked out over the forest in the South and the stone yard and road to Manton in the North.

"Is there anything I might do for you, my lady?" I asked.

She ceased to cry, stood, smoothed down the blue velvet of her skirts and pushed back the mousey brown hair from her forehead. She then swung a long, thick braid over her shoulder and beckoned to the maid to come and re-plait it for her, for it had come loose in her exertions.

"I am sorry I have disturbed you at your work, Sir Aumary," she said. "There is nothing you can do. I am doomed."

"Surely, my lady, that's a little harsh."

"No, sir. There is nothing. Unless, of course, you can convince my father and mother to let me return to Amesbury Abbey."

"I have not that influence, sadly, Lady Matilda."

"No, no one has…it seems." Her gaze seemed far away.

She took a deep breath, wiped her eyes on the back of her hand and dabbed her nose. She tilted her head, and I was treated to the gap-toothed smile.

"There is something you can do for me. Please can you escort us to the church? We wish to pray."

"Certainly." I offered my arm, and she took it shakily.

She was shaky all the way down the stairs, the keep steps and into the courtyard. She tripped a couple of times, and I saved her from a light fall by catching her by the upper arm. She smiled that gap-toothed smile at me again. The tiny maidservant followed us.

The chapel was in darkness, save the winking of the sanctuary light. The sun had not yet gained the windows. Lady Matilda de Neville knelt at the altar steps. Her maid retired to stand a little way off and watched her mistress carefully. She said not a word.

I learned later that she could not, for she was mute. I backed away from the altar and opened the chapel door to exit.

I heard a whispered, "Thank you", and then, "It will not be long till our wedding day." And that was all.

Two days later, I was talking to my two men at arms, whom I kept at the castle at my own expense, against the time when I might be called to muster for my king and country or simply to accompany me when I travelled, for the country was not safe everywhere. The presence of a couple of armed men was usually more than enough to keep even the most tenacious brigands and lawless men at bay.

We were laughing and joking a little about a small wager that one of them had made. Stephen Dark, a stocky man with a profuse head of dark hair, was boasting of his bet with one of the grooms at the castle. "An' I said to 'im, I said...well that don't make no difference to me 'coz I ain't got nuffin' to stuff in em anyway!"

A lewd joke, and we guffawed like ten-year-olds.

Then, without a by-your-leave, a bay horse came careering around the corner of the chapel. I made a grab for Peter's woollen gambeson to pull him out of the path of the hooves and caught him by his neck cloth. Stephen dived to the floor, rolled the other way, and was up again in one movement. He shook his fist at the horse and rider and dusted himself down. The horse flew on.

"That was a close thing," said Peter, stuffing his coif back on his head. "Thank you, my lord, I might'a been worm fodder if you hadn't got hold a' me."

"You're welcome, Peter."

Stephen was swearing under his breath.

I looked back over my shoulder at the young man riding the horse. He had pulled up at the wall and was now turning it round to come back the other way. Before he had the chance to do so, I jog-marched up and grabbed the reins.

"What?"

"You will not do that again, sir. If you must ride at breakneck speed, go out of the bailey."

The young man was of medium height with two very sharp eye-teeth, blond hair swept back over his forehead, and a permanent sneer: Guy de Saye.

The irate face coloured red. "And who are you, sir, to tell me what I cannot do in this castle?"

"I am Sir Aumary Belvoir, under-constable of this castle and warden of the Forest of Savernake, and by the power vested in me by our sovereign Lord John, I command you to get down and walk your horse whence he came."

Two nasty eye-teeth appeared as the youth tried to grimace a smile at me. "You know who I am then?"

"I do indeed, and it makes not a jot of difference. Take your horse away."

I heard Stephen say under his breath, "Arrogant puppy."

Guy de Saye's eyes blazed. "Come here and say that, you putrid, poxed peasant."

Stephen adjusted his belt and was about to step up. My hand on his shoulder stopped him.

"I would not tangle with my men if I were you, Sir Guy. They are seasoned fighters and can have you on the ground and begging for mercy in the time it takes for your fancy horse to fart."

"I will appeal to my father-in-law."

"As yet, he is not your father-in-law, and I have no doubt he will say the same. Besides, he is laid up, and I am the law in his stead. I have no wish to anger you. We may all part friends now, if you will dismount and lead your horse away." I patted the horse's neck. "He's a beautiful creature. He deserves better treatment. There are too many obstacles in this bailey, especially with the building work going on here. Best you take him down to the Salley Gardens to run him, or up onto the downs. I would hate to see such good horseflesh hurt."

That sobered him a little, but he was still, as Stephen had said, an arrogant puppy.

Guy threw his leg over his horse's head, narrowly missing my own and I had to duck as he jumped down.

"Walk him, I will…" His face was surly.

He began to walk past me, leading the beast by the reins. As he did so, he purposely jostled the horse so that it sidled, and I had to step out of the way to avoid being trodden on by a shoed foot.

In a flash, Stephen extended his leg and caught Guy on the back of the knee. The lad tripped, went over and landed arse-first on the ground. There was a second of inaction, then, "Oh dear…do forgive me, m' Lord de Neville,"— though this title was not de Saye's to claim, and Stephen knew it well—" A nasty accident. Please allow me to 'elp you up," and he extended his hand, smiling in a gesture of fellowship.

Guy was up in a breath and brushing himself down. He slapped Stephen's hand down. He made a grab for the reins and, glaring seethingly at us all, walked the horse away. When he reached the corner of the chapel, he vaulted into the saddle from a standing start and was off around the corner at breakneck speed again.

"Nasty little pizzle, ain't 'e?" said Stephen

"We've made an enemy, there, I think, sir," said Peter, craning his neck around the corner to see where Guy had gone.

"No matter. He'll be off back to Oxfordshire when he is married. Only a couple of weeks, and we shall keep out of his way till then. Then we shall not see him again."

How very right I was.

Early in the reign of the Plantagenets, the king had established a mint here in the castle. This was part of the reason we were extending. We needed more room for the actual manufacturing for storage, and safekeeping of the coin. We had men at arms to guard it. We had to put them somewhere. Here, too, was the king's treasury, and latterly, the forest exchequer was run from the middle of the great hall. The castle was becoming a huge and formidable fortress.

As the castle grew, so did the town. I had known this little place on the River Kennet all my life, but as I matured, the town began to present a more affluent visage. It grew beyond the square by the church and the wide High Street. Houses now stretched almost up to the Common at the top of the northernmost hill and down to the river on the Newbury Road. A few houses had even begun to creep up the Salisbury Road towards the very edge of the forest. More houses stretched their gardens out to the castle, and another small church had been begun at the southernmost end of the town to serve the garrison and the outlying houses on the sprawling roads west and south west.

The whole place seemed to be a builder's yard.

One day in late June, when the flies were beginning to

plague the resting builders eating their mid-morning meal in the outer bailey, a royal messenger clattered over the bridge from the Winchester Road. He bowed to Hugh de Neville, lately risen from his sick bed, and then to me.

We escorted him up to the great hall and took the pannier, which he held out to us. I was asked to open it.

"There are two documents, sirs, both sealed by the king at Merton, but this is the copy, for the Great Seal has been affixed to the town copy, for it pertains to the rights of the town. His noble majesty believes that, whilst he is granting a special boon to the townsfolk, it would be politic to lodge a copy here in the castle."

I read the first line out loud, then the last.

*John, by the grace of God, King...Given at Winchester June 20*th *1204*. I stared at it. The messenger took the parchment from me and read it aloud.

King John had granted a charter to the borough.

The charter permitted an annual eight-day fair commencing on August 14th, the vigil of the Feast of the Assumption of Our Lady, in which "all might enjoy the liberties and quittances customary in the fair at Winchester." He also established that weekly markets may be held on Wednesdays and Saturdays.

Naturally, this came at a price.

Clever old John was selling liberties to towns so that he could raise money to pay for a professional army to move against Philip of France once more, and to regain the territories on the Continent that had been lost in 1203.

The town voted to pay, naturally. What else could they do?

But a fair, oh a fair. What a wonderful thing, for this charter exempted the town from tolls, pavage, pontage, passage and such like for the duration. Much money could and would be made.

The town merchants and tradesmen, hostelries, bakers, butchers and brewers rubbed their hands in glee and slavered into their beards.

In order to get it all organised by the required date, everyone had to work very hard at the administration, quite apart from the making of the goods to be sold, the brewing of ale, the baking of pies and the importing of special items not usually found in the town.

Much putting about of word had to be done. Few people could read, so all the advertising had to be done by word of mouth. It would begin in a relatively small way. Nowadays, of course, the fair is huge and famous throughout the South, but in those days, it was modest and relatively local.

Now people come from all over. In 1204, we were lucky to get a wine merchant from Winchester, a dealer in silks from Salisbury or a wild bird catcher from Wantage, but get them, we did.

Marlborough Town had come of age.

I saw Guy de Saye again a few days later.

He was standing by the hall door, deep in conversation with his future father-in-law, pouting like a child denied a sugar plum.

I was looking up, shielding my eyes from the glare of the sun, at a large crane moving stone blocks to the top of the wall.

I heard some of the conversation.

"She will come round. We shall give her a little longer."

"I am, my lord, in no hurry. She may take all the time she wishes. Marriage, I understand, is a great step for a girl," said de Saye. "Especially when she must remove to another county to live, away from kith and kin."

Well, well, I thought, he was thinking of someone other

than himself for a change. A cart passed between us, and I lost the next utterance.

"We shall postpone the wedding, then, for a couple of weeks. There's more than enough happening with the fair and the building."

"As you wish, my lord." He bowed.

I turned as they walked away in separate directions and I watched the smirk gather on de Saye's face.

Hmmm. I don't think this wedding is quite to his liking either, I said to myself. Well, well.

Early June had been chilly. Late June had improved. July was baking and we laboured in our shirt sleeves to get the town ready for the fair and for the wedding. The field to the south of the small church, being built outside the castle walls and dedicated to St Peter, was mown by a team of men, ready to house the many booths that would be set up there. Carpenters in the town were asked to make a few simple huts for those who did not bring their own business premises and these could be hired out for the eight days the fair was to be open. Then, they would be dismantled and stored for the following year.

One hut was to be hired by our friendly shoemaker, Master Cordwainer, who, when he saw me riding past one lovely evening, hailed me from across the street and stopped me to chat about this and that.

I dismounted and hooked my reins over a peg protruding from the wall of the priory. "Good evening, Master Cordwainer."

"My lord." Gilbert tugged his forelock. "Have you a spare minute for a beaker of my finest?" He tipped his head towards his door, his eyebrows rose into his fringe, and he smiled his perfect white smile.

"Aye…why not."

The leather cups and the flask came out from under his counter.

We leaned against the door post and watched the bustle of the street in the golden evening sunshine. People were taking advantage of the fine and warm weather to complete tasks late in the day.

Gilbert took a swig and swallowed. "Grrblubbrrrr…" he shook his head and then scrubbed his hair till it stood in peaks like a cock's comb. "That's better."

I laughed. He had such winning ways.

"How goes it then? What do you think about this new fair of ours, Gilbert?"

"There's many in the town as isn't happy. Foreigners, they say, coming and taking our dues. The shops will suffer, traders from other counties taking our business away."

"And what do you think?"

"Me…? Weeeeeell, I'm thinking if you can't beat'em, join'em."

"That's the spirit!" I slapped him on the back.

"I shall hire one of the small town booths and be out there on Southfield. Leave me apprentices and the wife here to manage those who might come to the shop. Two chances at commerce, eh? Can't be bad." He tipped his leather beaker at me and drained it with a smack of his lips.

"How many others of the town might you persuade to join you out there?"

"Haha, m'lord. There's no flies on you…I have me cronies, don't you worry. I'll not be the only Marlburry man there. No other cordwainers, though. Nope. Can't have no other Marlburry cordwainers there."

This made me smile, for Gilbert was the only true shoemaker in Marlborough.

"I hear that one called Martin of Melksham, shoemaker,

is a-coming. I'll give him a boot or two up his backside, I can tell you. We'll see who the best boot maker in the area is."

"Good man!"

"Should be a good show, 'specially for the girls. They get their fingers on stuffs as they'd never normally see in Marlburry." Gilbert had two small girls.

"Spending the money their men make, eh?"

Gilbert opened his arms. "Well, what's it for, eh?" He chuckled. "I know my girls are looking forward to it. Ribbons and pins and combs and fabrics. They've talked of nothing else for days."

"Aye, if Cecily, my wife, were still here with us, she would be as happy as the rest of them."

"God rest her," said Gilbert as he crossed himself.

There was a little silence as I followed suit.

"No news about the boots yet, then?" I did not need to elaborate. Gilbert knew exactly what I meant.

"Nope…nothing yet. I have hopes. Them boots were too good on the feet to just disappear." Gilbert reached for the flask to refill the beakers. "Funny though, I am making another pair just like 'em. Special like."

"You are?"

"That prig, begging your pardon, sir, I shouldn't be so disparaging of me betters, but he is a prig, aye, and a pillicock…"

I chuckled. "Who's that then?"

"Young de Saye. Him as prances about on them fine horses. Came in the other week and demanded…demanded mind… I make him a pair of riding boots. I'd half a temptation to say I was too busy, go up the hill…" Gilbert cackled, "but then me business head got the better of me proud head, and I said yes. Loaded the price, though. Silly fool never flinched. Should'a done. More money 'n sense."

"That he has in very small amounts. Sense, I mean."

Gilbert stepped back from me and stared. "Ho, ho...you too?"

I grinned back. "Me too. Can't stand the overgrown brat." I drained my ale. "So he wanted a pair similar, did he?"

"Not just similar, the very same. 'Twas almost as if he had seen 'em and had made up his mind to have 'em copied. Described them to me to the very last stitch."

I frowned. "Now that is odd," I said, draining my beaker. I thanked him for the ale and his information and went on my way.

Chapter Three

*P*eople started to come into the fair days before it opened.

The town reeve had difficulty stopping folk from camping out on the High Street and in the centre of the road. Eventually, it was decided they could all go up to the Common and there was a steady trail of people ascending the hill to the grassy patch of downland and the old earthworks at the very top.

Carts trundled in from all quarters. Prefabricated booths were disgorged from wagons and the apprentices to the traders began to put them up in the south field by the castle. There was a cacophony of hammering to match that going on at the castle itself. In no time at all, the field was full of wooden booths, their window flaps pulled down and secured by chains or ropes, ready for bolts of cloth, leather work, food, haberdashery and other sundries to be displayed to the populace. Hooks were tapped into the wooden surrounds to hold ropes, flitches of bacon, and strings of sausages, caps, herbs and wildfowl. At night, these boards would be pulled up and the hooks emptied. The goods would be taken into the booths and the apprentices would sleep inside to act as guard dogs.

The inns in town were full to bursting with patrons who had travelled a few miles or many, and some of the more wealthy merchants with larger booths took rooms for themselves, for it was beneath them to sleep with their apprentices, journeymen, goods and gear.

The day of the fair dawned misty, which promised finer weather later. I just hoped that the field, which was heavy with dew and low-lying by the river, would stand up to the battering of thousands of feet. There was nothing worse than a quagmire to put people off sauntering amongst the booths. The weather had been very warm and dry lately, however. I need not have worried. I was out of my cubby hole, which counted as my office and sleeping place when I was at the castle, very early so that I could watch the booths opening and the first buyers. The sun shone and the mist cleared.

From the castle's southernmost wall walk, I could see almost the whole field, save that which curved around the river and behind a stand of willows. Most trees and vegetation had been cleared for the flooding of the castle moat, so the field was in plain view from my vantage point.

The whole place was a patchwork of colour. I spotted Master Cordwainer in his Sunday best, a rust red cotte and black hose, wending his way between the booths, one small daughter, holding his hand and skipping merrily beside him.

He stopped quite close to the edge and opened a booth. How clever, I thought, to choose one of the first pitches one came to and on the right, too. Most people were right-handed, so as they entered the ground, they naturally turned right. His pitch was not too near the entrance either, for those booths tended to be overlooked as one's field of vision narrowed as soon as you gained the field.

The field soon filled with people. I spent a good half-hour looking for folk I knew from the town and the forest.

I had given my forest folk and villeins permission to leave their work and visit the fair at any point in the eight days.

The gentry arrived a little later than the lesser folk. They did not stir themselves at dawn, especially the ladies.

Several high-born ladies of Marlborough, with their entourages, tripped over the little bridge over the River Kennet and into the field. There was Nicholas Barbflet's wife, Felicity, with what looked like her whole household. Next came Lady Millicent Mortemer, who was being helped down from her covered carriage. She was the wife of one of the biggest landowners in north Wiltshire, and she too had also brought a sizable retinue.

I moved to the corner tower and stared down the High Street and the junction with the Pewsey Road.

I watched as folk streamed in from the town. Then, my eye was caught by a flash of pale blue, a colour as bright as a summer's sky.

Matilda de Neville, head held high, came out from the castle gateway, closely followed by her little maid and three or four others, two of whom were men-at-arms, and marched along the roadway.

I watched her cross the bridge. She marshalled her folk around her, strode onto the field and plunged into the crowd. She reappeared now and again. There, in front of a booth selling gloves, and there, at another selling religious items. She bought a rosary, perhaps of carnelian, from what I could tell at this remove. She passed on and was lost to view.

I daydreamed some more, and then, there she was again at the edge of the field, talking to a cutler. She bought again and passed the parcel to the man-at-arms behind her. Then, she was off at a brisk pace to one of the wine stalls, where she tried a small beaker of wine. I saw her shake her head; on she went, followed by her parcel carriers. She bowed her head to my friend Johannes, who was passing by with what looked like a small rolled rush mat under his arm. I lost them both again in the press. Matilda de Neville then stopped at a booth displaying every hue of linen; she felt almost every bale, and she had the poor merchant pull out many of his cloths before shaking her head in disdain and turning away.

The ground dipped a little in the middle of the field and I saw her disappear into that dip and reappear at the furthermost side and stop abruptly.

Coming towards her was her bridegroom, alone.

Guy de Saye saw her. He, too, stopped. He bowed low and gave her his feral smile. She did not acknowledge his courtesy but turned quickly away as if she had not seen him and pointed to a booth some few feet away. Hanging from the hooks on this booth were caged birds. She approached and spoke to the salesman.

De Saye shrugged and passed on behind her.

Once he was past, she turned to look at him, and I swear that she shivered, though the day was already warm.

I turned away, too, and gazed down into the inner bailey of Marlborough Castle. Fairs, I told myself, did not really interest me. I sighed and ran down the steps. I had work to do.

That was the last time I saw Lady Matilda de Neville alive.

What did you say, Paul? Shivery down the spine? Ghosts? Well, maybe we will have a ghost or two later. You wait and see.

Two days into the fair.

There I was, as usual, in my little cubbyhole. Now I was signing documents requesting enough platters and pitchers from the town to feed the wedding guests.

Twenty wine coolers, ten large meat plates, two hundred napkins... Naturally, we had some of these at the castle, but we were expecting a great influx of people and needed further items.

I heard voices as some people passed by my open door, but I didn't look up.

Then I heard, "Lady Matilda, please. I must speak with you alone. It's important. To us both."

I did look up at that. Just outside my open door, though unseen, Matilda de Neville and Guy de Saye were speaking to each other. This was the very first time I had seen or heard them do so. I put down my pen.

I heard a rustle of skirts as Matilda turned. "What can you possibly want to say to me?"

"I think it is important that we are both clear about how we feel about our situation. Please, can we go somewhere quiet to discuss it?"

"I must have my maid with me. We may be affianced, but..."

"For propriety's sake, yes. I know."

There was a little silence as she seemed to think.

"Come up to the tower room. It is quiet there, and we shall not be disturbed." They moved away.

Shortly after, I heard Matilda say something to her maid. The door above me opened and closed. I heard booted feet cross to the middle, where there was a table. No doubt de Saye was pouring wine from the covered jug placed there daily for that purpose.

A chair was dragged from the window recess to the table across the boards, its feet screeching on the polished planks. There must be a protruding nail in the bottom, I thought.

I shook my head. Some poor servant would have to repair that scratch damage tomorrow. Low voices began to burble.

Then I heard distinctly and loudly, "I do not wish to marry. Ever. You know that!"

"And neither do I. Well, I do not wish to marry you. Why would I?" Booted feet paced. More indistinct voices.

"We must...the king has willed it."

Matilda began to cry.

"Mistress, please take a drink and calm yourself."

The boots crossed the room again, and I heard the sound of the chair leg once more, pushed back as if in haste.

Matilda was screaming at de Saye. "You are a foul creature. I hate you. I cannot bear to be in the same room with you, let alone the same bed. Oh my God!"

De Saye made placating noises. Then I heard, "Why do you say that? You know we will not ever obtain a divorce..." sobbed Matilda. Her voice was louder and higher in pitch and more easily audible.

"Once we have been together a while..." said de Saye.

"NO! NO! NO! I cannot."

"Then we must marry and live apart," he said.

I could not hear the answer, for it sounded as if Matilda was sobbing into a kerchief or through some material. Perhaps she had come close enough to sob onto his shoulder, though I doubted it.

There was a period of silence and then a retching as if someone were choking and gasping for breath.

"Lady, lady, please," said de Saye. "Calm yourself...You will make yourself ill. Here..." The rest of his words were muted. "Try this...it will ease you."

More soft words. I took up my pen again. Their quarrels were none of my business.

More inarticulate screeching: Matilda. More soft, placatory words: de Saye.

Matilda yelled something like, "I feel ill!" But the words were indistinct and blurred.

De Saye crossed the room. I looked up to my ceiling, mentally shrugged and bent once more to my lists.

De Saye shifted booted feet on the floor, very slightly. I heard the heels clip.

Then, there was a strange, strangled cry. I looked up at my ceiling again. The booted feet staggered a little, it seemed, and then there was a thud. De Saye yelled, "What are you...?"

Matilda muttered something to him. She cried out an inarticulate screech.

He yelled back, "What...?"

Matilda answered him. I know not what she said.

De Saye yelled in frustration, "Oh my God! No!"

Then she began to sob again. The chair leg screeched once more, and there was a wooden bang.

I heard sobbing and retching and a slight drumming.

I furrowed my brow. All was silent, and then the chair was dragged again, its leg screeching on the boards.

An instant later, there was a small splash, a tiny far away sound. It was like someone plunging their hands into a bowl of water. What seemed like a metal wine cup fell on the floor and rolled and rolled side to side until it was still.

The chair was dragged again.

Gradually, the sobbing ceased. Then there was silence.

Perhaps, just perhaps, I thought, they have made it up. I continued with my checking of lists.

Perhaps the time it takes to say eight Paternosters afterwards, there was a small plop. A red blot appeared on my manuscript. I frowned. I took a rag and tried to blot it. It smeared.

I was not using red ink.

I looked up. There on my ceiling, between the planks which made up the floor above, was another red droplet ready to fall. I stood.

It fell. I raced out of my doorway, around the corridor and up the stairs. The little maid was crouched at the bottom of the chamber door. She was wide-eyed, snivelling and shivering.

"No one has come out?"

She shook her head. I lifted her up.

"Stand there. Do not move." I pushed her to the stair opening.

I tried the door. It was locked. I rattled it. I peered through the keyhole.

"Go for the officer of the watch. You will find him in the gatehouse. Bring him here. His name is Andrew. Understand?"

She nodded, picked up her skirts and was flying down the stairs at a dangerous speed.

I yelled "My lady Matilda! Can you open the door?"

No answer.

"De Saye...open up. It's Sir Aumary Belvoir."

Silence.

I worried my lower lip with my teeth.

I ran quickly to the roof. One more flight up. I scanned the inner bailey.

Yes, I was right. My two men, Peter and Stephen, were half-heartedly practising quarterstaffs in an open space, laughing and larking about.

I yelled over the roof top, "Bel-voir...to me, to me!", which was our customary battle cry. The two of them looked up, dropped the staves where they stood and pelted for the keep steps.

It seemed an age before they got to me, but it was really only a matter of a heartbeat. Peter rounded the stairs first.

"You all right, m'lord?" he asked breathlessly.

"Yes, I'm fine. We need to get into this room. Quickly."

Stephen bent and put his eye to the key hole. "Key's in the lock, sir."

"Yes, I know."

"Can't you just ask them to open it, sir? Thems as inside, I mean," asked Stephen.

"No...I can't...I can't raise them."

Stephen lifted his booted foot and kicked hard. The door simply rattled.

He looked at his friend, Peter.

The three of us counted to three... just as the officer of the watch, Sir Andrew Merriman, came up the last step, and we kicked together.

One more hard push from a shoulder, and the door opened.

It opened so quickly that it hit the wall behind and bounced back. I caught the rebound with the flat of my hand.

The key fell on the floor with a tinny rattle. Stephen stooped to pick it up.

"Come in with me, Andrew," I said. "I may need a witness."

My boys stayed outside the broken door. The little maid, I noticed, was peering round the top step of the stairwell. She had been crying again.

The room was much as it had been when I first spoke to Matilda here a couple of weeks ago.

The table was still in the middle of the room.

Over it was sprawled Matilda de Neville. She was half sitting upon the chair. Her right arm was outstretched as if she had been reaching for something. I glanced past her. There, on the floor, was Guy de Saye. He lay almost on his left side, one leg drawn up, the other outstretched as if he had fallen gently to the ground in two movements, one to the left knee and then to his side.

I remembered the thud.

That must have been when he fell to his knee. I had not heard a second sound of him hitting the floor with his body.

His right arm was lain quite straight on the top of his body. 'Strange,' I thought. 'Men do not lie so.'

I crossed the room and felt for a pulse on Matilda's neck as Johannes had taught me to do. It was very, very faint. "Call for the doctor quickly, and the priest."

Peter clattered down the steps.

It was obvious de Saye was dead, for his lifeless brown eyes stared out at me accusingly. Whatever had done the damage may only have been small, but it had done enough, for it had severed the blood line which runs up a man's neck. The knife or sharp item had been pulled out. Blood had poured from the wound and pooled beneath him. Gradually, as the pool widened, it had seeped through the floorboards, through my ceiling, and onto my document.

I groaned. Oh, if only I had paid attention. If only I had acted earlier, the man might still be alive. There is no doubt my few moments of inaction had allowed the lad to bleed to death.

Andrew looked at me inquiringly. "By all that's Holy!" he crossed himself. "What's happened here?"

I lifted Matilda's head gently. She had a crusty froth around her mouth, and her breathing was shallow, very shallow. I could see no outward damage. No knife wound. I checked her neck. There were no bruises, so she had not been strangled.

I called to her gently. Her eyes opened drunkenly. She could not focus.

"Who did this, Matilda? Tell me."

Andrew came close and took her hand. She did not know, I think, that he was there.

"It's Aumary, you remember me. Tell me, what has happened here?"

Her eyes widened. Her pupils were tiny. I thought she said, fuzzily, "killed him", or perhaps "kill him", and then the light went out of them.

"Who killed him?" asked Andrew as I laid her head back down on the table.

"I don't know," I said.

I scanned the room. Stephen, standing in the doorway, crossed himself.

"The room was locked from the inside and the key was in the lock. It's a very long way down for anyone to jump once they had done the deed. I doubt they could squeeze through the window. Nowhere at all to hide. No curtains, no cloths, no furniture where someone might conceal themselves. No one hidden behind the door. As it opened, it banged the wall. No one there."

I turned to look at the door again. I saw the lines of scratches from the window to the table, four of them. No doubt the leg of the chair.

I hunkered down and looked at the base of the chair leg. I could just see the point of a nail.

"No shelf above the door where a killer might hide, as there are in some of the rooms in the castle. No garderobe," said Andrew.

I looked up. "No chance anyone might be hidden in the rafters, for there are none. The ceiling is the floor of the roof above. Flat." I added.

"No furniture in which to hide," said Andrew, his thoughts running along the same track as my own. "No chests."

The castle doctor arrived. He took in the scene and he too crossed himself. He listened for breathing and tutted. He shook his head and left, saying, "I will fetch her father. The Lord above knows how we shall break it to him."

I went out into the stairwell and called for the little maid. "Tell me what you heard happen?"

She shook her head.

Stephen had followed me.

"It ain't no use asking 'er m'lord. You'll 'ave to do it with signs and such. She's as mute as a fish."

I sat on the top step and beckoned her to sit beside me. "Now, Pixie. Your mistress and the young de Saye went into that room together. I heard a little of what was said from my room downstairs. I shall put a scene before you. Can you nod if I am right, please?"

She nodded, and I patted her little hand.

"Good."

I thought carefully.

Before I could begin, the castle priest, Father Columba, came up the stairs, pushed past me, and entered the room. I acknowledged him with a nod.

"They asked you to stay outside?"

She shook her head.

"You volunteered?"

She shook her head and lifted one finger.

"Your mistress asked you to stay outside?"

She nodded. I digested that.

"They argued."

She nodded and then moved her hand in a sort of wave pattern.

"They spoke to each other, and then they began to argue...?"

She nodded.

"I am right, am I not, when I say neither of them had much care for the other? Neither of them wanted this marriage."

She shook her head violently then.

"Your mistress, for example, wanted to be a nun, did she not?"

Pixie smiled. No, she did not.

"But she wanted to stay at Amesbury Abbey?"

Yes.

"As a permanent guest then?"

Pixie nodded.

Hmmm, I doubted if that would be allowed, but Matilda was very young and perhaps did not realise that she might not be permitted to live a life of pampered luxury in the abbey forever.

"Let's go over what you heard and see if it tallies with what I heard.

I could hear voices at the foot of the stairs, distressed voices, calling on God and asking questions. I heard Peter's voice, gentle, kind, deferent. Oh God, I thought...here comes her father.

I ploughed on.

"They argued. Then I heard de Saye yell as if someone had come up behind him and struck him."

She nodded furiously.

"Matilda said she felt ill. Yes?"

Again, the nod.

I shook my head.

"But why did Matilda not cry out? A name, maybe. She MUST have seen the murderer approach. De Saye would then turn and fend off the blow."

To this, I had no nod or denial.

I stood. There was a red-faced Hugh de Neville panting from his run up the mound steps and the keep stairs.

I nodded to him and stood. "Sir."

His eyes bored into mine. "Tell me, Belvoir. My girl... she isn't dead? No!"

"I'm very sorry, sir. I don't know what to say."

"Dead?"

"Yes, sir, and her fiancé with her."

Hugh de Neville rubbed his hands over his face. "Oh, Almighty God. Christ Almighty."

"I am so sorry for your loss, sir."

"Has she killed herself?"

"No, sir, I don't think so. I cannot say in truth, but I don't think so."

He looked up at me sharply. He was not a tall man, and as I've said, I am a full six feet. Besides, he was standing on the third step down.

"And I have spent a bloody fortune on this damn wedding. Fortune. Bloody, bloody wedding! All for nothing. Christ. Stop all the work…now. Bloody Hell."

He turned and stomped down the steps. There were no tears. Nothing.

He never even went in to look at his daughter.

Once the priest had gone, I locked the door and kept the key. The hard-working crowner would have to view the bodies with his jury. Andrew and I were the first finders and would give evidence.

I took the little maid, whose proper name, according to Stephen, was Agnes, to my room and gave her a beaker of he castle's best Gascon.

She sat on my chair and drank it, two hands clasped around the metal cup. Her feet didn't reach the ground. She wriggled backwards on the seat like a child does when it sits in a chair too tall and big for it and smiled her thanks at me.

Suddenly she caught sight of the blood-blotted copy of my list lying on the table top, and she looked up quickly at the ceiling. Her mouth formed a perfect 'o' but there was no sound.

"Yes, that is how I knew something was amiss," I said.

Her eyes came slowly back to my face.

"Agnes," I was not sure how I was going to put this to her without seeming harsh. "Agnes, you know that some folk might say that you murdered your mistress and Sir Guy de Saye?"

She nodded once and then fiercely shook her head so that her chestnut curls bounced on her shoulders.

"No, I know."

I perched on the edge of my work table. "You do not have the height or the strength to overpower de Saye, I know that. I do not think you can pass through a locked door either, though some might say..." I ran my hands through my hair, "Some might say that you managed it by supernatural means."

Her large brown eyes became larger at that, and for the first time, she looked scared.

"No! I do not believe it. You are not, forgive me, like other women, and I know you are not a child. I have no doubt you are as normal as I am. You are no witch or shapeshifter, of that I am sure."

I filled the beaker for her again and fetched another for myself.

"We must make sure that any stories are stamped on immediately. I will not allow you to be taken for this murder, should some wish to blame you."

I could tell by her expression this was not something she had thought about. The horror of it sank in, and her eyes filled with tears.

"Some will seek to blame those who are," I sought the right word..."Different." I smiled down at her. "I will do everything in my power to help you should it become necessary."

She nodded once.

"Will you help me?"

She nodded again, a smile playing around the edge of her lips.

"Let us go through what we heard again."

I removed my blood-stained parchment and took up another sheet. I searched for a piece of graphite I had laid on the table.

"We shall make notes."

I lifted a stool nearer to the table and sat. Even though I was a good two feet taller than the little maid, standing and the stool placed me much lower than Agnes, I still towered over her it seemed. "The noises I heard. Will you tell me if you heard them, too, outside the door?"

A little nod.

"First, I heard what I thought was de Saye cry out."

Yes

"And then a thud, perhaps as he hit the floor?"

Yes

"He was still able to speak, for I think he said something like - 'What are you?' Or perhaps it was 'Who are you?' "

A nod.

"Matilda was able to scream then, I think. Do you think that might have been when the murderer struck de Saye?"

Agnes shrugged.

"And the Lady Matilda collapsed onto the table. I think I heard her drop or knock a cup to the floor, a metal one."

Yes.

"Now, I could not hear what Lady Matilda was saying much of the time unless she was screaming. Her voice was weak. Can you recall what she said?"

Ah, this was going to be difficult.

"How are we going to get you to unburden yourself? You cannot tell me what she said." I screwed up my nose and pinched the bridge of it in frustration.

The little maid smiled up at me and, turning the parchment towards herself, she reached for my graphite.

"I can write." She scribbled.

I laughed. "Of course you can."

Quite a while later, we had pieced together much of what we thought had been said and done in that room, but we were none the wiser about what had really happened. We had plenty of speculation but no hard facts.

That same amount of time also brought Johannes into my cubbyhole, and Stephen and Peter back into the keep from the tasks I had set them. Peter had gone with The Lord de Neville to make sure he was all right, even though he seemed more concerned about the fact that the wedding would not now take place than by his daughter's untimely death and Stephen had fetched Johannes from his workroom at the other end of the town.

I told Agnes that she was to go to the place where her mistress and herself had been staying and sent Peter with her to make sure of her safety.

Johannes and I went up to the tower room. I unlocked the door.

Johannes scanned the room, and then his eyes met mine. "Well...this is a fine mystery."

I walked a circuit of the room. "I heard much of what was said, Johannes, from downstairs. Little Agnes filled in a little of what she could hear and I could not, from her place outside the door. None of it makes sense."

We walked through the scene as it was played out as I sat in my little room. We searched the room. We found the metal cup. Johannes sniffed it. He went down on his hands and knees and checked the floor where the cup had fallen. A few dregs of something had spilt and dried on the boards.

"I shall need to scrape that up," he said.

He lifted poor Matilda's head and sniffed her breathless mouth.

"Wine."

He checked the crusty froth around her lips. "And I shall need to take some of this too."

I nodded.

"Her right hand is a little bloodied. Perhaps she fought the attacker and was nicked?"

Then he turned his attention to de Saye.

Both of us put our heads close together and looked at the little knife wound.

"He was right-handed. Either he pulled it out from his left side with his right hand..." I said, "Or he pulled it out with his left..."

"Or the murderer did..." said Johannes.

We puzzled.

"No, it cannot be. His hand is still placed on his side, see."

"Someone came up behind him? The knife in the left hand? A very accurate plunge. One blow," said the doctor.

"I heard him fall to one knee...quite a thump," I said. "He does not seem to have clutched at the wound to stop the bleeding as one would instinctively do.

"No...It's as if he just fell, toppled over, pulled out the knife or the knife was pulled out, and he stayed there to bleed to death." He looked around again. I could tell that Johannes was extremely perplexed.

"The murderer took the knife?"

I shrugged.

"Matilda did not help de Saye?"

"By then, I think, the murderer had got to her too."

"How?"

"I hate to say this to you of all people, Aumary, but..." he grimaced. "I think it's poison."

My wife Cecily had been murdered by poison in 1200.

"Poison!"

Once the coroner had finished with me and with Andrew Merriman as first finders and his jury had pronounced the deaths in the little locked tower room, murder by person or persons, unknown, I was free to go. I told Sir Thomas Bourne, the coroner, what Johannes and I had found, but his was not the job of fact-finding, his job was merely to pronounce the manner of death. He politely listened, then turned and left for home.

I, too, could go home, home to Durley, for the first time in several weeks.

The building work, the fair and the wedding had claimed much of my time here at the castle. Now, there was to be no wedding, so there was little for me to do, beyond my ordinary daily duties and the supervising of the taking down and storing of the specially built staging, now not to be used. That took me and my team of carpenters all of four hours. 'Why does it take so little time to demolish and so much time to build?' I thought.

The first Marlborough fair was slackening off. On the last day, fewer people could be seen visiting and buying, and those were mostly of the lesser sort, who had waited to the end to get a bargain as the traders began packing up. Deals were being struck for the last of the items left for sale. Why cart goods home—except, naturally, one's nicely fattened purse or strong box—if items could be sold off at a bargain price?

I strolled around the grounds in the last few hours. No crowds now, and the field surface had lasted except in a few places where boards had been laid over the churned-up mud nearer the river. I bought a tan brown leather belt, a fine one sporting a good pewter buckle and with well executed chasing, an image of a running dog with a matching metal aiglet, on which was etched a deer.

I was happy with my purchase, turning it over in my hands and was making my way out towards the bridge when I heard my name called with some urgency. I looked back over my shoulder to see Master Cordwainer frantically gesturing to me from his partly emptied booth. I jogged over.

"M'lord Belvoir, sir...there, over there...the boots...man with lank brown hair and light jerkin. Got'em on his feet, so he has!"

And he pointed to the other side of the field, where a man was negotiating with a leather trader for a small flask. I threw my belt at Master Cordwainer and was off after our booted man. They were indeed the tan leather boots with black turned-over tops and a high polish.

The man turned. He had heard us and he was off like a hare, throwing the flask to the ground in my path. The stall holder of the leather booth yelled and vaulted over his counter, banging into me, slowing me up a little.

There was something familiar about our running man which, for the life of me, as we sprinted and ducked round the remaining stalls, I could not recall.

I yelled, "Harrow! Harrow! Felon!"

This was supposed to aid the hue and cry, for all folk within earshot were beholden to aid me and give chase. There were few fleet-footed people about, but there were a couple of young lads from the castle who were helping to dismantle the town booths, and they took off after our man.

He reached the centre of the field. There were few ways for him to go. He dithered: into the river, over the road where I stood, thence into the moat, over the town bridge and eventually, to the Pewsey Road. That was the way he took now, by way of the willow trees of the salley garden and along the riverside path towards Manton.

The two castle boys drew level with me. I panted

instructions, "One to the field gate, one to this end of the leat. I shall try to drive him to one or the other. If he draws a knife, let him go. I want no heroics."

I pursued the man towards the castle mill, which sat just in from the riverbank a furlong ahead. He would have to leap the mill stream, which was diverted towards the mill, from the River Kennet, and that would be no mean feat, for it was eight feet wide.

He was running hard now as if he knew he had little chance of escape. I remember wondering if he was not a Marlborough man, for he seemed not to know the lie of the land. He feinted towards the field gate. The fleet-footed blond-headed lad stationed there drew himself up and glared menacingly. Our booted man approached the mill bridge and doubled back towards the leat just as I drew level with him but still quite a few feet away.

"Stop!" I cried, "We mean you no harm. Stop and throw down any weapon you have."

He ran on, and I watched as he drew a knife from the scabbard attached to his belt. He did not discard it. So, he meant business.

My eager young helper by the millpond was closing on him.

"No, lad, leave him to me." I slowed and walked forward

"There is no escape." I panted, "Come back to the castle with me..." But he wasn't listening. He was casting around for a way out.

The lad from the gate came up to my side. He had picked up a formidable branch and was waving it around like a staff. Our felon feinted a knife pass at him, and the boy jumped back. Behind me, I could hear the voices of Stephen Dark and Peter Devizes, my men-at-arms, as they jogged up the Pewsey Road and came across the grass, both of them with drawn swords.

The man in the boots made up his mind. He turned and ran almost to the edge of the stream and, screwing himself up to coil like a spring, he leapt.

I was fast behind him. I reached out and caught his light-coloured leather jerkin, but it slipped from my grasp, oiled as it was with mutton grease. It was enough to foil his leap, though, and instead of scrambling for the other side of the water, he splashed into the furthest bank and slid in the mud. There was a frantic scrambling as he tried to grab the plants growing on the bank. None of them were secure. No trees grew here, for this was a man-made stream, and it was made with one purpose in mind: to channel water to the mill pond and thence to the mill wheel. He fell back into the water.

I could hear the wheel turning on the side of the mill building with a rhythmic clatter and splash. Our booted man went under the water, then surfaced and splashed about coughing. I extended my hand but got a knife scratch for my pains.

"Lad! Go to the mill...this side, and yell for all you are worth. Stop the wheel. You won't get over the bridge in time."

The bridge was back towards the road. There wasn't enough time before our man was swept along into the head race.

I yelled at him, at our booted man,

"Run in the water-like this," I demonstrated treading water. "It will save you from being pulled. It might slow you..."

But he was not listening. He went under several times and came up panicking, spluttering and splashing. His knife had gone.

I lay down and extended my hand again...he reached, but though our finger tips touched, he swept on past me.

I jumped up. I could hear the blond-headed lad yelling, "Stop the wheel, Master Miller! STOP THE WHEEL!"

Stephen had gone back to the bridge and was running, legs pumping, over it to gain the furthest bank and enter the mill by the main door on the other side of the building.

Mills are noisy places. I doubted Master Miller could hear us.

I kept pace with our booted man all along the leat. He went under several times.

I saw Stephen disappear around the corner of the building just as our felon was swirled into the head race. His eyes were huge and round now. He knew what was coming.

It seemed an age before the huge mill wheel slowed, and the green moulded slats flapped free and dripped into the pool.

The whole wheel ground to a halt with a terrible groaning and ceased to turn abruptly.

I knew why.

Our booted man had been trapped underneath.

He would not now need the leather flask he had purchased at the fair. Neither would he need his fine boots.

What, Paul? Yes, it was a shame. They were extremely fine boots. Completely wet, mangled and ruined. They'd never be quite the same again.

It took us a very long time to get the man out. It was going dark by the time we managed to manhandle him into the castle mortuary. He had drowned, yes, but he'd also been mashed and beaten by the huge paddle of the mill wheel. There is much power in these great man-made things.

Stephen had recognised him as he followed us into the mill field before the man jumped. No one might do so now, for his head was crushed and mangled.

"Gerald... Gerald of Broughton, one of de Saye's cronies," said Stephen. "One o' them 'orsey sorts from Oxfordshire, some sort o' groom, I think."

Ah, that was where I had seen him.

It was too dark, and I was too tired to go home that night, so I bedded down on my pallet in the corner of my office and slept the sleep of the exhausted. On my way home the next morning, I called at Johannes' house and told him we had found the man with the boots—and lost him again.

"Gerald of Broughton, palfreyman. I made inquiries at the castle. Came in with the de Saye party for the wedding. Not noble but a hanger-on. Bit of a right-hand man for de Saye, with his horses. Quiet, kept himself to himself. Slept in the hall or with his lord in his accommodation. No one knows about the boots. Never seen them on him before. They were all due to go home, minus their master, of course, today. This was his last walk about town. He tried to buy a leather flask at the fair, for the journey, I suppose.

We shall probably never know, now, why he had the boots."

"No...oh yes, talking of boots."

Johannes got up from his work table and reached into a box on the floor by the hall door. "Matilda's shoes. I filched them from the body when no one was looking. The coroner knows I have them, though. They will have to go back. Notice anything?"

I took them by the two sides and pinched them together, right and left, with one hand. They seemed very small. They were dainty, light-coloured shoes to the ankle, made from very soft leather and with soft soles which, when I turned them up, were marked with a brown stain.

"Blood?"

"Aye. She walked through de Saye's blood at some point. Just a little, not much, perhaps the very edge of the pool. There were some part footprints going towards the window on the north side of the tower of the keep. Hardly there, really."

My brow was furrowed in puzzlement. "Have you any idea what that means?" I handed the little boots back to him. "Why she might do that."

"None whatsoever," he said, dropping them once more into the little wooden box.

On my way home, I turned and turned the murder of Matilda and Guy over in my mind.

The words of Master Quimper, my brother Robert's tutor, dead now some years, came into my head.

Quimper had been a very clever fellow, much learned in languages, history and natural science. A long time ago, when I was puzzling out another murder, he had repeated the words of some Roman called Cicero to me. "Cui Bono?" he had said. "Who benefits?"

Well, who did benefit?

Not the murdered pair, certainly. Not Matilda's father, for he was seriously out of pocket and had no other daughter to marry off in her stead. Not de Saye's father either, for he was as set on the marriage as was King John, and he had lost his son and heir.

Who else? Did we have a secret lover, one who was in love with the objectionable de Saye and wished to kill Matilda to clear the road ahead? I could not imagine anyone wishing to marry him, though some older noble girls might take him to prevent them being left on the shelf.

Matilda? She had no desire to marry at all. I had heard

that from her own lips, and I had no reason to disbelieve her.

I suppose if she had discovered someone pretty of face but an undiscerning lesser noble, perhaps a younger son who was not too fussy about the girl herself but who was in need of the dowry that came with her, she might fall in love and be content. I crossed myself. That thought was unworthy. The girl was sixteen and had lived in a nunnery almost all her life. She didn't strike me as the sort who would give her heart away just like that. When I had met her in the tower room that first time, it was not a book of gushing love stories she had thrown at the door but a delicately illustrated breviary. Perhaps, had she been able to live longer, she would have decided to take the veil at Amesbury.

When I reached home, weary with thinking, John Brenthall, my right-hand man in the forest, came running down the hall steps.

John was a quiet man of forty, very controlled, with short dark hair and a clean-shaven but shadowed chin. He was small and compact, with a serious expression most of the time.

"Nice to see you home, sir," he smiled as he took my horse from me and walked it to the groom, Cedric, who had emerged from the stables.

"Matthew has a good pie baking for your supper. With some of those leeks and peas you like so much."

"Lead me to it then, John," I said jokingly, rubbing my belly. A mountain of correspondence was piled on the hall table, and as I entered, I spotted, right on the very top, a letter with the seal of Hugh de Neville.

Why was he writing to me here, personally, when he could have called me into his chamber at the castle and said what he wanted to say to my face?

I opened the missive. There was the usual preamble then, this.

The de Saye group had delayed their departure from Marlborough by a few days, he said, in order to wait for Guillaume, Guy's father, coming from Oxfordshire to claim the body of his son and take it in a lead-lined coffin back to Witney.

There was a further amount of burbling about Joan, his wife, who was back in his manor in Lincolnshire and how upset she would be by the death of her daughter and then came the real reason for the private letter.

"The king, his Gracious Majesty John, has told me that you are possessed of a good mind, Belvoir."

'Well, thank you, John, I am touched.'

"He tells me that you once performed a delicate task for him, one concerning a heinous murder and that you acquitted yourself well in Normandy."

'Well, yes, I did. I couldn't argue with that.'

"I write to ask if you might perform a similar task for myself and for Guillaume de Saye. We are both at a loss as to understand why this thing happened to our most beloved offspring and would bring the perpetrator to justice. I have written to his noble majesty informing him of the terrible crime committed here at his castle of Marlborough and have asked that he sanction your intervention on our behalf."

I chuckled to myself. The parsimonious old ferret probably wants to get his spent wedding money back from the murderer.

"I am informed that you…", he went on, "were privy, in a small way, to events in that terrible locked room."

"Oh, has he at last been up and taken a look for himself," I asked out loud.

"Please, Belvoir," I don't think the old badger had ever said please to me in the whole time I had worked for him, "Please use your considerable intellect to discover who has done his foul thing." There was a little more, mostly flattery and another heartfelt plea for help.

I folded the letter again.

Well! It looked as if I was destined not to spend much time at home after all.

I took the solar steps at a run, two at a time. My daughter Hawise was there with her nursemaid. She was five years old and the light of my life.

I took a run towards her and she jumped up and ran towards me. She vaulted up from the floor towards me and I caught her under her arms and her knees and swung her round. She giggled and yelled,

"Dada!"

I kissed her forehead. She wound her arms around my neck. I hugged her close.

"Matthew Cook says we are to have a huge pie for our supper. I knew you would be home when he said he was making a huge pie!"

I laughed. "He's a witch!" I said and set her down on the floor. "And he knows I love huge pies!"

She grabbed my hand and pulled me forward. "Come and see what I have been doing."

That evening was taken up with looking at sewing and reading—yes, I was having my daughter taught to read, despite the fashion for girls being raised in ignorance—and playing ninepins along a cleared place in the hall.

I was knocked out of the game quite early. My senior man-at-arms, Hal of Potterne, a gruff man with a beard almost to his navel and a love of bright clothes, played on with Hawise and let her win. He loved my spirited daughter as much as he had loved my son Geoffrey, dead by another's hand in 1199. He was wonderful with the younger children of the manor. He could always be relied upon for a game, a story or a whittled wooden toy.

I sat and sipped my wine and watched and laughed with the rest. Then I thought, if my daughter had lain dead in that tower room, would I have been worried about the money she had just cost me for her cancelled wedding? No, I would want justice. I would want to see the felon hanging by his neck and going to hell.

I vowed to myself to do what I could to bring the murderer of Matilda and Guy to book.

Chapter Four

I spent a few days at Durley catching up on my work there. John Brenthall was a very capable man, and much could be done without me by my staff here at the manor and in the forest, but some things were mine and mine alone to deal with. I also spent time with my much-neglected daughter and we rode about the nearer forest together, she on her small pony, Felix, and me on Bayard, my roan gelding.

I was very much in favour with Hawise, for I had bought a few pink almond paste pigs from the fair, and I had given her one each day. She had squealed with delight. I suspect she would have Matthew, my cook, making these for her before long.

The time came for me to leave and return to Marlborough, but I promised to return soon and bring one of Hawise's little friends to stay for a while. Petronilla was the six-year-old daughter of Michael, the Lord of Snap, a small village near Ramsbury, who had a fine town house on the High Street in Marlborough. The whole family would come to stay in the town for months at a time, and I knew they were in residence at the moment, having come for the duration of the fair. It was the price for me being allowed to leave Durley.

I jogged at a swift pace back to town. It was a beautiful morning. The sun was showing the trees in all their glory. It was September 9th, but it was more like a summer's day, for the temperature was already climbing.

Two things told me we were on the doorstep of autumn, though: the robin was singing his winter song from deep in the brushwood at the side of the road, and the swallows, once I reached the outer buildings of the town, were gathering in numbers on the ridges ready to disappear to wherever it was they went for the winter. Everywhere was looking parched for we had had no rain for quite a while. There would be early autumn colour in the forest this year, I thought. My mind ranged back to last autumn when the wind and the rain had devastated many of the forest trees, to the night when I had nearly lost my life to a stone thrown from a sling. I was meant to drown that night. I crossed myself and emptied my mind of that memory. It would do me no good to dwell. I was here alive and in good health, thanks be to God.

These musings, of course led me to the recent deaths at the castle, and as I rounded the church yard, I had a fancy to talk to Johannes, if he was free and at home, about the request from de Neville and de Saye.

I would, there was no doubt, be glad of his help in this quest.

I slid from Bayard's saddle and walked him into the small yard at the back of Johannes' house, where he kept a compact stable for his horse and pack mule.

I was about to enter the building by the back door when I heard singing. I pivoted to try to work out from whence it was coming. Not the church, a mere few yards away. It was a woman's voice, sweet and low, and the song, I recalled, was a French one, the Lark in the Morning, and it had a beautiful melody.

Then, as if by magic, I heard Johannes join in, his rich baritone underpinning the song with a long series of notes held on just some of the words. They have done this before, I thought. It's too practised to be just a little ditty strung out of the moment.

My mind raced to remember whether this was an Agnes Brenthall day. No, a foolish thought. Agnes was a soprano and not as accomplished as this female voice. Besides, she had waved me off from Durley this morning with a flap of her apron as she crossed the yard.

The next verse was beginning. I peered around the kitchen door so as not to be seen. There, standing at the table, a slickstone in her hand, was a woman smoothing a shirt.

Johannes was singing and watching the fire at the back wall, his hand leaning on the wall, and I realised he was preparing the next stone in the flames. When the stone the woman was using became too cool to iron, he would snatch the next one from the embers with a gloved hand and pass it to her with a cloth wrapped round the handle.

The song came to an end.

I stepped from my hiding place and clapped.

"You should both go and sing in the street. People would pay good money to hear you."

The woman jumped as if she had been slapped, and the slickstone in her hand leapt from her fingers, landing with a crack on the flag stone floor.

Johannes turned in the action of stirring the fire's embers with a poker.

"Oh no." The woman put her hand to her breast and stared in horror at the broken stone. I leapt forward, not thinking and tried to pick it up with my bare hand.

What was I doing?

In truth, the beauty of the mystery woman had taken my senses from me, and I had reached for the red-hot iron without thinking. There was no sound as it made contact with my skin, but I yelped and drew back, shaking my injured hand.

In one stride, Johannes was by me. He grabbed my wrist and plunged my hand into the butt of water, which always stood by the kitchen door.

"This is not a trial by fire, Aumary," he laughed. "We know you are innocent. There's no need to prove it."

I tried to pull my hand out. He held onto me.

"No, keep it there for a while. It will save your skin. Then I shall put a salve on it. Right as the adamant in no time."

The woman was staring at me. I was rudely staring at the woman. Johannes was in the middle.

"Allow me to present Lydia of Wolvercote, widow of Edwin of Wolvercote by the town of Oxford, and my well-beloved niece. Lydia, this is my foolish friend Aumary Belvoir, who does not know how hot a slickstone is."

He put his hand to his mouth in a conspiratorial way and whispered loudly, "You can tell he never does his own ironing!"

I felt a fool, but, keeping my hand in the bucket as requested, I gave the best bow I was able to, in the circumstances.

Lydia of Wolvercote curtsied.

She was, there is no other way to describe her, simply the most ravishing woman I had ever seen. Her beauty took all the pain from my injured hand.

Her large eyes were a pure dark violet colour and framed by long, dark, and lustrous lashes. Her skin was as white as the shirt she was ironing. Her hair, held back from her face by a barbette and small white veil, was jet black and fell down her back in a thick plait. Her perfect eyebrows were curved and dark. Her gown, which was a rich murrey colour, was covered by a black embroidered supertunic of the same colour and she wore a full apron of white linen over it.

Her pale skin was now flushed by a very becoming blush as she realised I was staring at her.

I burbled my apologies and took my hand from the bucket.

Johannes had now retrieved the broken glass and tossed it on the table. He leaned over and looked at my palm.

"I'll go and get some salve," and he was off through the inner doorway to his workroom. There was another silence.

"Forgive me, my lady. I did not mean to startle you," I said, nursing my dripping, injured right hand with my left one. "I am punished for being so inconsiderate, but I could not help but be entranced by your song."

Lydia dipped her head. "Thank you, that is kind. Johannes and I have sung together since I was a child."

Her speaking voice was as charming as her singing one.

"I cannot sing. I try to do so with my daughter Hawise, but..." I laughed deprecatingly. "She tells me I sound like a donkey braying!"

A very fetching smile played around the perfectly formed rose-pink lips, "How old is she?"

"Five...and a very good judge of singing."

She laughed a tinkling laugh. "No daughter thinks their father can sing at that age. I am glad to hear that you do sing with her. Many men feel it beneath them and leave the job to their women folk."

"Sadly, Hawise no longer has a mother to join her voice to hers. I have to be both mother and father to her,"

"She is blessed," she said as Johannes returned to the room with his pot of salve.

"Sit, my young and impetuous friend," he said.

I pulled a stool from under the table and sat.

After wiping his hand on a wet rag, kept by the water butt, Johannes, bending over me, began to slick the greasy substance on to my palm, which had now blistered in white bubbles. I peered over his shoulder. The damage was not great.

There was another silence. I raised my eyes to Lydia's face. She smiled at me. It began to be a little uncomfortable, and at last, Johannes said, "There. Take the pot and slather it onto your hand often until the stuff has all gone in. Keep doing it. Keep it open, don't cover it, but I need not tell you to keep it clean."

"Yes, sir," I said with a smile.

Johannes straightened. "Sir Aumary is the warden of Savernake, Lydia, and Lord of Durley, not to mention under-constable at the castle." He reached for his wet rag again and wiped his fingers. "Far above me in station."

"Pah!" I scoffed.

"But somehow, over the years, we have become the firmest of friends and the most equal of men."

"We have," I nodded. "And partners in crime..."

Johannes harumphed. "That too." He reached for a jug, set aside on the kitchen pot board and fetched three cups from a shelf close by.

As he poured, I told him what I had read in de Saye's letter. I could see that Lydia was fascinated. Her eyes never leaving my face, she pulled a free stool to the table and sat.

"I heard from a neighbour that a man had drowned in the mill pool," she said, "Awful, just awful."

"He need not have died." I said quickly, "He was trying to resist arrest, or not strictly arrest. I merely wanted to ask him some questions. There was something in the way he fled and then defended himself, which shouted 'guilty' but guilty of what, I can only guess."

"Of what did you suspect him, my Lord Belvoir?" she said

"Of stealing a dead man's boots. It may seem but a minor crime, but the dead man was found in my forest, and he had been murdered. The man who steals is often the man who kills. Though in this case, I do not know."

Johannes sat with us at the table. "News of the residues I took from the locked room, Aumary," he said. He pushed a parchment towards me.

I read out loud. "Aconite."

Johannes caught my eye. "Matilda had all the symptoms of poisoning by aconite. Her pin-prick pupils, the breathing, vomiting a little. Numbness and tingling in the mouth. You say she spoke but that it was indistinct?"

"Yes, Andrew and I thought she said, 'killed him', but she spoke like a man slurring his speech with too much ale."

"The aconite was in the small metal cup we found and in the dregs of the wine spilt on the floor. The poison had been ground down from the root, the deadliest part. There was enough in that small cup to kill an army of Matildas."

"De Saye took no poison?"

"No, his cup was still on the table and was free of it, so the aconite was not in the jug of wine that had been sitting in the room all day, with plenty of chance for adulteration by anyone, I might add. He had had little chance to drink from his wine cup, it seems, as it was almost full. It was definitely in one cup alone: Matilda's."

Lydia shivered. "It was well planned, this murder."

"It was," said Johannes with a finality that was chilling. "However, we still have no idea why anyone would wish to kill the bride and the bridegroom so close to their wedding."

"Some evil person, jealous of their happiness perhaps," offered Lydia.

"No, I think not. Neither of them were going into this marriage willingly. It was a match made by their parents." I said.

Lydia smiled ruefully. "Matches made in heaven are as rare as pigs in flight," she said lightly.

Johannes reared back on his stool and folded his arms to look at her laughingly.

"Your marriage to Edwin was a good one, was it not?"

"I was married at seventeen, as well you know, by a father who wanted rid of me, out of the house so that he might marry his dead neighbour's wife."

"Aye, well…"

"Your brother, Johannes?" I asked.

"My elder sister's widower."

Lydia continued, "At first, I was very unhappy. There was, after all, twenty-six years between Edwin and myself, and a great gulf of class. Edwin was Lord of the Manor of Wolvercote, and I was the daughter of an Oxford book seller. It was not easy. His manor people resented me. He tolerated. I learned. Over time, I did come to love Edwin, for he was the best of men, the best of husbands."

"Do you not inherit the manor?"

"His son, Eustache, he has it now. His son by Edwin's first marriage. We were childless. I have my dower."

"And that leaves you…where?"

Lydia got up from the table smiling and grasped Johannes' shoulder, linking their arms together.

"It leaves me here in Marlborough as housekeeper, helpmeet and herbalist to a very much loved uncle."

Johannes beamed up at her.

"Well, I for one…" I said, "am very glad of that."

Lydia blushed again.

The rest of my journey to the castle was accomplished in a light and happy mood. I nodded to all my acquaintances.

I 'hallooed' to all my friends with a friendly wave.

I passed under the gatehouse and shouted "Good day, Andrew," to Merriman, the officer of the watch, for his turn had come about again.

He returned the 'Good Day' and added a 'God keep you' and came leaping down the steps to meet me in the outer bailey.

"Aumary, I'm glad you are here. I have something to show you."

I dismounted and gave Bayard over to the groom who came to deal with him.

"Come into my room."

I followed him into the gatehouse, throwing off my cloak, for the day had become quite warm. Autumn days can begin chilly, and by Terce, it can be as hot as a day in the desert.

Andrew was rooting around in a wooden box on a corner table. "Here. Mind how you handle it."

He turned and, opening out a square of rough cloth, put it and the twist of parchment paper lying in it into my hand.

I stared at it.

"Found it under the body of de Saye when they lifted him into his coffin. It was not spotted at first as it had become wedged between the planks of the floor. One of the men who came to take the body prised it out with a knife and gave it over. I knew immediately what it was and told him to wash his knife and his hands."

"The poison."

"I heard Johannes say that it was likely that Matilda was poisoned, and I began to wonder where the stuff had come from."

"You have done very well, Andrew."

He beamed at me. "I have done even better, Aumary. There were a few tiny bits still left in the paper—don't worry,

I used old gloves, which I then burned. I know Johannes says that poison can be deadly even in tiny amounts."

"Aye, it can. It can creep into the skin by insignificant cuts and then into the blood and do its damage that way. It doesn't have to be ingested."

"Well, ingested it was."

I looked up, horrified.

"Not…"

"Castle rat…Piece of cheese." Andrew made a cutting motion. "Dead in a heartbeat."

I chuckled. "Andrew, you are a genius."

"You'll think I am even more of a genius when you hear the next bit."

"You are not going to tell me that in its death throes, the castle rat told you who murdered…?"

Andrew tutted and raised his eyes to heaven. "I can tell you where it came from."

"The rat?"

"The poison, dammit."

"Sorry, Andrew…I am flippant today." I composed my face. "Carry on"

"I recognised the paper, the twist it was carried in."

"And?"

"Master Gallipot, the apothecary in Chute Alley."

I frowned.

"The mean old bastard re-uses bits of old receipts. He gets his apprentices to cut them up, and then he twists powders and such like into them. Saves him a fortune on vials and pots. He sometimes gives back the request you go in with."

Master Gallipot looked at me under wide silver eyebrows. "I am not in the habit, my Lord Belvoir, of handing out poison will-I-nil-I to all and sundry."

"No, Master Gallipot, I am not suggesting that, but..."

"When I do give over a poison, I record it in my book and..."

"You have a book?"

"Naturally..."

I was about to ask if I could see it when Master Gallipot rode over me with, "And under no circumstances would I give it to one of my clients in a," he sniffed, "paper twist. Most unprofessional and downright dangerous."

I put on one of my riding gloves. I fished in my purse and brought out the piece of hempen cloth in which Andrew had wrapped the paper twist. I opened it very carefully.

Gabriel Gallipot looked down his nose at the piece of paper. He obviously had difficulty seeing things clearly. He screwed up his eyes.

"Is this one of your pieces? It appears to be part of a receipt for a compound used as a laxative, does it not?"

The master apothecary lifted his hands in a gesture of impatience and then peered closely at the script on the paper. "Yes. It is mine. It is indeed a purgative. It was written by Doctor Johannes of Salerno for one of his patients. Naturally, I am not at liberty to tell you who...even if I could remember which, sadly, I cannot."

"That isn't important, thank you, at the moment."

He straightened and looked at me once more under his copious eyebrows.

"Might I see this book of yours, please?"

The apothecary sighed, and, leaning behind me, lifted a little bell which sat on the counter.

An apprentice appeared from behind a coarse blue curtain.

"James, the book, please."

James came back with a folio of papers stitched loosely

together with twine. Master Gallipot turned the pages.

"Here."

I scanned the parchment. "Aconite root. Powdered." I ran my finger along the line. There was the date that the last batch was delivered. There was the amount of poison sold. At the end, the amount due.

"Brother Francis, Marlborough Priory of St Margaret of Antioch," I said aloud. There were many such entries for the priory.

The apothecary closed his papers and shook his head. "You wanted to see the book. Now you have seen it. However, I could have told you who the aconite was destined for, for so much of it always goes to the same place. I sell very, very little to anyone else."

"The priory?"

"To the kitchener, Brother Francis."

"Why do they need so much, so often?"

Master Gallipot sighed. "It's a large site, as you know. They have many buildings close by the river. There are numerous places where the rat population is a hazard. The aconite is for the use of the kitchener and also the cellarer, Brother Fabian. It is also used in the infirmary by Brother Petrus in very small doses, you understand. It can be effective in cases of anxiety and restlessness; acute sudden fever or symptoms from exposure to dry, cold weather or very hot weather; tingling, coldness, and numbness, fevers with pain in the limbs, or colds with congestion; and heavy, pulsating headaches. It can also… "

"Yes, thank you, Master Gallipot." It sounded like he was reading, he had the list to heart so well.

I put away my little twist of paper carefully and wound my glove into my belt. I would clean it fully later, just in case.

Now for a visit to Johannes to show him our find and

to ask about the paper. I would be pleased to be seeing him again so soon.

No, I was not to fool myself. I was happy to be returning, for Mistress Wolvercote—or, should I say, Lady Wolvercote—would be there. I smiled to myself.

"Thank you, Master Gallipot."

"Pleasure, m'lord," he replied, though I doubted it very much.

> *Yes, Paul, I suspect you still do have aconite at the priory. You be very careful. Though I doubt you will encounter it. You are not, I suspect, called upon very often to prepare food, look after the sick or deal with rats as a scribe. As far as I know, it's not used to make ink. Don't worry, you're safe.*

As I passed out of Master Gallipot's shop, which was at the bottom of a small alley leading off Kingsbury Street, rounding the corner more than half way down, I bumped into one of my manor workers, my housekeeper, John's wife, Agnes Brenthall. She was hurrying around the corner from the main road.

"Oh, m'lord," she set her head rail straight again, "I'm so sorry, I wasn't looking where I was going."

I steadied her with both hands, letting go of Baynard's reins. No matter, he would follow me without me holding them anyway.

Agnes was a small woman with a cheerful face and two red apple cheeks, which made her look like a child's painted doll.

"Agnes...are you come from Doctor Johannes' house?"

"No, sir, John was out with the small wagon, so I took the opportunity to come with him to run some messages in the town and...I am visiting my mother who..."

"Ah.

She shifted the basket on her arm. I thought she looked a little flustered.

"You have business with Master Gallipot, then?"

"Yes. We are overrun at our house with rats since poor Cuthbert was flattened by that cart and the rat man, Cenhelm, died."

Poor Cuthbert had been one of our manor's best ratting cats.

"I was coming for a little poison to deal with them."

"Aconite?"

Agnes looked horrified. "Oh no, sir, never. We can't have that at the manor. Ours is a much lesser mixture." She shook her head and once more righted her head cloth again. "We none of us would feel safe with that stuff about the place. Bearing in mind what happened to poor Ol' Colmar, an all."

My cook Colmar had been poisoned by aconite a few years ago.

"Yes indeed."

She made to go past me.

"Agnes, has Doctor Johannes told you that he has managed to get help around the house and surgery?"

"Yessir. He sent a message yesterday along with the finest box of little almond paste eggs you ever did see, especially for me, for me, sir, to say thank you for all I had done for him. They are almost too good to eat. They look so pretty, all coloured and shaped like the real thing, only smaller, of course."

"That was very thoughtful."

"Aye, it was. Wherever he can have got such things, I don't know. He's a real gentleman, sir."

"At the fair, I suspect, Agnes."

"I suppose so. Oh, and that lady niece of his. She is so beautiful, m'lord. You should see her. Like a goddess, my

John says she looks. I do wonder, though, if she isn't too refined to do cooking and housekeeping and such like, with her..."

"I think you have no need to worry on that score. I have met the lady, and I have cause to know that she is excellent with a slickstone on a shirt." I showed her my palm.

"Oh, sir...how ever did you...?"

"One day, Agnes, I will tell you," I said and changed the subject.

"Hello!" I shouted as I came up to Johannes' door and scratched on the wood.

His workroom door, the first on the right of the passage, was closed, which meant he had someone with him.

"Hello!" I shouted again.

Lydia Wolvercote came tripping from the kitchen. Her apron was a little splattered, and she was holding up two bloodied hands to prevent the drips from going onto the floor. In one of them was a skinning knife.

"Oh, my lord," she said, bobbing her head.

I leapt forward, "Are you all right?"

"What...?" she looked at me strangely, then laughed her tinkling laugh. "Tsk. Oh, sir, you must not think that every drop of blood means murder." She turned back to the kitchen. "I am merely skinning and gutting a few rabbits to make some stew."

She went out of the back door to a large water trough that stood in the courtyard and rinsed her hands.

No, Agnes need have no worries that Dr Johannes would not be well looked after.

"He is busy at the moment, the doctor, but do come and take a cup of ale," she said as she re-entered. "And wait for him. He won't be long."

I don't know what made me say it. I am not a man for flattery or, for that matter, boldness with the ladies, but I sat and said, "No matter. I am more than happy with your company, my lady."

Lady Lydia flushed that becoming pink again and turned away.

Oh dear, I thought. That was a mistake. I tried to make amends by quickly entering into the reason for my visit.

"Some good news: one of my friends has discovered the source of the poison."

She looked over her shoulder. "Oh?"

"Yes, the poison was carried in a twist of paper, and it was found under the body of the young man Guy de Saye. The paper was part of a request made by Johannes for a preparation to be made up by the apothecary Master Gallipot in Chute Alley.

"Johannes has mentioned him, but I have yet to meet him."

"He's a dour and exact man, not one for conversation. You are not missing his company," I joked.

She turned and smiled at me.

Johannes came through the kitchen door, rubbing his hand over his forehead. "I swear, one of these days, I will commit murder and swing willingly for it." He sat down heavily at the table.

"Do not become a doctor to wealthy and demanding old ladies, Aumary. They will drive you into an early grave."

"The sort who demand purgatives at every consultation?"

"Ah, I see you have come across the type already."

I smiled. "No, just this..." and I fished out my hempen scrap and the piece of twisted paper again. "I need not tell you to be careful with it."

Johannes took it from me. "My handwriting."

"Yes, yours," and I told him how it had been found and

what the apothecary had said.

"So, a receipt of mine for a laxative, no name to the person who took it." He turned the paper about carefully. "Could be one of many."

"Gallipot couldn't tell me, and he didn't know what was put into the twist originally."

"No."

"So this piece has been reused to carry an amount of poison to the castle tower room, where it was emptied into Matilda's cup by...someone."

"Gallipot says the aconite he makes up is mostly sent down to the priory. It's used in the kitchen buildings and the out-buildings to control rats and in the infirmary to cure...oh, all sorts." I chuckled, "He gave me a lecture."

"I do know," said Lydia, "that it is sovereign, in small doses, in helping with headaches."

"We shall make a doctor's assistant of her yet, eh, Aumary?"

I smiled. "I was hoping you might come down to the priory with me. They know you well and me not at all. I'd like to know how the aconite got from the priory to the castle, if it did."

"No time like the present," said Johannes. "Leave Bayard in the back. We might as well walk."

As we walked, we talked about the murders again, as if going over it once more might turn up some inspiration, but it did not.

Brother Porter let us in at the wicket gate, and Johannes clasped the arm of the diminutive monk.

"Might we wander through to the infirmary, Mark? We have business with Brother Petrus."

The little monk waved us on.

I had never been into the priory of St Margaret of Antioch. As a lad, I had scaled the back wall and scrumped apples from their orchard and had been cuffed around the ear by one of the monks and sent on my way, but I had never been in any of the conventual buildings.

Johannes knew his way round, for he came often to help in the treatment of guests and to consult the books housed in a little room which passed as a library; works begun to be collected and copied some ten years ago, when the priory was newly founded, by the then abbot, Adam of Malmesbury.

Yes, Paul, it was before your time, of course.
Now you must have many more wonderful books
in the library.

The infirmarer was a man in his sixties, slow of step and deliberate of action, quietly spoken and with a natural tonsure, a fluff of white hair around his shining pate, which obviously never needed shaving.

He took us to his little room and offered us refreshment, which we declined.

"Petrus, you have probably heard about the murders at the castle and the accidental death of one of the de Saye servants at the castle mill. This is my friend, Sir Aumary Belvoir, Lord of Durley. You know him as the warden of the forest and as under-constable at the castle.'

Petrus nodded slowly, "And I have also heard that he has been asked by the families to look into the matter."

I sat up at that. "How did you learn this, Brother?"

"Why, from the family itself."

I looked in perplexity at Johannes.

He snapped his fingers, "Of course, they would stay here with you. The de Sayes. In the guest house."

"Naturally. There is no room at the castle, and begging your pardon, my Lord Belvoir, it is not a place where one might be comfortable for any length of time."

How right he was there.

"Especially for the ladies and with the building work…"

"No, quite."

I took over the questioning. "We have come to ask if you have seen this before. Please do not touch it," and I explained the story of the finding of the little twist of paper and laid it before him.

"It's a receipt of mine, Petrus," said Johannes, "given to Gallipot in Chute Alley to make up. A remedy—we do not know the recipient—was contained in here first, and then when the original contents were gone, the paper was reused to hold a small amount of aconite, which was the cause of Matilda de Neville's death. We know that aconite is used here at the priory.

Might someone have stolen a little from you or from the stores of the kitchener or Brother Fabian, the cellarer?"

"No, I don't recognise it. Steal it from me? No. My aconite is kept under lock and key." He shook his head. "From my colleague, Brother Kitchener, likewise. From Brother Fabian, however, perhaps."

"He is less scrupulous about his poison stores?"

A smile played around the elderly monk's mouth. "No indeed, not normally. It's just that his duties require him to be more liberal, shall we say, with the stuff."

We must have looked perplexed, for he went on.

"He had the job of baiting the boxes we use for the killing of the rats. Since the death of Cenhelm Ratman last year, the town has had no official rat catcher. He was a boon to us here, was Cenhelm, living so close to the river, but sadly…"

"Gone to God," said Johannes. We all crossed ourselves.

"A little left over rancid food was put in the boxes, and then some of the poison. We must be careful, very careful, where we leave these boxes. The rats come in, eat the mixture and go elsewhere to die. We see a few floating in the river. As you know, the wall of the priory and our salley port backs onto the flow." Petrus smiled. "Others just die where they are, and we burn them."

"Hmmm," I said. "Anyone then might have access to these boxes lying around the priory?"

"Only in certain places, where the rats run," said Petrus. "But yes, many know where they are situated."

"Might one of your guests know what these boxes are for? Might they have taken out some of the powdered aconite and dropped it into the twist of paper?"

Brother Petrus deliberated for a moment. "If they had seen Brother Fabian at his work or had asked him about the poison, yes, they would know."

"Might they be able to do this without being seen?"

Brother Petrus assented. "Yes, they could," he said. "Some of the store houses and further buildings nearer the river were not frequented much by the priory inhabitants. It would be quite easy."

"May we speak with Brother Fabian, Petrus?" asked Johannes.

"Sadly, you may not." He shook his fluffy white head.

"He is from the priory at present?"

"He is from the priory for ever, m'lord. He died on Thursday and is now resting in the bosom of our Lord in our cemetery. He was nearly eighty, you know."

I looked sharply at Johannes.

"Was he expected to die?" he asked.

"Doctor Johannes, how many men do you know who are over three score years and ten who are not expected to die?"

"He was not ill?"

"Not as such, but he was very old, and he had started to be, shall we say, forgetful."

Johannes sighed. "Then we shall trouble you no further..."

I put out a hand to stop Johannes from rising. "Wait… you say that of late Brother Fabian had become a little forgetful? How was this manifest?"

Brother Petrus looked at me under his eyebrows. "Yes, young man, I see where this is leading."

"Had he begun, perhaps, to forget where he had left the powder? Perhaps he left his store unguarded, did he maybe…?"

"I cannot comment, my lord," said Petrus sharply.

I looked at Johannes. I think that in that sharpness lay our answer.

"Thank you, Brother Petrus," I said. "You have been most helpful."

The iciness disappeared. He bowed. "It is good to see that even little apple thieves can turn out well, m'lord," he said, rising and putting his hands into his sleeves. "Good luck in your quest."

I stared at him. Yes, I realised, once, this gentle old man had been able to run as fast as my much younger self, and he'd had a very good aim and a hard hand."

I beat a hasty retreat.

Our next visit was to the hosteller.

The two monks were as different as May is from December.

Brother Wilfrid was sharp and quick, young and eager, with an abundant energy manifest in a restlessness about his work.

He fetched his record book and quickly turned over the pages.

Yes, almost the whole of the de Saye household who had come for the wedding had stayed at the priory and in other priory properties around the town—five young noblemen, including Guy and two cousins and two best friends, plus hangers on, it seemed. The rest of the family were due to travel and stay on the day before the wedding. All was ready for them. A hasty and sad message had been sent home to them, telling them not to come, save for Guy's father and his men, when Guy had been found murdered.

The lesser folk, too, had been accommodated in the priory, but in the dormitory bedroom. The high-ranking folk had had rooms to themselves.

Occasionally, Guy would bed down in the castle hall if he were too drunk to get back to the priory. They missed him a few nights at curfew, said Brother Wilfrid.

I suddenly had a thought. "His man, Gerald of Broughton, did he stay here at the priory?"

"He did." Wilfrid consulted his book again. "He ate communally, too, in the guest hall with the others. He stayed in the room with his Lord Guy when they were not at the castle."

"How did he seem?"

"Seem, my lord?"

"Yes...did they get on? Did they argue? Was de Saye a good lord to him? Did Gerald seem content with his lot? Do you know?"

Wilfrid smiled. "They were like brothers. Both mad for the horses, too, I hear. Close as kin, though they were none, de Saye being noble. I thought at first they were brothers, for they were...you know, very familiar. The servant imitated the master, I think."

"In what way?"

"Well..." he scratched his chin. "Clothes...they liked similar clothes, though naturally, the lord was the finer dressed."

"Thank you, Brother. You have been most helpful."

I turned to Johannes. "I think, just a little...but I think...I have chink of light shining through this dark business, my friend," I said.

Chapter Five

We walked back to Johannes' house, each deep in his own thoughts.

I could not yet share mine with my friend as they were too muddled, and my conclusions were not fully formed. I needed to write everything down, my customary way of sorting my ideas. Johannes looked tired, and I thought he plodded wearily up the slight incline to his house.

"I will leave you to your dinner and the tender ministrations of Mistress Wolvercote, Johannes," I said.

"You are not coming in to sample her good rabbit stew then? She is, despite outward appearances, a good cook."

"I have no doubt she is."

I was sorely tempted and not simply for the stew.

To feast my eye on the lovely Lydia was a meal in itself to me. I would devour her, for there is no doubt she had touched my heart and mind.

One day...that is all...one day. I felt as if I had known her forever.

"I shall be at the castle, ordering my thoughts," I said. "Shall I see you tomorrow, perhaps?"

He stretched and yawned. "Aye... God willing."

"God be with you, Johannes."

I collected Bayard and walked him to the road. The sun was still bright in the sky, but the afternoon chill was coming in, and a slight mist was rising from the river below the houses to my left. I looked down the wide main street of this sleepy little town, with its slight bend to the south west. The buildings on the right, stretching away to the castle and the new church of St Peter, were on the slight rise of the hillside. Those on the left were a good few feet lower. Here and there, were little alleyways running between these houses, many of them leading to yards for those trades that needed water for their manufactures.

The town water mill was here, too. Fulling mills were situated on this side of town and also further upstream, slightly out of town, in the area called Elcott to the East. Cloth was becoming an important industry here in Marlborough. I owned some sheep, which I farmed out on the downs, the gentle chalk hills surrounding the town. In my father's time, many of the fleeces were sent right out of the area to be carded and spun—I also owned a spinning industry in Collingbourne, out on the Salisbury Road. Newbury town, 19 miles further east, was the centre for the collection of the wool packs, and laden mules plodding along the Ramsbury Road through the forest were a common sight. Here, the merchants would gather, coming from all over the country and even abroad, to get their hands on our good English wool, which was prized throughout Europe. Lately, my wool factor Tom Herder and I had negotiated to keep some of our spun wool in the town, and now it was woven into cloth, fulled and dyed right here in Marlborough.

My stomach grumbled. I realised I had had nothing to eat since my meagre breakfast, and the smell of Johannes' dinner, the rabbit stew, was tantalising to me.

I moved off quickly towards the castle, walking Bayard the short distance down the High.

Half way down, I met a party of three riders in the middle of the wide road, with a string of about six horses, beautiful, proud creatures with long, slim necks and sturdy but elegant legs. Guy de Saye's stable of racing horses, I thought, going home without their master.

The lead rider waved his thanks as I led Bayard round the posse. I looked up at the man.

"Where do you take them?" I shouted.

He tugged his forelock. "Master Guy had a stud out at Baydon, sir. We are to go there till the Lord de Saye decides what to do with them."

I nodded. That was information I would squirrel away.

With a small chuckle, he said, "Have you a fancy to buy one then, sire?"

I looked them over.

Had I? I was as appreciative of horseflesh as was the next man, but a horse just for racing? There, in the middle, was the beautiful bay stallion that Guy had been riding the day I met him in the castle bailey. He was a fine horse worth many pounds. His coat shone, his black mane was combed to perfection, and his long tail was held proud. I caught Bayard's eye. I swear it narrowed. He snorted. I patted the beautiful beast's neck.

"No, I think not," I said, "This sort of horse is as expensive a past time as a mistress. I don't expect I could afford either of them."

The man laughed, called a blessing to me, and they passed me by.

Deep in thought, I skirted the southern end of the new church, dedicated to St Peter before, bending with the road, I headed towards the castle gateway. A voice hailed me. I turned.

There, coming through the doorway, was Master Cordwainer, a rolled-up cloth under his arm. How many others were going to keep me from my dinner this day?

"Good afternoon, m'lord!" he looked up at the sun, "Ah yes…still afternoon, just, and not evening quite yet, I think."

"And me not had a bit to eat since I broke my fast this morning." I grumbled.

Gilbert smiled. "About official business, are ye? Never enough time for food when on official business," he said laughingly. "And so, sir, in your long-winded and dinnerless investigations, what have you discovered, eh? If you may confide in this friendly and humble cordwainer of the town, that is," and he bowed from the waist, a twinkle in his merry eye.

What could I tell him? I told him about the poison, and I gave him a first-hand account of the death of the felon he had spotted at the fair. Well, Gilbert had been the one to alert me to the fact that Gerald of Broughton had been wearing the murdered man's lost boots. He had heard of the death naturally, on the town grapevine, but to have it from one who was actually there was gossip he could not pass up. Gilbert had sent my hastily discarded, newly purchased belt up to the castle for me, but I had not seen him since the end of the fair.

"Hmmm, so Alan of Didcot must have known our drowned boot thief."

"I suspect he did, yes. He was, you told me, very much involved in the racing of horses up on the downs. Gerald of Broughton was de Saye's right-hand man with his race horses."

"A falling out of thieves, perhaps?"

"I've no reason to think our limner was."

"No, seemed a decent sort to me, apart from the drink, very talented with his brushes. Nice man when he wasn't drunk."

I tilted my head to look at Gilbert Cordwainer sidelong. "Gilbert, you told me you didn't know him well. Now what do I hear?"

The cordwainer snatched his hat from his head and fingered his curly hair, "Weeell, I didn't know him proper well, you understand. Just on a business footing." He scratched the side of his nose.

"Business...what business...more boots?"

There was a little silence as Gilbert made up his mind to confide in me. "No. Oh...um...well...oh, come on, you better come with me, and you can see for yourself, sir. I was trying to keep it a bit quiet, like. Don't s'pose it matters now as it will never be finished."

He turned on his heel and went back through the west door of St Peter's. The place was aglow as the sun shone through the windows, but there was little light for they were but narrow lancets, long small slits, rather like the castle keep's lower windows and orientated south and north. Indeed, the same masons who worked on the new castle building worked here when they could. The only light came from a wider window at the eastern end.

Everything seemed whitened with stone dust, but the closer one got to the eastern end and the place where the altar stood, the cleaner it was. It was all very pristine and new, for indeed, it was new and not yet quite finished. We picked our way over bits of stone and discarded blocks and around a wooden saw horse and several planks which had obviously, at one time, made up the scaffolding.

It was a very plain little church. Round columns marched up the nave, relieved only by a few simple stone leaf decorations to the top. The floor was flagged. The arch to the chancel was high and narrow, almost in the Saxon style, and all around it were dog-toothed designs executed in brown-red paint, very exactly painted.

I turned to look down the nave.

I gasped.

Up on the west wall above the outer door, in what I think is called the tympanum, was a painting.

A man was kneeling and praying, and a woman was standing behind him with clasped hands. Two small children were drawn roughly into the plaster, but these were not yet filled in with colour. Above these were three angels in glory, hovering in the air, beautifully executed with every feather of their unfolded wings outlined in detail, their faces smiling, sensitive and kind. Around the scene, were little flower patterns made into a simple twining border. They were flowers I recognised, flowers which could be found on the downs around and about us: field pansies, cinquefoil, scabious, orchids, field poppies, vetches and the pasque flower. Even in the gloom, I could tell it was lovely.

I marvelled at the beauty of it, and whilst I took in the colour and the lifelike poses of the people and angels, Gilbert was unrolling the cloth he carried under his arm.

"This is the complete design here, just in drawing, you understand. It was so nearly finished and then he had to go and get himself killed."

I looked down. There on the floor, weighted down with four bits of stone, was a drawing, the design for this painting.

I looked from one to the other. There were to be radiating lines of sunshine behind the heavenly bodies and grass around the earthly ones. The children, both girls, were to be gazing up into heaven. No, it was not quite complete, but it was wonderful.

"Gilbert, it is wondrous," I said.

He shuffled his feet. "Aye, well…"

"And this was all executed by our dead limner, Alan?"

"Aye. It was to be a secret till it was done." Gilbert lowered his voice, "My wife, Grace, doesn't know I commissioned it. I wanted it to be a surprise for her. The limner worked mostly in the evening when everyone else had gone. He was, they tell me, often to be found here in the night by candlelight, painting on as if he had forgotten the time of day."

"Even as it is, it will be a fine gift for her. His was a great talent. We have lost a very clever man," I said, still staring at the ingenious way in which Gilbert's face had been rendered in paint.

"You, Grace and the girls." I peeled my eyes away from the painting. "Most paintings are just scenes from the bible or patterns...like those." I turned and pointed to the dog-toothed designs. "How did you get him to execute such a portrait as this?"

"Aye, well...it did cost me a sack of silver."

"A humble cordwainer, with pennies to spare for things like this? Have you been waylaying folk travelling through my forest and relieving them of their goods and gold?" I asked, half joking.

I did wonder how he had afforded such a thing. And where Alan's money had gone. He shuffled a little, and I realised that he was embarrassed to tell me the thing he was about to say.

"Well, m'lord...it's kind 'a' like this. Alan wasn't the only one as liked the horse-racing on the downs."

"You, too, won money on betting?"

Gilbert flushed at that. "Aye...once or twice. I didn't do it often, but it seems I have the knack for picking the winning horse. No idea how I do it. I don't know much about the beasts. Never owned one, never ridden one. But win I did. Enough for this," and he gestured to his drawing, which he rolled up again. "Anyway, they've gone now, so there'll be no more racing."

"Yes, I saw them move out through the town today."

I stared again at the painting. Grace was elegant in a light pink gown with a pale yellow bliaut and a fine tan belt falling almost to the floor. Gilbert was wearing his Sunday best, the tunic and cotte I had seen him wear to the fair the day we apprehended Gerald of Broughton. A white shirt of linen showed under a tunic of black, and a grass-green cotte was over them all, with a turned-back hood lined in black. All was beautifully rendered in paint.

Grass-green.

Green paint.

My memory clicked into place.

Johannes and I had seen that colour on Alan's hands shortly after we had brought him out of the forest.

So, this is where he had been shortly before he had been murdered.

Gilbert sighed and strolled off, throwing a goodbye over his shoulder, his rolled-up drawing clutched lovingly under his arm. He muttered to himself, "I come to look at it now and again. 'Spose I could show Grace now." His voice disappeared into the gloom and out of the door. "Good day, m'lord. God keep you," it echoed.

"And you, Gil," I said.

All was silent save for a few noises filtering in from outside. The door banged.

I looked around again. So, if our limner had been in here, where were his paints and equipment? Were they here, too?

I started to search. After a hundred heartbeats or so, I found them, stuffed haphazardly into a canvas sack and pushed into the space behind the altar, a solid block of Caen stone. I fished it out.

I opened the bag. No self-respecting artist would keep his tools in such disorder. Many of the items inside were a complete mystery to me. I checked and puzzled: brushes and tiny hammers, spatulas, little pots, solid lumps of what must be minerals, and a small pestle and mortar with which to grind them to powder. There was birch bark paper, naturally, and some charcoal and graphite. A further small bag was at the very bottom. In it was a tiny book. Well, I say a book. It was just pages sewn together with looped string. Hundreds of minute drawings sprawled over the pages to the very edges. No space was wasted. I smiled. The man had had a wicked sense of humour.

Here was a knight and his lady held upside down by a very large hare binding their feet with twine. Dinner, I thought. I turned the page and laughed out loud. Here were two children being poked in a hot skillet by a very competent cook, who just happened to be a hairy pig.

I turned the book upside down, for the drawings were scattered will-I-nil-I. On one page, an armoured rabbit was fighting a snail. This would keep my daughter amused for hours. Ah, perhaps not this one. Two people in bed, and they weren't sleeping! I turned the page again and rotated the spine to the top. There, drawn in perfect detail, were two men. They were standing, embracing each other, lip to lip, kissing, and when I looked carefully, I recognised them both.

I came out into the evening sun and shaded my eyes. It had been cool in the church, but now it was quite sultry and there was no breeze.

Bayard was cropping the grass across the road to the side of the castle moat, and John Brenthall was hurrying towards him with a worried expression on his face.

He saw me and relaxed. "Oh sir, I wondered where you had gone?"

"Not like me to visit a church then, John?

He smiled.

"I thought you would be long gone home with Agnes," I said.

"Yes, I was…did…but I came out again quickly on Old Fenrir, to the castle, looking for you. We have trouble at the manor."

"Something you can't deal with, John?" I couldn't imagine anything he couldn't handle.

"Aye, sir. It concerns Peter, and I have no real power to intervene."

We galloped speedily back to Durley, John on the fleetest horse we had besides Bayard, a black stallion we called Fenrir, for he was as bad-tempered as the wolf of the legends.

John gave me a breathless version of the events happening at the manor as we trotted along the High so that when I reached the road into the village, I was well incensed and ready to do battle.

I threw myself from Bayard's back outside the church lych gate and, in the fading September light, for it was now coming up to vespers, I pounded up the path to the church door.

'Make an entrance,' I said to myself. 'Assert your authority,' and so I threw open the door with such force that it banged on the wall behind. John caught it and entered. I took it from him again and slammed it.

About fifteen people were crowded into the nave. Many were shouting, and some of the women were crying. They were all silenced.

I strode up the nave.

"Stop this and stop it now!"

There was a further silence, apart from the snivelling of the women.

Agnes, John's wife, flew to him and buried her head in his shoulder. He stared over her head and round the crowd and nodded to me, directing my gaze.

There, on the floor, in front of the altar, arms stretched out in the shape of a cross, his back bare and crossed with red lines, was Peter Brenthall, his thirteen-year-old son. He was stoically gritting his teeth.

Hal of Potterne was standing over Peter, glaring angrily at our new priest, Father Swithun and Hal was holding a whip, the sort used by priests and monks, penitents in particular, to scourge themselves.

My man-at-arms looked up at me and closed his eyes in relief. He stepped over the prone Peter and gave me the whip.

"Glad you're 'ere now, sir. Maybe as you can talk some sense into his thick'ead."

Father Swithun's chin jutted, but he said nothing.

Agnes left John's side and went to kneel by Peter. Peter got up shakily and bravely faced the Durley priest.

One of the women put a cloak softly around Peter's shoulders. His eyes filled with tears, but he would not show weakness in front of the assembled people. Later, in the privacy of his own home, when his mother had dressed his hurts, he would probably cry his heart out.

"You have no power to do this thing, Swithun," I said, and my voice rang to the rafters.

"The power vested in me by..."

"NO! Punishments must, as was agreed by us all here at Durley a long time before you came here, be discussed by the village tithings, and then I must be given the facts. I will then decide if a punishment is necessary. I most certainly must be present when that punishment is carried out. I am Lord here, not you."

Swithun took a step towards me. "You are the lord

temporal. I, however, answer to a higher power and must carry out corrections as I see fit, for I am the Lord's instrument, His right hand, His scourge, and I must discipline my flock as I see fit."

"You may not do it without my permission, do you hear me? And I WILL NOT AND DO NOT GIVE YOU PERMISSION."

I was shouting at him. It is not my way, but I was so angry.

I moderated my tone. "You may, as is your right, expect your flock to perform any penances you deem fit for any spiritual transgressions they confess to you, but you may not take it upon yourself to administer physical punishments."

I beckoned Peter to me. I wanted to put my arm around his shoulder, but at the last moment, I remembered his bruises and cuts.

"Sit, Peter."

There was one bench at the side of the nave for the elderly and infirm to rest when at devotions. The rest of us had to stand.

"Sit, Father Swithun, here." I gestured to the other end of the bench.

He would not sit.

"All those who have nothing to say about this matter, please leave now."

Ten or twelve of the folk left, passing by Swithun with furious looks.

"Now I will listen to Father Swithun first. You will all keep silent until he has had his say."

The priest sneered at those of his flock who were still present and swirled his black cloak around him. The man loves the histrionic gesture, I thought.

"How did this begin?"

"Peter has charge of the bees in the orchard, as you know."

There was no 'sir' or 'my lord', no deferential tone, and so I exercised my right and said swiftly, "My lord…"

Swithun's eyes narrowed, and the skin around his nose became white with fury. He breathed hard.

"Sir," he said.

"Carry on."

"It is the right of the priest of this place to take for his own use fruit from the orchard. Indeed, with past usage, Father Benedict, the previous…"

"Yes, we know."

"He had charge of the bee skeps and the honey therein and was entitled to it."

"Benedict managed the bees himself, Swithun. Peter was his apprentice and help-mate for the last year. No one else in the manor had the skill or indeed more of a desire to look after them better than he."

"They are the property of the church. The bees should come to me as the next priest."

"They were willed to Peter by Father Benedict."

"They were not his to give."

The assembled people shuffled their feet. One man, our village blacksmith, Hubert, tutted and said under his breath, "Knows all about bees, does he?"

"Have you proof that the bees in their hives are the property of the church? A document, perhaps?"

Swithun was silent and stared me out.

"I have lived on this manor for thirty years. Some folk present have lived here longer. We do not remember the bees belonging to anyone but Benedict. In fact, I think I remember my father, Sir Geoffrey, who was born here and who lived forty years on this land, saying that there were no bee hives until Benedict came and that his knowledge with them was a boon to the village, for he shared willingly, the produce with every man, woman and child."

I folded my arms.

Swithun glared at me. "What was the priest Benedict's should now fall to me as my property."

I turned to Peter. "So what happened that you must be punished so, Peter?"

He stood, but I waved him down again. He was a good, brave, respectful lad who had proved his worth to me over and over.

"Sir," he began, looking swiftly at Swithun."

"Father Swithun came into the orchard this morning as I was looking at the skeps. He would not stay away as requested. You know how the bees can be angry if they are approached in the wrong way or by a stranger..."

"I am not a stranger."

I put up my hand to silence the priest. "We did not interrupt you. Please have the decency to reciprocate."

Swithun was incandescent with rage, "I have never been so insult..."

I shouted, "Stay longer and behave as you do, and you shall be!"

Some of the crowd tittered. I let the noise die down.

"Peter?"

"I asked him to stand away. He would not. I warned him. One of the bees stung him, and in his fury, he kicked over the whole hive."

"Foolish," I said.

"Then, when I had managed to right it and placate the bees, he told me that the bees were no longer mine and that I was not to come there any longer. I told him, as you have done, m'lord, that Benedict willed them to me and that I would not, begging his pardon, do as he requested, for, save a chap in Collingbourne, there was no one else to deal with and look after them."

"That is the right of it, Peter," I said.

"The orchard is for all of us, is it not, sir? We collect the produce, store and share it out, including the honey from my bees. Father Swithun has no right to forbid any of us to walk there, take our ease on the grass or for him to take the orchard into his own care. It is not his. It belongs to you, and you allow it for us all.

"Save his tithe, yes, his one-tenth," I said. "Which the village has always delivered willingly to the priest, time immemorial."

"I told him so. Then he struck me with the flat of his hand and told me to wait in the church."

People were nodding and muttering at this.

"He came in here a moment later. Some of the women were here, sweeping the floor and dusting, as they do."

There was a lot of nodding.

"He told everyone present that the orchard was out of bounds and that from now on, the bees were his."

"Who was here when this was said?"

Three women put up their hands.

"I ran out and fetched Father."

"He did not close the door and..."

"Silence, Swithun, you will have your turn."

John took up the tale. "Shall I speak now, sir?"

I nodded.

"In his hurry to fetch me, Peter left the door to the church open. When we returned, Father Swithun was frantically screaming that there were now birds in the church and that it was defiled."

"Swallows?"

"Yes, sir."

"But the swallows and the bats are always here. We just leave the door open for them to go out again. They can, after all, come in through the open windows should they wish. And they do now and again. It is no awful thing."

"They defile the Holy…"

"They are God's creatures, Swithun."

"Their excrement…"

I put up a hand to silence him.

"Ladies," I addressed my womenfolk. They tittered at being thus called by their lord.

"Is it a hazard or an onerous task for those of you who clean the church to rid it of the offerings of these small creatures?"

"No, sir…not at all, sir," they murmured together.

"You, I take it, Swithun, are not going to take it upon yourself to start cleaning the church?"

He drew himself up. "Certainly not."

"Then why do you complain? It is done for you. Go on, John."

"Some of the men had come in wondering what the shouting was. One, I think it was you, Edwin, said that the creatures were all belonging to God, for had He not created them all and saved them from the Flood with Noah."

"I did," said Edwin, who was a village elder of the village and a respected man.

"Then you, Tom, said that we were to have the animal blessing soon and that all God's creatures would be taken under the blessed wings of his angels for one more year, so what did it matter?"

I nodded.

Many churchmen went around the village at some time in the year blessing the animals, domestic, companion and kept animals, such as the sheep, chickens and pigs. It was something Benedict had done since I could remember.

"Father Swithun then said he was not going to do it, for animals had no souls, and there was nothing to bless."

Bessa, the woman in the village who kept the few cows we had here, scoffed at that. "Well, I know me cows give more milk when they are blessed, for sure, an' Old Blackballs the Bull, 'e is better at it when..."

There was a general lightening of tone as everyone laughed, except, of course, Swithun.

"That is your right, Swithun," I said eventually. "You can choose to bless or not bless as is your whim."

"But, sir..."

"No!" I silenced them all.

"If Swithun will not do it, I am sure that Father Godfrey from Bedwyn will do it for us. He is a kindly man," and I glared at Swithun.

They were more happy with that. They all nodded.

"So how did Peter come to be punished so?"

Peter's voice sang out again, echoing in the little church. His voice had broken last year and was now much more steady.

"I ran out into the churchyard after that and was going to go back to the manor when your hound bitch, sir, you know, the one who is a bit disturbed because she is so old..."

"Alceste?"

"Yes, she doesn't see so well now...and wanders a bit."

"Yes, she has milky eyes, but she is safe enough in the courtyard and the hall. What happened?"

Peter looked daggers at the priest. "She came out of the yard and for some reason, she thought I was you, I think. She reared up and greeted me. I gentled her ears and she went past me into the church, where she heard voices. I think she realised it wasn't you after all...by the smell, I should think... I think she thought you might be in the church."

"And I took exception to such a beast in the holy place," said Swithun, righteously.

"Sir priest" I said, beginning to be very angry indeed now,

"Alceste has been my faithful friend these past twelve or so years. She has always been allowed in this church. None of my beasts foul the house-places. None have ever fouled in here. They simply would not. They have been well trained. Why do you take exception to this animal coming into God's house?"

"It is just that...an animal." He looked down his nose at Peter.

I pinched the bridge of my own nose.

Peter could see that I was at the end of my tether. It was growing very dark now in the church.

"I came back in to fetch her out, for I knew he would be angry, and Father Swithun, he... lashed out and kicked poor Alceste."

"And Peter took a swipe at the priest because of it, sir," said John.

"Is Alceste all right?" I addressed Peter.

"Well...she yelped and whimpered, but I got her away from him, for he was kicking and kicking her."

There was a chorus of nods and noises of agreement from the assembly, who had seen this thing happen.

"The priest said he would discipline me. I was quite happy to take a few extra penances for poor old Alceste, sir. I took her back to the manor house, sir, and then the priest marched me back here and locked me in the robing room. I have been there some of the day without food and water."

"That is when I came for you, sir," said John. "His mother stayed here, and I came to find you."

"You did the right thing."

"After a long while, Father Swithun came and let me out. I thought that was it. Then he made me lie on the floor before the altar. I was there ...oh maybe till well after nones, and he prayed over me-that I would see the error of my way."

"That is when I came back, sir, to see Peter and found the priest preparing to beat him," said Agnes. "I ran out for some witnesses, for I thought that was the thing to do. This lot here, now, came in with me. He only managed three or four lashes, sir, thanks be to God, before Good Old Hal, here, came in and snatched the whip from him."

"I tried to talk some sense into the fathead," said my irreverent man-at-arms, Hal of Potterne. "Di'n't work. 'E screamed an' yelled and frothed at the mouth, the stupid fella...beggin' yer pardon,...well you know as 'ow that doesn't do much with me, sir. 'E might be a priest, but..." He preened his long, forked, grey beard.

"No, indeed, Hal." I tried not to smirk or chuckle.

"An' in you came, sir, then. Right as a bucket o' blood."

I let the silence run on a little. Then, I moved up to the altar. I stood on the little step before it.

"This is my word," I said. "The orchard remains for us all to use. The bees will remain in Peter's care. I will talk to the Bishop of Salisbury and examine the manor records to see if the bee skeps are indeed the property of the church. If we find that they are, Swithun is welcome to them."

There was a collective gasp.

I raised my voice. "If they are, and the village loses the bees, we shall set up our own skeps elsewhere and ensure that there is sufficient blossom for them, even if this means planting another orchard. Peter will be our apiarist."

The company sighed.

"As to the animal blessing. I will speak to the priest of Bedwyn. You all know him. He helped us out before Father Swithun came to us. He will help again, I am sure."

People were nodding, and you could tell things were returning to normal.

"As to my dog, Alceste, any one who mistreats her will answer directly to me. She is, I am sure, not long for this world. I would have her end times with us as happy as we can make them. Peter, watch her carefully. Do not let her into the church again. Tell everyone to watch out for her."

"No, sir. Yes, sir."

"The swallows will be gone in a few weeks. I will think hard about what to do about the problem of them getting into the church so that we do not have a repeat of this fracas next year. I am about to have glass put into the solar window spaces. Perhaps I can do the same here. Also, I have thought for a while now thought that a porch on the church might be a good idea. We shall discuss it and see if this is something we might build."

There was a general muttering, and I saw Father Swithun's head nod.

"Father," I turned to address him specially. "This manor is run by and for people who have the welfare of each other at heart. Our systems work. Our hierarchy works. We are happy with it, and we discuss all changes to be made in our village committee, a group of ten elder men-headed by Walter Reeve. I suggest if you wish to keep the peace, you would do well to remember that. You cannot and will not take to yourself any corporal punishment without first consulting the committee and myself. Is that clear?"

"I will appeal to my bishop."

"Please do. He is my godfather," I turned away. "Peter, I know why you did it—and, I admit, the provocation was severe—and you are now punished for it. Never again strike the priest. Please apologise."

Peter looked defiant and then faced Father Swithun. "I am sorry, Father," he said weakly.

Father Swithun scowled. "Father, please apologise to Peter for striking him."

There was a collective indrawn breath as all those present swivelled their eyes to the priest.

Would he do it? A churchman apologise to a boy of thirteen?

"I will not." And he stalked off out of the church and slammed the door.

Now I know why Henry the Second, our present King John's father, was so vexed by the church. His words...those he is supposed to have said aloud, came into my head: "Who will rid me of this turbulent priest?"

I shook my head, No. I could not think like that. Look where it had got Henry.

My stomach gave a huge grumble. I really would go now, and have some supper.

After my supper—a good thick soup of quail and partridge, birds which abounded on the downs, some white loaf and some wonderful plum syrup made with plums given to us by my dead wife's mother and Hawise's grandmother... ah, so she had been in today to see my daughter—I took out the little sketch book again. I scrutinised the drawings made by Alan of Didcot. No matter how I looked at that little scribbling, I could not make it anything other than two men in a passionate embrace and kissing.

In my youth, there had been stories about our Good King Richard. How he had taken lovers, discreetly, yes, but that he was one who preferred the company of a man. I knew that this kind of behaviour went on back into the times of the Romans and Greeks, for I had heard it called the Greek disease. To me, it was no disease. It was merely a preference for one's own kind, though I dared not say it aloud, and I only write it here because I am an old man and will be dead before anyone can worry about what I think.

Oh, do not worry, Paul, my scribe. All you need to do is write this down for me. You will not be thought wicked because you have written it. After all, these are my words, not your own. What? You think that some of the brethren at the priory...no, Paul, no, do not even think of it. It is their business and not yours, though I have to say, with so many men locked up together down there, I would not be in the slightest bit surprised.

Those churchmen who railed against it as being against the laws of man and God, *peccatum contra naturam*—sins against nature—obviously did not know anything about the natural world, for man was not the only beast to indulge in such practices. I had known foxes and rams who yielded to such behaviours, and I am sure there were many other animals that did.

What de Saye and Gerald of Broughton were or were not to each other was none of my business.

Except it could be a motive for murder.

I sat long, sipping my wine and staring at the flames that night. Gerald and Guy had been seen. Yes, perhaps Gerald of Broughton, feeling that he was about to lose his lover to her, might have acquired some poison and somehow got this into Matilda's wine cup in that little locked room.

Why, though, was Guy killed? That was not what Gerald wanted.

Had Alan drawn his little picture as evidence of their affair and then shown it to them to extract money? Was this why he was killed? If that is the case, who hid the bag and book, and why did they not destroy it? I would.

And where was the murder weapon which killed Guy?

That question would be answered before the next day was out.

I rose to a fine misty dawn and vowed to sit in my office before I broke my fast.

As promised, I went through the manorial records looking for references to the bees in the orchard, but could find nothing before the time of Benedict, who had come to the manor in 1171 as a young man. Not what Father Swithun wanted to hear.

I also wrote a letter, which I would take with me to the town later that day, to my master glazier. Perhaps he would kindly come out to Durley once more and tell me how much the church windows would cost to glaze.

The porch building would have to wait.

I packed up my horse once more and sailed into Marlborough, resisting the urge to stop at Johannes' house to speak with Mistress Wolvercote again.

Today, I wanted to look at the little locked room once more. There must be something we had missed.

The room was no longer locked, the door had not yet been mended and the key was in the door. I took it out and looked at it. It was an ordinary iron key about three inches long. I set it in the lock on the inside. I jiggled it. I turned it. I fiddled it. There really was nothing special about how the door was locked, as far as I could tell.

I walked around the walls, my eyes carefully scanning every tiny undulation of the plastered white painted stone—nothing. I lay on the floor and scanned the wooden boards.

I rose, dusted myself down and walked to the window on the courtyard side. There was the space where Stephen and Peter had practised staves on the day of the murder. I was one floor down from where I had spotted them; I could see no more from here, but just over the rooftops, I could see the forest up the Granham hill. I turned about and walked to the other small window. This window faced north-west. It was a long drop to the slippery grassed sides of the motte and the water of the moat beyond it.

It had been a very dry year. The little rivers which populated the chalk downs shrank to mere trickles in such years, and some dried up altogether and, it was said, disappeared underground. The Kennet had been shrinking by the day. It was never a really deep river anyway, along all its journey to the Thames. In Marlborough and all along its length locally, it was broken up in places into several different streams, dividing, forming islands, and joining again, merging with the Og just past Marlborough town. It spread out into boggy places and trickled over gravel where it was easily fordable. There were one or two deeper parts, but in the main, it was a shallow river. The Kennet had been diverted for the moat of the castle. The water passed right around the outer bailey, in a square shape, under the bridge and circled the round motte upon which the four-storey keep stood.

As the river dwindled, so did the castle moat. There were sluices to prevent this, but we were living in peaceful times, and no one had thought to apply them.

I looked down at the green waters, sluggishly sailing by. I imagined a siege here with me pinned inside. Would the moat save us? Was it deep enough to deter even the most accomplished swimmers? Might the besiegers be able to fill in the depth with rocks and cross dry-shod? Might they build a small fortified bridge? The inner bailey, which was quite narrow, would be yet another obstacle to achieve, even if you managed to scale the outer walls, and missiles would be raining down on you.

But here, just here, the wall was so close to the motte. There was a matter of just two feet or so between the edge of the water of the moat and the wooden paling surrounding it, and then the twenty feet of water.

I opened the shutters as fully as I could. I hoisted myself onto the sill and wriggled my shoulder sideways out of the window, holding on tight with my thighs to the 'V' shaped aperture. I looked straight down.

Yes, it could be done, a boat perhaps. A rope up to the keep. But AH how would you get in?

I was tall, not a hugely built man, but bigger than many. From the inside, I could get myself partly out of the aperture. My shoulders were well developed. There was no way a man could get in from the outside, for the gap was a mere twelve inches wide on the inside. Even a tiny creature like Pixie or Agnes could not do it.

As I deliberated, my eye raked the daily receding waters of the bank. The plants here were kept down so that men who might manage to swim the moat would have no purchase to drag themselves up. The green water sailed sluggishly by.

There, on the very edge of the moat, was a white speck. I rubbed my eyes. The white speck became something which looked much more interesting. It was certainly a foreign object on the bank of the moat, but not a piece of detritus washed up, not a plant or stone.

I wriggled back, and my feet felt for the floor.

I careered down the steps and into the room below next to my own cubbyhole. Several scribes looked up as I entered.

Again, I squeezed into the window embrasure.

Yes, it was interesting.

"Sorry, lads," I said as I sped past them again and down one more flight of stairs.

The next room down was a store room. The windows here were even narrower. I could just see out at the edge of the moat.

I cried aloud, "Yes! It's there!" and a sleepy head poked

round a large tun of wine.

"Hello Ansell," I said. "Sorry to disturb you."

Ansell was the castle victualler. It looked as if he had been having a nap. By rights, he should have been checking stores, measuring, weighing and taking delivery of goods destined for the kitchens, but not today.

"Hello, sir," he beamed. "Can I do something for you?"

"Yes, poke your little head out of that window, look straight down and tell me what you think you see at the water's edge."

Ansell looked puzzled, but he did as he was asked.

His shoulders were not as well developed as mine, for he did not practise with sword and buckler every day as I did with my men-at-arms.

"It's…" wriggle, "I think," squirm, "Yes… I think it's a piece of ivory or bone, sir."

"Yes! I'm right!" I yelled to myself and sped out of the storeroom, calling, "Thank you, Ansell!"

I ran down the keep steps and into the outer bailey. I pelted over the bridge, dodging a couple of people coming in with packs on their backs. I ran onto the road in front of the Church of St Peter. I careered around the corner into the area known as the Barton, for there had been barns there long ago, and I fell foul of a party of nuns trudging down the narrow path. I politely waited for them to pass, and then I was off again.

I skidded to a halt and the keep reared up above me. I screwed up my eyes and scanned the further bank just below the wall and the windows out of which I had looked. I counted to make sure I had the right place.

My eyes passed down the white plastered surface of the building.

There, about twenty feet away, was a knife, hilt up in the mud of the bank. Then, it was a mad dash back to the gatehouse and the officer of the watch.

Why was I running? I slowed as I reached the bridge. Unless it rained and it would not today, I was sure, my knife was safe in the mud. I could retrieve it.

Sadly, the officer was not Andrew Merriman but a much slower man called Edouard Picot. I explained that I needed a small boat and someone to row it.

I explained why.

He perked up. This was more exciting than watching folk with packs and carts come in and out of the castle.

He disappeared into the depths of the gatehouse and came out with a young lad of about twelve. I recognised him.

"Hello, my lad," I said. "Fancy helping me again?"

It was one of the boys who had been dismantling the booths at the fair and the one who had helped me catch Gerald of Broughton.

"For another penny, sir?" he asked.

"You drive a hard bargain. You are...?"

He grinned. "Perkin Fisher."

Picot said, "He has a skiff. He'll fetch it for you to the bridge, then he'll row you round. I'll follow on foot and meet you there, sir."

I waited on the bridge, and Perkin brought his unsavoury little craft to the edge. I carefully lowered myself into it. Yes, I could swim, but I did not wish to get a dunking today, thank you. Edouard walked around on the bank with us.

Round the keep, we rowed. The water level, I could now see, had dropped by about eight inches. The level was visible by the dryness of the bank and the mud left at the edge by the receding water.

"Stop!" I pointed. "Now there...row me there."

Perkin manoeuvred his little boat close to the moat edge.

I leaned gingerly out of the boat. My hand closed around the hilt of a small knife with an ivory handle. Apart from the fact that it had been submerged in the moat and stuck in the mud, it looked quite new and unharmed.

"Got it!" I cried out to Edouard.

We rowed back, and I paid my debt.

I took the little thing to the horse trough and washed off the mud. Edouard watched over my shoulder, as did Perkin. No blood was on it now; it had been thoroughly cleansed by its sojourn in the moat. It was still quite sharp, though.

"It's an eating knife...the sort a lady might use to pare an apple," said Picot.

"Sweet little thing, ain't it?" said Perkin.

"Yes," I answered quietly, "and a very nasty murder weapon."

Chapter Six

I wasn't prepared to let the coroner know that I had possibly found the weapon which had killed Guy de Saye just yet.

I needed to show it to Johannes.

I wiped it carefully on a rag. It was about six inches long, easy to secrete in the hand or up a sleeve. The ivory hilt was carved into the shape of a tiny woman holding a stringed instrument. I couldn't make out what it was.

It didn't look old, for the dress was of the fashion worn today and the hair of the woman was rolled up either side of her head in two curls like a ram's horns, held in place by a sort of net, the latest fancy for high-born ladies, I was told.

This was not a thing disposed of lightly. It was, for one thing, no cheap item. Anyone who had lost it would be most upset and would no doubt do everything in their power to retrieve it.

There, in the moat, it had lain for quite a few days.

I was, for some reason, convinced that the little eating knife—for I agreed with Picot as to its use—was not lost accidentally but thrown deliberately from the window. I needed to ask Johannes if he thought the wound on Guy's neck might have been made by this little creature.

I wrapped it in a rag and set off on foot down the High Street.

I rapped with my knuckles on the wood of the front door so I might be heard from the kitchen. Mistress Wolvercote was away from home this time, no doubt visiting some of the shops in the town, and the usually open front door was closed. This also meant that either Johannes was away from home with a patient or his doctoring room was not functioning today.

It was the latter, for he came striding down the passageway from the back room. I heard his distinctive tread on the flags, and then he flung open the door.

"Ah, come on in," he said. "I am looking for a drinking partner."

"Hmmm, drinking alone is no fun," I chuckled.

Johannes slid himself onto a bench and put his booted feet up on a stool. He prised them off his feet, one with the other. "Had a hard day, and it's not yet dinner time. Well, to be truthful, I have had a hard night, and I haven't been to bed yet."

"Called out in the middle of the night?"

"You have it right." He swirled the wine in his cup round and round and looked morose.

"It didn't go well?"

"No." He stood and replenished his cup.

"I hate losing patients, Aumary," he said. "Especially young ones. Somehow, I feel I have failed them personally, but we know so pitifully little, it is sometimes hard to know what to do for the best."

"That is all you can do, your best, Johannes," I said quietly.

He looked up. "Aye."

Putting down his cup, he ruffled his hair, now greying at the temples a little, which he had let free, for he normally wore his hair long and tied back in a queue. Then he re-tied it with a black leather thong.

"So, what news do you have for me?"

I took out the little knife and showed it to him, giving him a shortened story of its discovery. He held it in his palm.

"One of those little moments in life in which you wonder why you did what you did, until it all becomes clear later."

"That's true...I have no real idea what made me look out of the window with such diligence."

"Some would say it was the hand of God guiding you."

I smiled. "My own insatiable curiosity. I was wondering what it would be like to be besieged in the castle and wanted to see how well the moat, as it stands, would protect us in the keep. Just a thought that came into my head for no reason. That, and I was wondering about putting glass in the church windows at Durley..."

"Wha..."

"It's a long story which I will tell you sometime soon. And I was looking at the apertures and wondering if they were about the same as ours at the church. I saw the hilt, a fraction of it, poking out of the mud. It occurred to me that if someone had thrown the knife from the upper window, it might have landed about there, when there was water to cover it. Of course, the moat has receded in the drought."

"Which accounts for the small splash, only a small splash you said you heard, for it landed in less water. It hadn't been flung out into the middle of the moat, and, of course, it was stuck in mud."

"I remember everything had gone quiet just at that moment in time," I said. "No one upstairs was speaking. My table is close to the door, which I leave open, or I would need candles every minute of the day. I have no windows, so I don't always hear what happens around and about. The nearest window is in the corridor about five feet away. I do hear things coming through there, for it seems as if the sound is funnelled into the passage and thence into my tiny room."

"And, of course, you hear what goes on above you."

"I do. I'm one floor down and nearer the mud," I laughed.

Johannes turned the knife over. "It's an expensive item. If it is our murder weapon, then someone was surely desperate to rid themselves of it in such a fashion. Many would have done the deed, hidden it on their person and hastily made their exit so as not to lose such a valuable and, I must say, pretty thing."

"Except, of course, no one came out. No one went in. The room was locked from the inside. Two dead bodies and a knife and a slip of poison and no one upon whom to fasten our murders."

We lapsed into silence.

Then I remembered my other piece of news.

"And then there is this..." I rummaged in my purse for the little sketch book and held it out to him."

"What's this?"

"I have found some of the limner's tools. This was with them. They were stuffed into a bag and concealed behind the altar at St Peter's. I had cause to go in there and found that he had been executing a private commission on the west wall there for Gilbert Cordwainer. Green paint. There was an abundance of the right colour green paint there, too; the paint we saw on Alan's palms and in his fingernails when we brought him in dead. So, my mind naturally progressed to the question of whether the tools were still there. I searched, and they were. Or maybe some of them were."

Whilst I had been talking, Johannes had been flicking

over the pages of the little book, smiling at some of the images there, just as I had done.

"He was quite the jester, was he not, this clever painter? Do you recognise some of the people he has drawn? I do." He turned the book towards me. "Here is Master Gallipot... hahaha, as a lizard." He flicked the next page, "and Mistress Magda Fuller as a swan. Very apt, that one." Johannes turned another page and tilted his head to look. "And well, I never, Nicholas Barbflet as a fish! Oh, how comical."

"There is one which is not so funny," I said. I took the book back. "Here."

Johannes frowned and then looked. His eyebrows shot up into his hair. "Is this what I think it is?" Johannes whistled.

"Sir Guy de Saye and his palfreyman, Gerald of Broughton? I believe so. Yes."

"They are very good likenesses, even if they are almost in profile. Of course, I saw de Saye about town a few times, but I am less familiar with Broughton."

"It is them."

"Well, you would know."

He turned the book again. "Well, well, what do you know...it's ME!"

"I craned my neck.

"Me as a ...the cheek of it...a leech!"

I smiled...well...he was a doctor.

"Look at my teeth, Aumary. Are my teeth really as awful as that?"

"No, not at all," I said confidently.

After a while, we laid the little book aside and digested the information gained from it. Both of us believed that it was certainly something which could be used to blackmail the two men. Enough for one or both to commit murder? Alan of Didcot was obviously aware of the relationship between the two men.

We sat in silence and we heard Mistress Wolvercote return to the kitchen and bustle about.

"So, do you think that little knife was the weapon used to stab de Saye in the throat so that he bled to death?" I asked eventually. "We cannot now go and compare the wound with the blade. He is nailed down in a lead-lined coffin, ready for his last journey home, and lies in the castle chapel."

Johannes stared at the knife. "We shall never know for certain, but yes, I think it might be the murder weapon. Yes, I do think it."

We parted, and I looked in quickly at the kitchen just to say hello. I did not linger, though I dearly would have loved to, and I fancied that Lydia's face fell when I said that I had to leave.

There was one more task I had to do, and I had to do it quickly, for the bodies were ready to go home.

I slipped into the chapel at the castle. It was a small building sturdily constructed with lancet windows only a little wider than that of the keep and so quite a dark place.

Before the altar were two coffins on trestles. At least they were lying together now, I thought, almost side by side, de Saye and Broughton, except one was laid in fine wood and on a white embroidered cloth with gold work and tassels to the edge, and the other was plain deal and was laid on a sagging black cloth, which had faded to brown and which had definitely seen better days.

There were black candles burning on the altar, however. Expensive, I thought, and probably bought by de Saye's father. Matilda was not there. She had been removed fairly quickly, I recalled, and taken to St Mary's at the top end of town.

De Saye's coffin was closed, Gerald's was, as yet, still open, but the body was wound round and round with a cloth as a shroud, covering every piece of him, and I could see nothing. I checked the chapel; there was nothing there that did not belong.

I hailed the cheerful Edouard as I left the chapel and asked him the whereabouts of the possessions of the dead man, Broughton.

He scratched his chin thoughtfully, making a rasping sound in the bristles.

"I think they went, yes...they went into the store to be sold when next we have a sale. His lord didn't want 'em, he said."

"A sale?

"Stuff as is lost in the castle and not claimed or has got nowhere to go—like his stuff—well we collect it all together, and then we has a sale of it all, amongst us, the garrison at the castle, and we sends the money to the priory for the poor." Picot puffed out his chest.

"Very commendable," I said. Under my breath, I said, "Do you hell as like!"

"Have you his stuff somewhere now?"

"Should be under the stairs. Hang on a moment, sir."

And the little man bustled off somewhere into the depths of the gatehouse. He came back with a sizable pack. "This was 'is, I think."

"Might I use your table, Eduoard?"

He dumped the pack on to the scrubbed board.

I undid the straps. Everything was stuffed in haphazardly as if someone had picked up everything the man had owned and just pushed it in with no thought or method. Naturally, when the man had been pronounced dead, someone had had to deal with everything he owned, and they had just grabbed it and got rid of it.

There was nothing of value: a moth-eaten blanket, smelling of horses; a wooden plate, rough-hewn; and a bit of metal, which looked like some accoutrement for a horse, but I had no idea what. The pack itself was of good quality, and the leather was supple.

What the man had of any value, no doubt, had been pilfered by the garrison and maybe his companion horsemen before the rest was stuffed into this pack.

There were no clothes, for example, no spare hose or shirts. The man was not so poor as he couldn't afford a spare shirt.

There were no bits and pieces as a man collects over his life; even a man none too wealthy but one who was a valued member of a noble household and well thought of. No belt. No spare shoes.

"Where are his spare clothes, Edouard?" I asked

"Ah, they went to the priory for the poor straightways. We knew he was dead, and there wasn't no one to claim nothing. As did them he was drowned in sir."

I thought about the ruined boots. I would look about town for those, I thought.

"And there should have been some money. No doubt you never found any money, did you?"

"Money...?" he sucked his teeth. "No, no money, m'lord."

I dug deeper. There was another bag. I pulled it out.

Here was the rest of Alan of Didcot's painting equipment. Most of these were carefully packed in a roll—tidily, as Alan would have packed them, no doubt—kept in place by ribbons and string ties. Whoever had gone through the pack had missed these or had not known their worth or understood their meaning.

"He had little of value," I said.

"Just a silly little book thing with drawings in...made us laugh it did when we saw it."

My ears pricked up. "Where is it now, this book?"

"Oh, is it not in there then?" He leaned dramatically

over my shoulder and the pack and stared in. "It were with a load of pens and inks, though why he had those I dunno, he couldn't read nor write. 'Spose it were to do them funny little drawings. Really good they are."

"That book did not belong to de Broughton but to the murdered man, Alan of Didcot, the painter who was found in my forest. I would like it back," I said strongly.

He righted himself. "You would?"

"I would, and I would be willing to pay for it."

"How much then?"

The book was in my hand. It was the sister piece to the one I had left with Johannes. This, I think, was a newer one, for the pages were not so filled up, and there were some blank ones at the end.

Here were more drawings of people. I recognised de Neville with his slight paunch looking for all the world like an owl, even down to the tufts of hair which came out of his ears, and the garrison priest, Father Columba, with his spiky tonsure, was tricked out as a hedgehog.

I smiled. Oh, what a talent had been lost.

There were no salacious drawings at all. Why did de Broughton have this one and not the one with his picture in it?

Perhaps this was the only one he could find. Perhaps he thought this would be the incriminating one and found too late that it wasn't. I did not look carefully through the whole book.

One thing, though.

If de Broughton had the rest of Alan's painting equipment in his pack, it meant that he had either waylaid the limner coming home through the forest from Hungerford or found him in the town somewhere when he returned.

Alan had taken some equipment with which to work to that town and it had come back with him, for we know none was left there. Nothing was found with the body.

What was de Broughton doing with the painter's tools?

I suspected he'd pilfered them from the church.

Did he think he might sell them when he reached home in Oxfordshire, far enough from the scene of the crime not to connect him to it? There were enough scriptoriums in the locality to take such stuff. Oxford was a mere thirty-two miles away as the crow flew. The place was stuffed with scribes and limners. Wroxton Abbey was a few miles away. Yes, that was a possibility.

And he had the dead man's boots. He had gone to his death in that mill race, proclaiming his guilt. He had not needed to run at all. Certainly, he had not needed to draw a knife in anger.

That was enough for me.

The little maid servant Agnes had been living in the guest accommodation at the priory, but with her mistress dead and the body now on its way to burial in Lincolnshire, she was very much left to her own devices. By rights, she should have gone back to the manor with the body, but no one had given her any instructions, no one had contacted her, and she had been totally ignored. Servants are used to being ordered and marshalled. I had noticed before that if they must suddenly think for themselves, they were often at a loss as to what to do. If there had been any other women in the party, perhaps something might have been done for her, but they were all men, and men, it seems, do not give much thought to the role of a now redundant lady's maid.

Men from the estate came with a cart to collect Matilda's body. The de Neville party from the castle, all men, had gone with them early that morning, save a few who were permanently stationed in Marlborough castle.

No one here knew Agnes, for she had been at Amesbury Abbey with Matilda all her life and would have gone with her to her new married life, somewhere near Witney, I believe, where the young de Saye had a house. The priory really didn't want her. The castle didn't want her. She had nowhere to go.

I found her moping on the High the next day when I strode out of the castle gatehouse and into the sunshine of yet another beautiful, warm September day.

She followed me along the street a few yards behind, trailing her feet and twirling a strand of her curly chestnut hair around her finger.

"Do you want something, Agnes?" I asked.

She shook her head.

"Have you nothing you must be doing?"

She hadn't.

"Are you not going back to Lincolnshire with your mistress, maid?" I asked.

No.

"You have never been there, have you?"

No.

Suddenly, I heard the running of several feet and yelling. I turned quickly.

"There's the witch! Grab her!"

Two of de Neville's men from the castle and several from the town tried to surround us and they began to taunt Agnes.

I pushed the little woman behind me and drew my sword.

"Let no man touch this woman who first doesn't want to deal with me!" I yelled over the noise.

The yelling continued, but it was a fraction less violent. "What is the matter with you all?"

I singled out the two castle soldiers. "Gilbertson, Brooks, get back to the castle."

The two men stood their ground. "Sir...this woman... she's a witch. You know she was there when..."

"She is no more a witch than you are, Brooks. Do as I say...move off."

A man from the town I had seen working at the slaughteryard on the High Street stepped forward.

"She needs arresting, she does," he said. "She's a killer and a witch."

"She's a woman like any other and no witch."

"She got through that locked door."

"I was there, Gilbertson. She did not get through that door."

"But, sir. She must have. There's no one else. She looks like a witch. You can see she does."

"Oh, and how does a witch look, Brooks?" shouted a woman coming across the road. "You seen any lately? Familiar with 'em, are you? Your ol' woman a witch then?"

"Aye, she is a witch," said another man, pointing at Agnes. "She can shrink herself to go under the door like smoke and reappear the other side."

Agnes grabbed onto my surcoat and squeezed the material of it.

"If you believe that, then you are stupid," I said. "Are you stupid, Jonson?"

There was a little titter from some onlookers who had come up to watch the confrontation. They drew slightly closer.

Jonson jutted his chin but remained silent.

"This woman was maid to the dead Matilda de Neville. She has nothing to gain by killing her mistress, nor the Lady Matilda's affianced. In fact, it has made her homeless and masterless. Do you think a clever witch would do that? Gilbertson, Jonson?" I turned around, "Brooks?"

A woman who had come up from her shopping at the baxter's raised her voice. "Leave her alone, Hamon. You're just looking for trouble. Just 'cos she's smaller than you are!"

More tittering.

Two more women came up and stood by her. A second yelled coarsely at the slaughterhouse man. "You can't get yer own way and bully yer own women folk at 'ome, so yer try someone else, yer coward." She laughed, "Go on yer paltry pizzle. Go 'ome to yer wife. She's got a bigger pizzle than you 'ave!"

Hamon Jonson growled into his beard.

Folk laughed. "Fat lot of good you are to her!"

Gilbertson shouted the woman down. "She's a witch, I tell you."

"You'll all sing a different tune when it's you she's cursin' and your pigs that are dyin'," said the slaughterhouse man again.

Agnes violently shook her head. I felt her move closer behind me. I threw my arm over her shoulder.

"How can she curse yer, yer daft loon, when the poor chit in't got a voice to curse with?" said the same woman.

"God's teeth, Hamon, I really don't know how yer wife puts up with yer stupidity!" Another woman now became brave enough to join in. "There's only one person who does damage to pigs here, and it's you, Hamon Jonson." She made a gesture like someone cutting a throat.

There was another titter of laughter. The crowd was growing.

"Go back to the castle and back to your homes. There'll be no arresting of witches today," I said loudly.

The two castle men stepped forward.

"If you do not obey me, I will have you flogged!" I

shouted. "Do not doubt it."

They stopped and muttered.

"An' I'll be the one to do it! "said a voice coming up behind me.

"Hal!"

"An' I in't kind…oh no I'm not!" he finished.

He took out his sword deliberately and slowly.

We now had quite a crowd.

About seventeen people on one side were with the castle men, the slaughterhouse man and his friends, and twenty or so people were ranged behind me. Most of them, I have to say, were women.

Some men behind me had weapons of sorts: spades, billhooks, and sticks. One woman brandished a rather hard-looking loaf. I expect it was destined for a trencher. I looked around.

"Thank you, my good friends," I said, "but we need no help against these…" I turned back to the opposition, "misguided men."

Nick Barbflet, the town reeve, came running up. "What goes on here?"

"Master Barbflet, arrest that witch. She has murdered her mistress, sir."

Nick looked in disgust at the man who had spoken. "What…arrest that little thing? Why, she's no bigger than a child. You'd have me arrest a four-year-old, Philip?"

The women cackled in laughter again.

"You think this creature could overpower a knight?" Nick put his hands on his hips and laughed. "I'd like to see it."

Agnes drew even closer to me.

"Sir Guy de Saye was a young and deadly knight!" I yelled. "How could such a small woman overpower him?" I asked, taking up Nick's idea, though I knew in truth that Guy de Saye had been nothing of the sort.

"By magic, that's how!" shouted a townsman.

"That's ridiculous, Tom!" answered Nick, laughing derisorily.

"If this woman is a witch..." said one of the women defending Agnes, "Do you think she'd let you get away with the things you've said, Thomas Fuller?"

There was an immediate silence.

"Nah. She'd fly at you and tear out yer eyes...and there'd be nothin' you could do about it. 'Coz she'd hex you, she would." She pointed her hands out in front of her face and wiggled them.

"Aye, I think she wouldn't be standin' there with her mouth open, lookin' like she's about to piss with fright," said another woman.

The woman came up behind me and put her arm around Agnes' shoulders.

"If you're a witch, girl, my advice to you is to rise up in the air and make that man's pizzle shrink and drop off... that's what!"

Agnes' eyes were huge in her face. I don't believe she had ever heard such language from a woman, living as she had amongst the quietness and sobriety of nuns all her life.

There was no movement and no noise.

"Let's all go home and say no more about it," said Nicholas.

Some of the men at the back of the hostile crowd muttered and moved off.

"The constable has told you to go back to the castle. If you don't go...'e'll have you flogged," reiterated Hal with a nasty growl. "An' I know 'e's a man of 'is word."

"And the lock-up is empty. I reckon I can get about twelve of you in there," said Nick.

"Your wives'll have to bail you out, and you won't like that. Go home and back to your jobs. NOW!"

Another woman scoffed. "Nah! Plain evil. I'd never be parting with money for the likes of you!"

I looked at Nick. His face was furious.

His townsmen thought better of it and began sullenly to trickle away.

Gilbertson and Brooks sniffed, wiped their sleeves over their mouths and turned for the castle with a backward look, their eyes narrow and angry.

"You'll need to watch those two, sir," said Hal quietly.

He turned to the town's women. "Thank you, Mary, Gytha, Frida," he said and winked at them.

Agnes looked on, her mouth still open, but at least her colour was returning. The woman who had her arm around her shoulders now stood up straight.

"All right, Hal of Potterne?"

"All right, Yvonnet of Potterne."

The woman nodded. Hal winked again.

The woman curtsied to me and gave Agnes a pat on the shoulder. "You have any trouble with them poxed pizzles again, lass, you let me know." And she hefted her bread upon her shoulder like a pike and strode off down the dusty road.

I cleared my throat and replaced my sword. "Thank you, Hal. Thanks, Nick."

Nick watched the folk trickling away. "I don't like it, Aumary."

I shook my head. "We'll need to keep an eye out."

"I will," said Nick, backing off. He touched Agnes gently as he left.

"All right, Agnes?" Hal asked.

She swallowed and nodded.

"C'mon then." Hal put his arm over the tiny woman's shoulders, and we made our way up the road.

"Are you a free woman, Agnes?" I asked. If she were

not, she would be a runaway villein, and that would not be good for her.

She shrugged her shoulders.

"Can you not go back to Amesbury Abbey?"

She violently shook her head. It was obvious that the contemplative life was not for her.

I sighed.

"There may, I suppose, be a place for you somewhere here in Marlborough. Some of the women fancy themselves fine ladies in need of a lady's maid."

I turned and walked on, and she came up level with me.

"The richer their husbands become, the more money they make at wool, or spinning, or weaving, the finer these women fancy themselves. It might be possible to find you somewhere to live, though it won't be as grand, mind, as a fine house in Witney."

She grinned up at me.

"And we might meet a bit of opposition, like we have just now." I shook my head. "Come, I've a mind to ask you some more questions. I am going to Doctor Johannes of Salerno's House up by the church of St Mary. Will you walk up there with me and write me some answers like you did before?"

Agnes, her terror gone, smiled up at me. The little maid skipped a few times in front of me, then picked up her dusty skirts and ran on ahead of me a little way, leaving Hal chuckling behind us. She had recovered quickly. She turned in skipping circles.

I took that as a yes.

We sat in the kitchen of Johannes' house with four pots of newly brewed ale, while I brought the doctor up to date with my finds and with the frightening episode on the High Street.

Hal sat quietly in the corner and sipped his ale. "My word, you have been busy," he said. "Another book, eh?"

"But nothing in it to make us sit up and think...except the simple fact that he had it just proves that he took it from Alan the painter after he killed him. And, of course, his boots."

"Where did he kill him?"

"I don't think we shall ever really know. If it was in the forest, it could have been anywhere. There will be no evidence after all this time. I don't think he was killed where he lay, though. He was definitely hidden from sight. Perhaps he was waylaid coming back from Hungerford."

"Could he have been killed in the little church where he was working and his body taken out to the forest and dumped?"

"It might account for the concealed bag behind the altar. Maybe the two of them found him in the church and decided to kill him. In a panic, he hid the bag in the church, and then they found him, and... No, he took a second bag to Hungerford with him. He must have hidden the first before he left."

"How would they get the body out and away?"

I shrugged. "There are a lot of comings and goings to and from the castle. Would anyone notice if they had a sack or a bundle in a cart?"

While we were discussing the minutiae of the murder of Alan of Didcot, Agnes had been thumbing through the little book of drawings that Johannes had lain on the table top. We would hear her laugh silently through her nose as she recognised the various pictures of the few people she knew.

Suddenly, she sat up.

She flapped her hands at us both.

"What is it, maid? "asked Johannes.

She turned the book around to face me. It was upside

down. When I had first seen it, I had not, as I had with the original book, turned it this way and that. I had simply been looking for more drawings like the one in the first book: two men.

Agnes pointed.

There, under her finger, was a drawing of part of the church. The columns were drawn receding down the nave. Behind one of these nearer columns was drawn the back of a man. I could see the back of his head and his gloved hand resting on the pommel of his sword, his elbow jutting out behind him. Then came the back of his cotte and the heel of his boots.

A noble man, for he wore a sword and spurs.

On the other side of the column was another man, closely facing him. He wore a hooded tunic and was booted and spurred. No sword, but I fancied I caught the lines of a knife hilt, drawn stuck into a scabbard at his hip.

Above the drawing, there were tiny words.

I stared at them and then shifted my gaze to Agnes, who was nodding furiously. I read the words aloud. "Will have to die. Has heard us. We must kill him."

We stared at each other.

Alan had recorded this conversation in his little book.

"What had he heard?" asked Johannes.

"The two of them billing and cooing, I expect. Maybe they used the church as a trysting place. The cordwainer told me that Alan used to sit long at his painting, well into the night."

"Then let us imagine..." Johannes took his ale cup and mine. "This is de Saye, this Broughton. They are behind a pillar in the church." He reached over and picked up a rolled-up parchment and put it between them, balancing it carefully on its end on the table top. "Here is Alan at the west end." He reached for Agnes' cup and placed it further away. "Perhaps he has fallen asleep at his painting, up on his scaffolding?"

"Well, of course, how foolish of me not to realise. He cannot have painted the cordwainer's picture standing on the ground, can he? He must have had some steps or some boards on which to stand, for he is almost fifteen feet up from the ground."

"Precisely."

"Scaffolding. I saw the remains of it in the church." "Hidden."

"If he lies prone on his boards. He can see and hear everything that goes on. It is dark up near the roof beams by the west door. His candle has gone out. He wakes. He hears them. They may not see or hear him" I said.

"Right!"

"Ah but it would be dark in the body of the church. It is not yet consecrated. Not even a sanctuary light to give some form to the people. How would he see them?"

"De Saye and Broughton might have brought their own light. Perhaps a dark lantern?"

"Yes. Not a lot of light is needed for..."

"No...quite." Johannes nodded towards Agnes and cleared his throat. "And then he fled to Hungerford to hide there for a while." He gnawed his lip. "Alan of Didcot, it seems, had heard the planning of his own death."

"The master mason told me," I said, "That Alan went away to Hungerford quickly, all of a sudden. Escaping the wrath of those two?"

"Until the wedding was over, perhaps, and the participants had left for distant counties?"

"Then why did he not stay there until the wedding was over? Did he perhaps return because he suddenly thought of the value of the information he had, to those two? That he could blackmail them?"

"They did postpone the wedding, remember. Do you think he thought the thing done and them all gone and so he returned? And then, painting here one night or meeting them to blackmail them, he heard them planning his death. He then drew the little picture. Was he about to hide it when they caught him somehow and...?"

"A knife to the heart."

Johannes moved Agnes' cup to the 'column' and the other two cups to either side of it.

I took back my cup after a short while of staring at it and drained the ale.

"Something like that perhaps."

"And then a cart to the forest?" said Hal from his corner.

Agnes' eyes were huge. She had suddenly begun to understand the pattern of what we had been talking about. She blinked.

"Agnes, did your mistress know? Can she have guessed, perhaps, the nature of Guy de Saye's relationship with his Palfreyman?" I asked

Agnes quickly looked down at the table. She sighed. She closed her eyes and rocked her head.

Johannes asked, "Does that mean yes?"

"I think it means she is unsure, but she thinks Matilda might have guessed it.

Agnes nodded.

"It would account for the unbelievable hatred she seemed to have for him."

"Ah...yes..."

"She did despise him, didn't she?"

Agnes nodded again. She looked around for some paper on which to write and made scribbling movements.

"She can write, Johannes. Can she have something to write with?"

Johannes took the rolled-up parchment and flattened it,

held it down with the cups and then went to his workroom to fetch a pen and ink.

Agnes dipped the quill nib in the ink and wrote, "They first met at Witney. Her father had taken her there from Amesbury Abbey to meet her bridegroom. They... we, travelled fifteen miles on to the de Neville house at Abingdon. Matilda was very upset but not as upset about the marriage as she was when she reached Marlborough. She had more chance, I think, to watch Guy here. It was then I suppose she might have guessed."

"She said nothing to you."

"No."

"Did she confide in you at all?"

Agnes smiled and wrote, "I am not a good conversationalist, as you know, sir. She rarely spoke to me, except when she wanted something or I had done wrong, as she saw it. She was, forgive me, a nasty, spoiled only child with the temper of a three-year-old. God rest her."

I had had cause to see that sort of behaviour. I could vouch for that statement.

Agnes dipped her chin and parted the hair at the back of her head. She turned. There—she did not need to point as she did—was a large, red-raw patch of skin. Her hair had been wrenched out by the roots, and it had left a bald patch."

"She did this?"

"Often."

"Tsssoo. I can let you have some salve for that," said Johannes, ever the doctor.

Johannes went to the kitchen sideboard and fetched back some bread and cheese and more ale. Then, he went for a pot of salve from his surgery.

Agnes fell to the food with gusto. Poor child, I thought, she has probably had nothing all day and maybe the day before that.

"Agnes, can I ask you some more questions?"

She nodded, smiling and chewing at the same time.

"We know, you and I, that no one else went into the tower room that fateful day, for you would have seen them, and I would have heard them.

You also would have seen anyone exit. Indeed, they would have tripped over you as they fled."

"Yes"

"Why do you think your mistress left you outside the room?"

She shrugged and wrote, "She was a contrary creature. She changed her mind a dozen times a day. First, she wanted me there so she would not be alone with Master de Saye."

I read what she had written and answered, "Yes, I heard her say so."

She nodded and then wrote again, "Then, it was as if she made up her mind to be with him and talk, and she told me to wait."

"Where did she tell you to wait?"

Agnes smiled as if she realised that I had worked out that the instruction given to her had been ignored.

"A little way off. But I wanted to listen, so I crept and sat on the step by the door." She wrote.

I chuckled. "When they entered the room…did you see inside? Was it empty of people?"

"Yes."

"Who locked the door?"

The little maid frowned at that. "I think it was Master de Saye. He was by the door, closing it."

"Did your mistress realise he had locked it?" asked Johannes.

She shrugged.

"Why do you think he did that?"

"So that they would not be interrupted, maybe?"

Agnes' writing was quite large and not at all adult. I suppose she had not had a deal of practice.

"Did you learn letters and reading at the abbey, Agnes?"

She nodded. "Almost self-taught," she wrote.

My eyebrows rose into my hair. "Good for you," I said. "That skill has been most useful to us."

She had almost filled up one side of the sheet of paper. She wrote, "thank you," and turned it over.

Johannes yawned. Then he asked,

"Who used that room, Agnes, besides your mistress and yourself now and again?"

"No one in the daytime."

He nodded. "Your mistress liked it, didn't she?"

"She spent a lot of time looking out of the window," she wrote, "at the forest and the water."

"De Saye knew she could be found there?"

"I think he did, yes."

"And 'e might tell 'is lover, Broughton, that she could be found there too?" asked Hal.

She shrugged.

"No, we have no evidence that Broughton knew that," I said, and I continued, "Oh!" I put down my empty ale cup heavily. "This is most vexing! Suddenly, we think we know so much, and then we realise we know so little! The answers just throw up more questions."

I asked Agnes, "What do you think they were going to discuss in that room?

"I thought they would talk about how they might refuse to be married to each other, but they did not."

"No. They could not, for the king has had a hand in it. He would be most displeased if they refused."

Did she have any idea who had murdered them both?

She did not but offered an explanation, one which

she seemed a little embarrassed to confide given the confrontation we had just witnessed.

"A witch, maybe?"

I laughed. "Why would a witch want to kill two people she had never met?"

Her answer was quite logical, if spurious. "Because someone had paid her to do it. That is, after all, what witches do, isn't it?"

"Agnes, there is no such thing as witches. You know that."

She smiled and shrugged.

She had almost filled the second side of the paper with writing.

Then I asked her her own history. It took a while for her to write it all down, and her letters were cramped and the lines wavy.

She had been given up as a child to the Abbey of Amesbury, left on the doorstep. No one knew exactly where she had come from. There had been some itinerants passing by, some entertainers, a few days earlier, and it was thought that she had been an unwanted child of theirs.

Though fully perfect, it was obvious that she would never grow to the full height of a normal woman, so she was put to work in the abbey as a servant.

When she was about ten, one of the corrodians at the abbey, an older lady of good birth who had retired there, saw the potential in her, she said, and took her to be her servant. She taught her all about being a lady's maid.

When Matilda arrived at the age of six, her own mistress now being dead, Agnes was assigned to the girl to look after her clothes and person, her room and belongings, and there she stayed until she moved, with Matilda, to Marlborough for her mistress to be married.

I nodded and thanked her for her keen eyes and for

understanding the worth of the drawing in Alan's second little book.

I also told her that it was most unlikely that she was an unfree villein, tied to one place and one lord. She was free and could do as she pleased.

She beamed at me.

"She has nowhere to go, Johannes. Can she bed down with you until we find her somewhere?"

"The attic is empty. There's no bed, but I am sure we can find her a pallet and some blankets. For a while," he said

Mistress Wolvercote was asked to take little Agnes up to the attic and find her some things. She smiled at Agnes so sweetly that my heart took a leap. I must contrive to spend some more time in Lydia's company, I told myself, for she was the most wonderful woman I knew.

My mind instantly flew back to the day of my marriage when I was nineteen—my marriage to Cecily Congyre, who was the mother of my only daughter Hawise. My heart lurched again, and I felt guilty as I thought of her on that day, beautiful in her blue bliaut and flowery headdress.

I was now thirty years of age, a different person entirely from the nineteen-year-old who had married Cecily. I could not go back, and dwelling on such things was futile.

No, Cecily would want me to be happy, I knew. It was now four years since my wife had been murdered. I could not mourn her forever.

Johannes and I were left alone with Hal.

He stood and fetched the ale jug from its place at the other side of the board and gestured: did I want more?

"No thanks, I must be off."

He stood looking down at me.

"I hate to say this, Aumary, but..." he grimaced, "This little creature..."

"Agnes..."

"Aye, Agnes. Are you absolutely sure she could not have murdered her mistress and de Saye? She is the only person who…"

"Don't you start, Johannes!"

"He's not sayin' she's a witch, just that might she have killed them?" said Hal quietly from the corner.

"If we are looking for motive, Johannes, where is it? Her life with Matilda was not one of friendly companionship we know, but without her mistress, she is rootless and homeless. At least with Matilda, she had a roof over her head and food to eat. Secondly, she is too small to have inflicted the wound on de Saye."

"Could she have knocked him down?"

"He was a sturdy man, a knight. I doubt it. I didn't hear that sort of sound, I must say, and where is the motive?"

"Aye…where is it?"

We might as well have said that about anyone.

Chapter Seven

I could not sleep that night. I tossed and turned on the usually comfortable pallet in my little room.

Hal snored in the guard room.

I slept fitfully at last in the early hours of the morning, for I heard the bell at the Priory of St Margaret ringing for Lauds.

I dreamed of Agnes creeping into that small room at the top of the tower and jumping up onto the table to stab de Saye in the neck. There she was with the little ivory knife in her hand. Well, yes, that might be how she could have done it. She was, however, not tall enough to reach the window and throw out the knife.

The question would still remain: why? Why would she? He had had very little contact with her. She had no reason to kill him, and furthermore, how did she lock the door behind her afterwards.?

I had heard nothing of the sort from my little room here.

If she were contemplating murder, surely she would make sure that she was nowhere near when the body was discovered.

There she had been, when I found her, waiting, sitting,

and snivelling at the top of the stairs, as ignorant as I.

I jumped from my bed, rubbed my eyes and flung on my clothes and boots.

This was no good. My mind would not rest. I needed to walk about a little and think.

I crept carefully down the stairs so as not to wake some of the scribes who slept in their place of work, as did I.

I jogged down the keep steps and into the outer bailey.

It was pitch black. The sky had a few twinkling stars, but there was no moon.

I wandered down to the stable and looked in on Bayard, who whickered in his sleep and tossed his head.

"Sleep on, old friend," I said.

I crossed to the gatehouse. Andrew Merriman was there playing dice with another man I knew vaguely and remembered as Perkin Fisher's father. I had never known his first name.

"Out late or up early?" asked Andrew, tipping his stool on its back legs.

I smiled. "I cannot sleep, and if I do, dreams come unbidden. Not nice dreams.

"I only dream of dusky maidens under palm trees in the star-filled night of the desert near Antioch," said Andrew dreamily and jokingly, staring into space.

"You were out there then, with Richard the king in the Holy Land?"

"Aye. I was very young."

"I hear it is an amazing place, and you are never the same again once you return. You and Johannes of Salerno should talk. He was there too, as a young man."

"Yes...yes, we should."

I left them to their dicing and walked to the little chapel.

Everything seemed to be louder at night. There were no other sounds to mask those made by the tread of your feet or the door opening and closing, and the whole operation seemed loud enough to wake the entire garrison. I closed the door as carefully as I could, but I disturbed the person kneeling at the altar, for he turned round quickly, saw it was me and resumed his prayer. It was not long past Lauds. Amazing, I thought, how one's dreams seem to last forever but are, in reality, over in heartbeats. Hardly any time had elapsed between me hearing the bell, dreaming my dream, dressing, and coming here.

I stood and stared at the altar with its lit candles, now ordinary ones. The coffins had gone. All was back to normal. I tried to pray—for my little son, Geoffrey, and for Cecily.

Finally, the person stood up and somewhat stiffly made his way down the nave after genuflecting to the silver cross standing on the altar.

"Sleepless night, my son?" said Father Columba, the garrison priest. The light from the candles behind him made a red halo in his spiky hair, and I thought of the drawing made by Alan of Didcot.

"Just a lot on my mind."

"Not a guilty conscience then?"

"What man does not have something of a guilty conscience, Father?"

He snorted at that in a rather undignified way. "The number of confessions I hear here in this place, you would think them all saints," he said. "They are a godless lot!"

I smiled. "Yours cannot be an easy job."

"I thought you were a discerning young man when I first met you, Aumary, my Lord Belvoir, but now, I know it."

We chuckled quietly together.

"If you are able, come to the priest's room and take a cup with me. The days are warm, but the nights are chilly now we are in the middle of September."

We repaired to the little room where the holy vessels

and priest's robes were stored, built onto the side of the chapel, and sat at a small table just big enough for two.

"I heard that my Lord de Neville has asked you to look into the dreadful business up there in the tower." He tilted his head left, towards the keep. "Such devilry. The hand of Satan."

"The hand of man, I fear, Father, though as yet I have no idea why the two were killed."

He shook his head.

"Tell me, Father, were the de Saye party a godless lot, as you called the men of the castle?"

He put down his cup. "Some of them, yes."

"The young de Saye?"

He did not answer.

"I do not, would never wish, that you break the seal of the confessional, Father."

He nodded slowly.

"And his palfreyman, Gerald of Broughton?"

"I never heard his confession, no. I assume he went to St Mary's, if he went anywhere. Though, as you know, m'lord, one isn't required to confess every week. They came rarely to take communion; that's all I can say."

"Ah."

Isn't it the case that you often get the answers to the questions you ask, and surprisingly, some you do not?

I sighed. Despite my sleeplessness, I was tired. I stifled a yawn. "So, when the new church of St Peter is fully finished, you will be busy, Father, for I hear that you will be in charge there, too, as well as here in the chapel."

"You heard correctly, my lord. St Peter's has been built for the garrison here and for the houses growing up around the castle at this end of town. When we have a full complement of men-at-arms in the castle, this chapel is already too small for our services."

"Yes, I have noticed. We are all crammed in of a Sunday, aren't we?"

He smiled.

"It will be a fine church. I have noticed the paintings."

"Yes. Alas, we were to have further paintings in the chancel and side aisles, but …"

"Yes. Alan of Didcot was a fine painter. His is a great loss."

"I watched him sometimes…high up on his scaffolding."

"You did? How did he work?"

The priest quizzed me with his eyebrows.

"Did he stand, squat, lie…?"

"Oh…all those things. He had a platform at the top of the arch and would go quickly from one end to the other. He had little drawings to work from, but mostly, the things were in his head, I think. God was directing him in a mysterious way, I thought."

"I hear he could be found here at night, too, working by candlelight."

The priest snorted again. "Aye…but come morning, he would sometimes be found on his platform, dead drunk and sleeping it off, an empty ale skin by him. Heavens only knows how he did not fall off and injure himself."

"Yes, indeed."

"Strangely, too, he could still paint well whilst drunk. I used to berate him about his drinking here in the church. I know it was not yet fully a consecrated space, but God, I think, is still present, as he is everywhere. He could be messy, too. Paint dribbles everywhere on the floor under the arch. The workers would tread in it, and it would go all over!"

"I suppose that could not be helped," I chuckled.

"I gave him an old cloth to put under his scaffolding to catch the drips. He used it until the day he disappeared, and the mess was contained. Praise be to God."

I perked up a little to hear about the day he disappeared.

"I hear he just went with hardly a word to anyone. He told the master mason and that was all, that he was going to Hungerford."

"Aye," said Father Columba, "We waited for him for some time before we took down the scaffolding. He could always re-erect it. He had spilt a deal of red-brown paint on the floor cloth under the planks. It was dry and crusty, and I threw it on the midden, vowing to get him a new one when he returned. Sadly, he did not return, and now he never will."

"No." I tried to seem nonchalant about the floor cloth. "The cloth, Father," I said, scratching my ear, "did you drop it on the castle midden?"

"I did."

My heart missed a beat.

Early after dawn, saw me looking for Perkin Fisher again in the gatehouse.

His father, whose name I learned was Wat, was there taking instructions from the cook from the kitchen, and he told me that Perkin would be fishing in his boat on the river. He told me roughly where.

I ran down to the bank by the crack willows and hollered.

A voice answered, "Who wants me?"

"Sir Aumary Belvoir."

After a moment, the little boat came into view with Perkin rowing for all he was worth.

It was a Friday, and Perkin had been up early, fishing for perch, bream and brown trout in the river, for the suppers of some of the townspeople of Marlborough, for Friday was a fish day.

He leapt onto the bank.

"Do I earn another penny today, Sir Aumary?" he asked, grinning, tying up his craft.

"More than that, Perkin, for the job I'd have you do today is an unsavoury one, and I would not have you feel short-changed."

"Oh...sir...go on! You're havin' me on," he said, a little embarrassed.

"Will you root around on the castle midden for me?"

His face fell. "Oh, sir..."

"I know, and I will pay you two pence."

His eyes gleamed. He looked a little wary, but he spat on his hand and offered it. He was such a pleasant and willing lad, I had not the heart to disdain him, so I also spat and shook. He looked a little sheepish that a fully blown knight had shaken his hand in a bargain.

He grinned, picked up his fish and was off to the gatehouse. I rubbed my hand on the dewy grass. It stank of fish.

Once he had stowed his fish away—I know not where—we made our way around the wall to the midden. All castle rubbish ended up here, and it was cleared periodically, when the smell had grown too high for us all to manage it any longer, by a carter in the town. What he then did with it, I have no idea.

Poor Perkin looked at the mound, then at me.

"Here," I said, "put this cloth around your nose, it will stop the worst of the smell."

I told him what we were looking for. He scrabbled up to the top of the mound like a little mouse. I gave him a stick to poke around with.

Luckily, we found it quite quickly and were not asphyxiated, for it was quite a big piece of cloth and not so deeply buried. He handed it to me on the end of the stick.

"Excellent work, Perkin," I said. "A well-earned two pence."

The cloth was splattered with green paint, with yellow and black in smallish splodges, and with other colours in lesser amounts. It was obvious even to me, who had never held a brush, that these were spots that had fallen as he worked high up on his platform. They were all in the same place on the cloth, about a couple of inches in from the edge, and they were in a line as if he had ranged the length of his plank and the paint had fallen between the wall and the edge of his wooden walkway.

Then, there was a large splodge of red-brown, almost in the middle. This, I knew, was not paint.

"Another halfpenny if you will run up to the doctor's and ask him to come here to me, Perkin. Tell him it's important."

"Doctor Johannes? Right away, sir," and he was off with the enthusiasm and the legs only a youngster possesses.

I went back to my office, leaving the noisome cloth just outside my doorway. It smelled of everything that had been piled on top of it on the midden. The smell from it was beginning to permeate the room when I looked up to see Johannes staring at it on the floor.

"The cloth Alan of Didcot used to protect the new flagstone floor of the church from paint," I said as I got up from my table.

I donned one of my riding gloves and picked up the cloth, spreading it out on the floor of the passageway in the light under the window for Johannes to see. I told Johannes how we had come by the cloth.

"Paint, paint...paint..." I pointed out, "and paint here."

"And blood," said Johannes.

"Aye ...blood."

Now we knew that Alan of Didcot had met his end in the

church of St Peter, underneath his painting platform. Our next task was to determine how his body got into the forest.

I was itching to go down with Johannes to his house and speak to Mistress Wolvercote again. The opportunity came that evening, for Johannes, once we had decided we must keep the bloody cloth, had invited me to supper.

I had no fine clothes with me at the castle. I would have to do as I was, though I did change my shirt and wash away the smell of the midden.

I rode Bayard out onto the common in the late afternoon and gave him a good run, for he was in need of some exercise. I decided I must get some of the grooms to ride him for me, for he was getting quite frisky, and I think he was peeved that I had not ridden him much of late.

Some appreciative workers, trotting home from their tasks in the fields, doffed their caps to me and commented on my fine horse, asking if I was going to race him.

De Saye might have left this earth, and his racehorses might have gone back to Baydon, but men here had begun to be obsessed with horse racing. It wouldn't be long, I thought, before some other enterprising person would take up where de Saye had left off and start to organise races again. No, it would not be me. I loved to ride Bayard hard on the chalk of the downs and feel the wind in my hair and the power of him underneath me, but I was not obsessed as many men were with the speed of it all and the betting. Besides, Bayard was not a race horse.

I trotted sedately back into the town and passed into Johannes' courtyard. I rubbed Bayard down with a wisp of straw and let him forage in the basket at the back of the stable with Johannes' old horse, Titus, and his mule, Mary. They were old, stable companions and happy to be together.

I washed my hands and face in the water trough and dried myself off as best I could with the hem of my cloak, ran my hands through my unruly black curls and made for the kitchen door.

"I thought I heard you come in," said Mistress Wolvercote, her back to me, her head almost in the kitchen fire. She backed out, and there in her hands, held out and protected by two rags, was a golden baked pie.

"I hear you like pies," she said.

I laughed out loud at that, for this sounded like my daughter's work for sure.

"Have you been speaking, Mistress Wolvercote, to my daughter Hawise?"

"I have yet to have that pleasure," she said.

I grinned. This was good news, for she was obviously thinking that a meeting between them was a good thing and about to happen.

"I will fetch her one day back to the town when I go to Durley," I said "and you and she can swap pie receipts."

"Ah...so she is a cook, your five-year-old daughter," she said, with a sidelong look, pulling the pie from its flat metal plate and laying it on the side to cool a little.

"No, she just tells my cook what to make, and he, knowing he is beaten, does what she says."

She laughed her tinkling laugh, and my heart lurched. Johannes came in, wiping himself on a towel. "Come in... come in. We shall eat tonight, I think, in the parlour."

Eat we did, and splendidly. Besides the pie, which was a fish pie with spices and herbs, we had darioles with a mashed vegetable filling, bream and eel pasties, and we finished with a frumenty, which was delicious. I could eat no more.

"I do not eat this well at Durley, and I have a professional cook, mistress," I said, leaning back and feeling as if I might undo my belt a notch but had not the bravery to do so.

Lydia blushed. "I do love to cook. I might be a little more restrained, were it an ordinary day, but when Johannes said you were coming, well, I thought we might have a bit of a feast, considering you have been living on the terrible food at the castle these many days."

"Aye, the food is awful," I said, "and everything tastes the same."

We all laughed at that.

"Where is our little maid?" I asked.

"Fast asleep, poor soul. I do not think she has felt safe these past few days and has not slept as a result," answered Lydia.

"That may be my fault," I owned. "For it was I who put into her head that some might blame her for the death of her mistress and her bridegroom and try to bring her to justice."

"Of course that happened, didn't it?" asked Lydia. "In the High Street."

"Yes. I am worried that it will happen again."

Johannes cleared his throat. "More wine, Aumary?"

I smiled. "I must be off... I have the night watch to see to. Since de Neville has gone, many of his duties fall to me."

"I do not know how you do it, Sir Aumary," said Lydia, a flush now on her cheeks from the wine I suspected. "You run the forest, you run the castle..."

"Ah, no. I must disabuse you. I have superb staff at Durley who run the manor and the forest for me, and likewise at the castle."

"But you, sir, are in charge."

"Well..." I scratched my head. "I am, I suppose, when de Neville is not there, but I have been doing it so long, it comes as second nature now. There was a time when I was young when I thought that I might fail in one or the other, and it would all come tumbling down around my ears.

"Oh," said Lydia, "but it did not."

"No. Like I say, my staff are sure-footed and good at their jobs."

"I think you are wonderful," she said in an unguarded moment.

I am not a blushing man, but I blushed up to the roots of my hair. Johannes sniggered into his wine cup.

I almost floated up the High Street on Bayard to the castle gatehouse. I scratched on the wicket door, for it was now past curfew.

Picot's eyes peered at me through the slit at the top, and he undid the gate and let me, now walking Bayard, through the main gate.

"Been a courtin', sir, have we?"

"What?"

He gestured to my cheek.

I rubbed my fingers over it. There was a pale pink stain.

Mistress Wolvercote had kissed me on the cheek as I bade farewell and left a little of herself behind.

I held my head high. "As a matter of fact…yes, I have," and I walked straight past him. I handed Bayard to a sleepy groom and said to myself, "Yes, I think I have."

The next day dawned grey and cool. It was such a change from the weather we had had all summer.

We were fast approaching the autumn equinox.

Oh, I thought, what should we do at Durley if Father Swithun banned our autumn festivities: our showing of the Belvoir regalia and the feast accompanying it? No, that was our harvest festival, and he could not ban it, for the church was given its tithe then. He would not pass that up.

However, he might not like the harvesting of our apples and the little lanterns we made of the larger ones for the children, as well as the bonfire and fun that we had on that night by dancing and making merry. Oh no, he wouldn't like that at all.

Well, we had a few weeks yet till the showing of the regalia, where we had a feast at Durley and all would come from miles around to see me use the regalia—the hunting horn, sword, saddle, belt and bridle given to my family by King William I to be a symbol of his authority over the forest.

If Swithun objected to that, then, I thought, I would lock him in his own priest's room for the day.

It was chilly for the first time in days, and I dressed quickly, though a glow came over me every time I thought about what had happened the night before.

I do think Mistress Wolvercote likes me, I said to myself, and I know that I like her very much. It was up to me to make more of it.

Meanwhile, I had a castle to run and a murder to solve. Nothing like practical action to bring one's attention from thoughts of love, I mused.

I had gone to the gate to see that all was well in the night and to take the guard's report, when John Brenthall came bounding over the bridge and under the gate.

He touched his coif when he saw me. "Mornin', sir."

"Good Morning, John. Though," I looked up at the heavens, "seems the good weather has broken."

"Not the only thing might be broken, sir."

"Oh...?"

"Can you come up to St Mary's, sir? There's a bit of a..." He sought for the right word, "altercation, going on."

"Shall we walk? Then you can tell me the nature of this fracas."

We heard the shouting long before we reached the churchyard.

We passed under the tunnel of the alleyway, which passed by the side of Johannes' house, and broke out into the churchyard at the back of his property.

Johannes was out there, too, with his arms folded over his chest. His yard backed onto the church cemetery. He looked around as I entered the churchyard.

"Wondered when you'd get here," he said.

Little knots of people had gathered by the south door of St Mary's. Some were Durley folk, for they had walked or come in carts to the Saturday market, which Marlborough was now permitted to hold. I recognised several of my people. Others were people of Marlborough; mostly, I recollected, those who lived a little way off down at the Marsh, the riverside area of the town just off from the London Road.

There, head to head with the priest of St Mary's, was Father Swithun. I groaned. What mischief was he wreaking now? He had no power in this church and no say in the town at all.

However, he was having his say. "She will not be buried in my ground, I tell you. She chose to leave Durley, and she should stay away in death as she did in life."

"She was a good supporter of this church, I agree, and loved it," boomed the other priest. He was a large man with a stentorian voice whose singing was much admired throughout the area. His deep bass rode over all the chatter of the women. "But I will have her wishes respected."

"Father Torold, what do we have here?" I interrupted.

He turned his head and then dipped it, the relief showing on his face. "A church matter, m'lord, but one in which you may feel you could become involved, as Lord of Durley.

"Anything concerning my priest at Durley is my business," I said to him as I smiled an open-faced smile such as often encouraged people to talk on.

Swithun whipped around and saw me. He scowled like the devil.

"What are you doing here, Father Swithun, away from your flock and your fold?" I asked. "Father Benedict, God rest him, never took it upon himself to trespass on another's piece of God's earth. He was always to be found dealing with his people on his own soil."

"That soil is about to be dug for one who should not lie there. She should lie here, where she lived twenty years. She chose then. She cannot change her mind in death and lie elsewhere till the last trump."

"It was her last wish," said Torold. "Her family lies at Durley. Her first husband. She wishes to be with them."

"We are talking about your mother, Agnes, aren't we?" I asked as I spotted her tearful and hidden face amongst some of my Durley folk at the back of the crowd.

She curtsied. "Aye, m'lord. Alys. Alys Fuller. But she was a Durley wife afore that. She married your father's chief groom, my father, Godwin Preshute."

"He died when I was what…eight? She remarried in Marlborough, didn't she? In my father's time?"

"Aye, sir, she married Nick Fuller, as lives down on the Marsh. She was freeborn and so could marry whomever she wanted."

I remembered her mother. Agnes was right; Alys's first husband, Agnes's father, had been a Durley man, and I fancy that this first short marriage was the love match that made Alys wish to be buried in Durley. Godwin Preshute had been kicked by a horse and killed outright when I was a youngster, and he lay in Durley churchyard.

"Is your stepfather still alive, Agnes?"

"Aye, sir…just. He's an old man now and bedridden. I visit him when I can, as you know."

"Ah, yes. I remember now." I stopped. "I was not aware that your mother was ill, Agnes."

"No, sir." Her eyes filled with tears, "She was taken quickly two days ago. There was no warning. And now the priest will not bury her at Durley as she wished," and she burst into tears.

John came round the back of the crowd to put his arms around her.

"You did not tell me…"

"I have not really seen you, m'lord, and…you have been very busy," she whined.

"No…it's true."

I stepped up to the front of the crowd. As I came fully into view, all my Durley folk curtsied, bowed or knuckled their foreheads, depending on their station at the manor or in the forest.

"I see no reason why your mother cannot be buried with her first husband, your father, at Durley."

I turned to Father Swithun. "Is the churchyard at Durley full, Swithun? Can we squeeze in no more folk? If so, we had better extend the cemetery and get the bishop, my godfather, up there to consecrate it for us."

"She is not one of my Durley flock, nor was she in life. She should lie here in St Mary's, for it was here she worshipped."

Father Torold was tutting at his counterpart's intransigence. "God does not mind where a body lies, Swithun. He sees all," he said.

"Then she should not mind either."

There was a general grumbling, and I heard the words "Devil" and "cruel" and "her spirit will walk if she is denied."

"Swithun, do not deny the woman the right to lie with her kin in the soil where she originated. Her daughter, no doubt, will also, when her time comes, forgive me, Agnes, be buried in our cemetery and will wish to lie with her mother at Durley. You cannot fragment the family like this."

"She is not a Durley woman, this Alys."

Suddenly, Agnes came pushing through the crowd. "You are a wicked and unkind man, and I wish you had never set eyes on Durley." Her eyes were blazing, and the crying had stopped. "I wish you'd go to hell!"

I came forward and gently took her by the shoulders. "Leave this to me, Agnes."

I looked into her face, and she nodded. Still looking at her, I said, "Swithun, if I had spent many years abroad—as some knights do, perhaps, as our good King Richard did—hardly spending any time in this country, and had died away from home, would you deny me burial in my own churchyard? A churchyard founded by my great-grandfather and built around the church he caused to be raised with his own money

I turned to glare at him.

Swithun simply glared back at me.

"Well?"

"I could not deny you burial, no."

"Then, I see no difference between that hypothetical scene and this real one. I was born and raised in Durley. I might have gone to Normandy as a young man and spent quite some time there, and I might have died there. Indeed, this time last year, I very nearly did." I stopped to let that sink in. "If I had died elsewhere, my body would have been embalmed and brought back to Durley to lie in the soil that had nourished me. Alys was born in Durley. She spent some time elsewhere, and she now wishes to return there. She may do so."

There was a collective sigh and a ripple of defiance.

"Thank you, my lord," said Torold.

"Oh sir...thank you..." said Agnes.

Swithun swirled his cloak and was gone.

I turned to Johannes. "You did not treat Alys?"

"I was not called. It was rather sudden, I fear."

"Shame."

Johannes was the only real doctor in the town, and he was well respected. It was known that he would treat the poor and the wealthy alike. He was a wealthy man himself, having made his money in the Holy Lands. Many's the time he would treat the poor of Marlborough for nothing more than a loaf of bread or a few eggs. Often, his work was free.

The crowd was breaking up. Some were smiling at me and nodding. I acknowledged those I could.

I turned to John. "John, where does the body lie now?"

"In the church, sir."

"Then we had better get a cart to come for her and bring her home to Durley, had we not? I will make sure I am there when she is interred. I don't trust Father Swithun."

"Yessir."

Then, I felt a hand touch my elbow. I looked over my shoulder.

It was Simon Smith, a man of few words and the mild-mannered farrier who lived just over the road from the church and Johannes' house. He was the man who'd organised the stone spilt outside Johannes' house to be delivered to the castle.

"Please, my Lord Belvoir, might I have the honour of taking Alys on her last journey?"

"Why should you do this thing, Simon? You are not family, I think."

He smiled, "No, but we have been near neighbours nigh on twenty years, and I was very fond of Alys. She helped me so much when..." He stopped and looked for the right words. "When my wife died. I was useless with grief. My children would have suffered greatly if it weren't for Alys.

She was a second mother to them. She helped me through the really hard times, did Alys. I would like to do this thing for her."

I looked at his boyish and open face. I had heard about his near brush with death and his attempted suicide on the untimely demise of his wife. He had, I'd heard, tried to hang himself. Many of us knew, and we all kept our own counsel, for self murder was a terrible sin. Not only that, it was also a crime for which one could be hanged.

Simon had thought to kill himself, but Alys had prevented him. For that, he was grateful.

I nodded. "Bring a cart to the church this afternoon, and we shall see her buried in the soil she loved later tomorrow."

He thanked me and was gone.

> *Yes, Paul, it is odd. It is written that God is the only one who can take away our life. We must not, ourselves, cut the cord keeping us tied to this earth before God sees fit to take us to Him. If one tries to kill oneself, it's a crime. If one fails in one's intent and one does not die, one is killed anyway. You are right. It is an odd way of going about things.*

A steady, miserable drizzle began in the afternoon. Lesser people, those who must be out and about in the rain, covered their heads with their hoods and added pieces of sacking, for it was the sort of incessant rain which soaked.

John came to me at the castle later and told me that Simon had been as good as his word and had fetched his cart to the church door. Johannes had supplemented Simon's donkey with his mule, old Mary—they were much the same size, and this meant that the slippery ways of the hill up into the forest might be more easily climbed in the wet. The corpse would be covered with a thick canvas cloth to protect it from the worst of the weather.

Our manor carpenter always had a coffin in his workshop. This would suffice for Alys once she reached her home village. Most people went into the earth wrapped in their shroud. Only the wealthy could afford a coffin. I would see that Alys had a wooden coffin.

John was now off to go with them, and I would see them all in the evening at Durley when I had quitted the castle. Simon would stay with us and pay his respects to Alys Fuller at her funeral the next day.

I had better have another word with Swithun before then.

I sat in my office and brooded.

It was plain that Swithun, with his bad tempers and his failure to understand the ways of rural life in the forest, was no fit priest for our little village and I deliberated over the letter I would write to my godfather, the Bishop of Salisbury, explaining just that.

With a draft of that letter written, I packed up my things and went down to the stable to fetch Bayard for the journey home to Durley.

It was a miserable ride. Where once Bayard had tolerated bad weather, he now complained at every step and his prancing and dancing as we rode through town splashed up so many puddles and streams of muddy water. He had been too long in the warm and comfortable castle stables with company and good hay and fodder. He was getting soft. Time, I think to get myself a new horse and train him to my ways, for Bayard was, as were we all, getting older. Bayard had been a present for my sixteenth name day. I was now thirty. He had been my faithful friend some fourteen years. There was much life in him yet, for he could live to twenty-five and beyond, but I needed to have a replacement for him ready and trained.

We splashed along and up the hill, remembering, both of us, I think, the journey we made at about this time last year when the weather had been atrocious and the forest trees were falling around us like bowling pins.

Once on the flat at the top of the hill, we picked up speed, but we were still riding cautiously, wary of potholes that could injure a horse and throw a rider.

At the hall, with a cup of spiced ale warming my hands and my daughter sitting demurely by me asking questions about Marlborough, the castle, the town and the shops, I beckoned Hal of Potterne. I asked him if he would be so good as to jog over to the priest's house and fetch him to me.

He returned some time later to tell me that Swithun was nowhere to be seen. "'E's not to be found in the village."

I cursed.

"Dada!" remonstrated my five-year-old. "THAT is a bad word."

"Aye, I know," I chewed my lip. "But sometimes, a man must use such words. They prevent him from getting up and bumping somebody on the head, hard," and I made a fist and tapped her on her crown.

She giggled.

"Do you want to bump Father Swithun on the head hard then, Dada?" she asked coyly.

"I do indeed."

John came in a moment later and took off his cloak, shaking it to rid it of water. He spread it out over a stool.

"Nowhere, no sign of him. I do know that Father Torold is coming to pay his respects to Alys tomorrow. Might we ask him to perform the ceremony if we cannot find Swithun by then?"

"I was thinking of a trip to Bedwyn to fetch Father Godfrey, if our own priest is still absent, John, but, yes, we shall ask Father Torold. He knew the woman well. It is, in a way more fitting, that he performs the obsequies."

He nodded. "Though God knows what Swithun will say when he finds that another has performed a burial and preached in his church."

"He will lie down in the rushes, eat them and foam at the mouth and call us all from hill to burn," I said with a grin.

He, too, grinned. Hawise giggled.

The next day dawned grey but dry, and folk tramped in from Marlborough town or came riding in carts with their neighbours from early morning to pay their last respects to Alys Fuller. Most of them were collected in the church, but I opened the threshing barn to them also and sent round ale and bread for them all.

"Your mother was well-liked," I told Agnes later that morning.

"Aye, she was," she answered, "but I think it's more to do with the scene created yesterday outside the church. Folk are curious to see what will happen. There is nothing like a near fight to make a funeral interesting."

There was still no sign of Swithun.

Father Torold was more than happy to perform the rites but did say that he was doing it under extreme circumstances and that he wanted it known and recorded that he had been asked especially. He did not want the wrong message to be sent back to his bishop. I promised faithfully that I would speak on his behalf to Herbert Poore, Bishop of Salisbury.

Alys Fuller was laid to rest in our little churchyard by the side of her first husband. The grey clouds lifted for a short while, and the sun shone again. Then, without warning, a rain shower drove the assembled people back into the church, and a rainbow was seen arching over the forest towards Burbage. The people took this as a good sign that they had done the right thing and drifted home.

Swithun returned to his house the next day. I did not talk to him. No one did.

One interesting thing came out of fetching of Alys's body from Marlborough. Simon the Smith, whose cart had been used for Alys's last journey, sought me out and thanked me for intervening and settling the argument between the townsfolk and the priest of Durley.

"It's not the first time I have had words with the man, Simon," I said.

"Oh?"

"He seems to think that he is lord of this manor and has tried to force his will on us all. He told me he would not bury the man we found in the forest, a poor murdered limner, in this little churchyard. Thank Heavens, we found out who he was, and he could be buried by our jovial Father Torold in the town."

"Aye, I heard about the murder of this limner," said Simon. "I wondered, once I had thought about it if I should come up to the castle and seek you out and tell you what I thought I knew about it," he said quietly, "but before I could do so, the young Sir Guy was dead, and the palfreyman followed him not long after. I thought perhaps I was wrong and so I kept my mouth shut."

"What is it you know, Simon?" I asked gently.

"Well," he turned away. "I don't know if it is…"

"Anything you can tell us will be of help, I'm sure."

He turned his face up to look at me, this gentle, quiet and obviously still troubled man.

"I was, I am, one of those interested in the horses that Guy de Saye had brought with him, his race horses. Horses, after all, fill a lot of my day, what with shoeing and making up tack and the like. I like 'em. I used to go up to the common and watch them racing. One day, I lost a deal of money up on the hill to the palfreyman, and he said that

I could pay him back in a different way."

I began to be a little worried for Simon then, for Gerald of Broughton had not been a good God-fearing man. What had he got him to do? He had been a dangerous man to deal with.

"If I would lend him my cart and say nothing to any man, he would forget the debt I owed him."

"And did you?"

"You would, wouldn't you, m'lord? It seemed easy. He fetched it and brought it back the same night."

"And that was it?"

"Aye."

"No questions were asked."

"None."

"No information was given?"

"None was asked for. It was their business. Then when the young lord died and then Gerald...well...I thought to keep quiet. Might I be next? If they...whoever did the murders, that is, thought I was involved."

"Thank you for telling me this, Simon." I turned to go.

"Sir...there is more."

My eyebrows rose.

"When I looked at the bed of my cart when they had brought it back, there was paint in the back, green and a bit of yellow and...also when I looked carefully, red... Only that wasn't paint..."

"It was blood," I said.

"Yes, how did you?"

I smiled. "Now we know how de Saye and Broughton got the body from the church, where they killed the painter, to the forest where we found him. Thank you, Simon. You have filled in the last hole in that mystery."

Chapter Eight

*H*enry Pierson was bustling about in his office. I saw him as I crossed the courtyard. He sat to count some coins into a purse, leaned forward and dropped it into a chest at his feet. He notched a tally stick, and then, for good measure, he marked a book on his table.

"How goes it, Henry?" I asked.

He stood bolt upright. "Well, sir. And you?"

"Tired. Do sit, please."

We sat together.

"Sir, there is something I must ask you, now you are here...a boon really, sir."

"Don't tell me you want to get married, Henry?"

He laughed, embarrassed at my joke. Well, he was now over the age, at twenty-three.

"No. It's Little Piers, sir."

"Our little thatcher? How is he doing? Over his nightmares now, is he?"

"Thank you, yes, he is a lot better except..."

He sighed. "He can't be a thatcher, sire."

"He can't?"

I pulled the book towards me and started looking down

the columns. Old habits die hard.

"No. We have found out that he cannot abide the straw thatch, sir. He coughs, and he wheezes. He can't catch his breath. It's terrible to watch him, sir, gasping for air."

I pushed the book away, totally satisfied.

I frowned.

"Your father was the same, since I think on it, wasn't he?"

"Aye, sir. So mother says. I don't rightly remember too much. Piers takes after Da in more than just a name."

I pictured my former steward as I had known him when I was a seventeen. I remembered him coughing and wheezing, fighting for breath, red in face and red of eye. It was no easy thing to suffocate in such a way, nor to watch a man do it.

Yes, Little Piers and Piers of Manton were very alike in colouring, facial features, mannerisms and stature. Henry favoured his mother.

"Yes, you're right, he does."

I recalled that Piers struggled when the manor was cutting the hay and reaping the corn. Even close proximity to the manor cats would send him into a sneezing fit. As to the threshing, I had told him to stay well away. He was to organise it with the reeve, and then retire somewhere safe. The day he had been killed, he was safely up in the manor, away from the reaping of crops in the manor meadow. Pah! Safely. And then he had been murdered!

"He must come home then. Will Giles release him from his indentures, Henry?"

"Aye, he will."

Little Piers came home two days later. He came home on the back of a tradesman's cart, grinning and happy to be home.

The cart had trundled from Marlborough castle. The glaziers had arrived to put the glass in the windows.

The glaziers set up their camp on the green in the middle of the village that day and began to unload their tents and cooking wares.

Fascinated, Piers helped them and was soon lost in their arcane talk.

I watched from the manor gateway. Perhaps we had found somewhere for him to go after all.

The making of glass, I had been told by the master glazier, Perkin Glazer, required two things in particular: wood ash—and beech wood was the best to burn for this— and river sand. The clean stream of the Kennet river bed would provide the sand, which was of uniform grit size and the forest could provide the wood. Beech trees grew well on the thin chalk soil, and over in The West Baily, beech trees were more common than in the rest of the forest.

When King John had decided to update and enlarge the castle, he had given permission for wood to be taken from the Royal Forest of Savernake for the making of the glass for the windows. Indeed, Master Glazer said, this type of glass was known as forest glass, for it was always made in places where forest and stream ran together. He himself hailed from The Weald of Kent, where glass-making was an established art. He had, as a master, brought his skill further west, and when he heard that John wished to add glass to the castle and chapel at Marlborough, he offered his services.

Out in the forest, the glaziers had built a furnace to heat the ash and the sand together. This required very high temperatures and was an exact art. When the glass was molten, it could be taken out of the furnace and blown into a cylinder. It would then be opened out and flattened to make a pane for a window. The master glass-fitter would then cut the pane carefully and fit it to a wooden or metal frame, and the whole thing would be sealed with a mixture of linseed oil and ground chalk, which was called putty.

I had watched the final pieces of flattened glass, protected by straw and sheep fleece, being trundled on a cart from the forest into the castle, and I held my breath with the rest of them as the last piece was fitted to the chapel. It was fragile stuff. It was a testament to the care the glaziers took over their job. Not one bit had been broken.

The following Sunday, we crossed the path and entered the church for the service. We opened the church door, and I stopped dead.

Father Swithun was at the eastern end, robed and ready to perform Mass. There were fourteen people in the church, all looking uncomfortable. These included my reeve and his immediate family, as well as John and his family. There were three or four of the old folk who were hobbled by their illnesses.

Then there was myself, followed by Hawise and her nursemaid, Felice.

The congregation consisted of merely fourteen manor folk. More than one hundred people lived and worked here and more in the forest.

"Where is everyone?" I asked with dread in my voice.

The place was normally packed and had been every Sunday when Benedict had officiated.

"Many have gone up to Bedwyn, sir," said the reeve, Walter.

"It is an insult to God." Swithun's voice boomed up to the rafters.

"No, Swithun, it is an insult to you, and you have brought it upon yourself."

He bridled at that.

"You must see what you can do to remedy the situation."

Part of me laughed at the antics of my people. They were making their feelings known in the only way they had open to them. Strictly, the tied peasants should have stayed at Durley, and if they had wanted to go elsewhere, they should have asked me. However, I was lord of the whole forest and overlord of all the villages within. Going to Burbage meant that they were staying within my land. I had no doubt this would have been their answer if I had quizzed them.

The freemen could go where they wished. They would not go to Swithun's church. He would lose, and the priest at Bedwyn would gain.

Swithun was seething.

What kind of man was Swithun?

To me, he was disrespectful, arrogant and humourless. To my manor folk, he was stringent, punishing, exacting, harsh and, by turns, lukewarm, disinterested and lax.

One never quite knew which was the Swithun of the day

Not long after the manor folk had made their displeasure known, an event which alienated them even further from the priest happened in the village.

He had been getting more and more surly, Walter told me. He thought, too, that he was not always as sober as he might have been. He could not be found when needed, neither at his church nor his home.

Did he wander off into the forest to drink?

One pair of my manor workers who had not gone to Bedwyn or worshipped at Durley church were the relatively newly married pair Ralf and Edwina Sylvestre. These two were my tied villeins who owed me their labour in my fields.

They lived in a small bothy amongst the trees on the Ramsbury road. Ralf sometimes helped out in the forest, hence his name, and was skilled at the making and repairing of hurdle fencing, as was his father, Fulke.

I knew that Edwina was pregnant and close to her time,

so I was not surprised that I did not see them at church that day, despite the poor turnout. I knew she would not be able to walk to Bedwyn.

Walter Reeve told me that she had gone into labour that morning and that the midwife had been sought from the tiny village of Buttermere on the other side of the Hungerford road. Ralf had loped off at a fast pace early that morning.

By the end of the day, God willing, I should have one more serf on my manor, albeit a tiny one.

The midwife was at church in Burbage, her nearest place of worship. It took Ralf some time to find her. Quickly, she gathered her things and made it on foot to Durley.

Edwina, I am told, struggled to deliver the child, and at last, twenty hours after her labour began, she was delivered of a daughter. The child was weak, and Aolfe Midwyf was worried that she would not survive. Nevertheless, that evening, she trudged through the village and up to the church in the dark, to find Swithun to ask him to come and baptise the little soul. He could not be found in the darkened church.

Walter told me later that Aolfe had gone to his house and called for him and scratched on the door. When there was no answer, the woman had pushed open the door and entered. The house was in darkness, but she found the priest. Swithun was rather the worse for drink, slumped in his chair.

He glared at her with a red eye and chastised her for entering his house without permission. She gave him the story and urged him to come and tend the scrap clinging to life down in the bothy on the Ramsbury road.

He would not.

Walter explained that after much pleading, Aolfe then ran back to the Silvestre house and baptised the child herself. This was a concession made to midwives. If they felt that a soul was in peril, they were allowed to perform a baptism themselves—albeit a perfunctory one—if a priest could not be found.

Little Mariot died just four hours later.

I'm told that her father and mother were beside themselves, as were the grandparents, who were also villeins on my manor.

I was absent that morning, but Walter told me that Edwin's father, Fulke, went to the priest's house the following day to arrange for little Mariot to be buried in the churchyard.

There was a furious argument. Swithun had not baptised the child—Aolfe Midwyf had—and he did not believe that it was a true baptism; how could it be proven? Mariot could not lie in the churchyard. She must be buried just outside and would not be given the opportunity—for her soul was unfit for Heaven, tarnished as it was, with the sin of Eve—to rise again at the Last Judgement. Fulke berated him for his tardiness in coming and saving the soul of his granddaughter. Swithun apparently laughed, still not quite sober.

What was one less villein?

When Walter told me of Swithun's refusal to bury little Mariot in our churchyard, I arranged with the priest at Burbage to inter her there, for her mother was a Burbage lass, and she had been transferred to my manor on her marriage. It was no bother to him, he said. Godfrey was a kind man. Before this happened, I would try to convince Swithun of his error.

I asked Walter to convey my severe disappointment to Swithun and my indignation at his words. I knew that Walter would give my words verbatim and imbue them with a certain venom, for Walter could be harsh when needed. I would speak severely to Father Swithun on my return from Marlborough later that week.

I did speak to him. He denied the midwife's right to baptism.

"Then why did you not come down as requested and baptise the child in its own home, yourself?"

"I was not asked."

"The midwife Aolfe says you were at your house and that you refused to come."

"She lies."

"Why? What does she gain by lying?"

"Why the opportunity to lapse into her pagan ways and speak foul words over the child. This village, nay, this forest, is rife with unGodly practices. The child has gone to the devil for all I know. The good church does not have a strong hold on this land, and I am surprised that you are allowing such backsliding."

"You will speak civilly to me, Swithun. I am, whatever you might think, your lord."

He stared.

"So, what practices are these that are so unGodly? I know you disapprove of the blessing of animals and the Mayday celebrations...what else?"

"The people go out to certain of the trees and tie ribbons and gewgaws asking the devils of the place to grant their wishes, when they should be on their knees in church, asking the saints to intervene."

"I think you'll find they do that also."

"They go to the pools deep in the forest and throw in offerings, that their prayers may be answered. This is not the act of a God-fearing..."

"So you have been lurking in the forest, watching my folk do these things, have you?"

"I must know what is in their hearts so that I can bring

them back to the ways of the Lord."

"Swithun, leave them be. These are harmless and time-worn rituals that mean nothing. I forbid you to go into the forest and spy on the manor folk."

"I am a free man."

"I am your lord, and I have spoken." I turned to leave him, then turned back.

"And leave the drink, Swithun. It is your duty to be sober and available at all times to your flock."

All these events had taken place as I journeyed back to Marlborough on the Monday morning, Hawise riding perched in front of me on Bayard. Naturally, she could not stay at the castle, and so she lodged with her little friend on the High Street at the home of the Lord of Snap. He was pleased to have her come and play with his daughter Petronilla.

That afternoon, she and I paid a visit to Mistress Wolvercote at Johannes' house.

Hawise sat pertly on the stool in the parlour in her best rust-coloured riding gown. Two strands of her beautiful, long, curly copper hair had been plaited to hold it from her face, all held in place by a black band embroidered with gold doves. Her belt was of the same pattern.

I wore my best cotte and, for a change, a capuchon in Lincoln green with matching chausses.

When Hawise realised that there were honey cakes and real cow's milk on offer, she sat up even straighter.

Mistress Wolvercote asked her to call her Lydia, but Hawise, I could see, thought that too much for her on a first meeting. She politely thanked Lydia for the cakes and ate demurely, one eye on me. I knew that I would be quizzed until I fell asleep with it all later that afternoon.

They talked about clothes, and Hawise was complimented on her choice of gown. Then they fell to talking about which colours suited them best. When they had exhausted that topic, they nattered on about stories they had heard. They talked about food and how to prepare it. I was amazed at my little girl's knowledge. Where had she found this adult conversation?

At last, the talk came round to me.

"Dada…" Hawise corrected herself, "Father said that he wanted to bump our priest Swithun on the head the other day. It was so funny. I would like to see that."

"Oh, so would I," said Lydia, chuckling. "From what I have heard, he is a foul man. For a priest, that is."

I smiled. Word got around in small places like this.

"There was no one in church yesterday. I tried not to laugh, but …I was so glad no one was there for him, the horrid man."

"Hawise, Swithun is our priest, and we must be respectful of him, regardless."

"You aren't," she said with a tilt of her chin.

"Well…"

"You told him off, and Agnes said he was an evil little man."

Lydia smiled into her hand.

"I am his lord; I am responsible for his village, and so I am allowed to tell him off. Agnes did not like the way he treated her poor mother, so she is bound to say that."

"What will you do about him, m'lord Aumary?" asked Mistress Wolvercote.

"I have written to the bishop. It may take some time to work its way up to him, but it will. I have asked that he be removed…ahem, elsewhere."

"Then some other poor place will get him."

"I hope that Herbert Poore will read between the lines and work out that he is not suited for pastoral work. He is too much of a zealot. He has no understanding of rural folk and their ways."

"He has no human kindness or understanding of people, and that is essential in a priest," Lydia said.

"You are very kind," said Hawise suddenly.

Lydia blinked. "It is sweet of you to say so, Hawise."

Hawise swung her legs on the stool, the flats of her hands on the seat beside her. "I wish you could come and be our priest."

"If it were possible, I should like that very much," said Lydia, blushing.

"You are very busy here with Johannes, so you cannot."

"No. Besides, the bishop would not think it right that a woman would like to be a priest, my dear. Priests are all men."

"Are they? Oh."

Here is my daughter now being her five-year-old self, I thought.

"Well, that is silly. I think ladies would make very good priests. They are good with babies and old people. They would keep the church nice and clean…"

"So do I…" I interrupted, "Think they'd make good priests, I mean."

Lydia laughed. "One day, maybe. Now, do have another honey cake. They won't keep, you know."

Hawise reached for one, remembered her manners at the last moment and offered the plate to Lydia. She took one. I declined.

"Will you come to visit Durley? It's a nice place," said Hawise, wiping the crumbs from the front of her dress. "I am sure Father will fetch you. You will, won't you, Dada?"

"I will indeed," I said.

Lydia smiled shyly.

"That would be too wonderful," she said.

The glass-makers were hard at work filling in the windows at the solar of Durley Manor house. I had left Henry in charge of them all and I was sure that they would work well under his guidance. When next I returned, I had every intention of talking to Master Glazer about young Piers. Henry told me he seemed very happy pottering about and fetching and carrying for them. He was not, of course, allowed to do anything like the main work, but there were small jobs that Master Glazer set him, to which Piers fell with a gusto. We saw he was happy, a willing worker and interested in it all and we vowed to talk about an apprenticeship for him. I realised, naturally, that this meant he must go with them if and when they moved on, for glass-fitters, like masons, were peripatetic, going where the work was to be found. However, Master Glazer hailed from the town and had a house here, too. There was beginning to be more work fairly locally.

I would need to talk to Piers' mother, who lived in the village.

Margaret Manton was a quiet woman who tended her little plot of land, raised goats, did a little weaving, sewing and mending, and looked after her two sons. When her husband had been murdered on my manor, I had felt an extra responsibility for the family, for Henry was only ten and Piers a mere year old.

As I have said, I took Henry under my wing and groomed him to take the place of his father. Their cottage was a little way towards the edge of the village and they were freemen, not villeins.

That Wednesday, I was walking about the town, off to the house by the high cross, which stood a little further up than Johannes' house. Here lived a cutler, and I was off to show him our little knife to see if he could identify it. He was the only worker of such metal things in Marlborough, though I doubted it was his work. There were a few Jews who lived on Silver Street, a little further up on the hillside, and they dealt in, amongst other things, precious metals and fine materials such as ivory. I might be wise to ask there, too.

I had passed the woman before I knew who it was. She was heading for the market, the new Marlborough market, which was only a month old and situated in the centre of the wide street, just beyond the shambles.

I turned as she stepped into the road. A cart was passing just a little too close, and the breeze was about to catch her cloak and whip it up. I made a grab for her arm just as the wheel passed, and her cloak flapped harmlessly, like a bird's wing, and was stilled again.

"Too close, mistress," I said.

Margaret jumped and came to again. "Oh...oh..." Then she realised who had hold of her. "My lord," she curtsied. "Thank you, sir. I hadn't realised he was going so fast. So close, I mean, m'lord."

I smiled. "Aye, too fast for this press of people and too near to the edge of the road where folk walk." I steadied her. "Are you all right now?"

She patted her head cloth and straightened it. "Yes, yes. I think so...Thank you."

"Come to the edge again and stand under Master Philbert's awning. You can sit on one of his boxes and collect yourself." Master Philbert was a fleshmonger. His shop was halfway down the High. "I'd like to talk to you."

Margaret perched herself on one of the cleaner boxes. It had, by the look of it, once held game birds, for feathers clung to the rough inside surface. She fanned herself with her linen apron.

"We are well met, mistress, for I had need of speaking to you about Piers."

"Aye, Henry told me that you wanted to talk to me, though Piers is fourteen now and his own man. He can speak for himself."

"Henry tells me he cannot complete his apprenticeship with Master Thatcher."

"He would be dead, and that is the truth, were he to have stayed. Dead before the year is out. His wheezing and breathing get so bad, sir."

"His father was the same, I remember."

She nodded. "His lungs were his weak spot, too."

"So I have a mind to make an offer for him to have a place with the glass-makers who are at the manor at the moment."

"Oh, sir...he does so like to be with them."

"I've noticed," I smiled. "The only thing is...the heat. Heat can often, I'm told, be as bad for the lungs as dust from thatch or corn."

She tilted her head, trying to understand my reasoning.

"I think we shall try him and then see how he gets on. It seems to me there are two kinds of glass men. Those who make the glass and those who fit it. Maybe we could get Piers a place to learn how to fit it."

She grinned. "Aye, that would be grand."

"Then, so I have heard, there is this fashion for coloured glass now. The glass-makers make the glass, but the artisans cut it and patch it together in patterns. I saw some in Normandy last year, in the church in Rouen. It is truly a sight to behold."

"Piers is always such a good lad. I am sure he will be very grateful for anything you can do for him. And we will pay whatever is necessary, Henry and me."

"Aye...well, I will see what can be arranged. Now, let me just see you across the road."

I took her elbow, and we passed between the jostling folk, the carts, and the horses. We stepped gingerly over and around the piles of horse, cattle and sheep dung that littered the street every market day.

Edith and Edmund Brooker were two of my villeins and were twins. This meant, unlike Margaret and Henry, they were not free and were feudal tenants entirely subject to me as their lord, to whom they paid dues and services in return for land. They lived, as their name suggested, by the brook in the last house in the village before the forest took over. It was a small house of one storey and two rooms, with a loft above. Their parents had died some while ago when our village had had an outbreak of dock fever.

They had been about sixteen when their parents died.

Neither of them seemed inclined to marry. Indeed, Edith had a sharp tongue and was known to be somewhat of a shrew; it would take a brave man to take her to wife. Her brother bore the brunt of her moods and evil tempers. I never understood how he could stand to be in the same house with her. When the wind was in the wrong direction, we could hear them arguing from the courtyard of the manor. Their nearest neighbours, poor Margaret and Henry, often used to complain about the Brookers disturbing their peace with their constant bickering.

I had spoken to Edmund a while back about building, perhaps, another small house in the village and letting him have it so that he might get away from the cutting tongue of his sister, but he declined and said that he was happy enough. Though she was indeed a nagging woman, she cooked, cleaned, fetched and kept the house for him, and if he moved, he would have to do this for himself. No, he would put up with her ill tempers.

I came across them now in the marketplace, arguing about a skillet that they must buy. Edmund was all for having their old one repaired; indeed, he had brought it with him in the hope of finding a tinker at the market who might do just that. Edith, on the other hand, wanted to spend their hard-saved money on a new one.

"Is there one here? Is there? No!" she screeched. "I cannot go any longer with such a piss-poor article as that," and she pointed to the skillet which Edmund was dangling from his fingers.

"We can ask about...see if..."

"No. I must have one now. I cannot cook on that any longer. There lies the ironmonger - I am going there," and she flounced off.

"I think you have lost that battle, Edmund," I said, coming up behind him.

He jumped and turned and knuckled his forehead. "Aye, sir, I think I have."

"She is probably right. That poor thing has been patched too many times to be useful."

"Yes." He looked at the skillet in his hand. Then he dropped it in a hessian bag and tied it with string. "It's been an old friend since before ma and da died."

"Many years now."

He sighed, "Aye."

"Are you selling at the market today, Edmund?" I asked, looking around for evidence of any surplus produce he might have brought.

"Nah. She won't let me, for she says it will be a hard winter, and we need everything we can lay down for ourselves."

"She knows about these things, does she, about the weather we shall have?"

"She's pretty good at picking the bad years, yessir."

"And this coming winter will be bad?"

"So she says."

I slapped him on the back. "Then we shall see... I will speak to you in the spring about how accurate we think she has been." And I went on my way.

On my way to the little lane that ran off the High Street and where lay the cutler's shop, I spotted some of the townsmen gathering by the high cross. Their manner was furtive and stealthy. I sank back into the shadows of a gap between two houses and watched.

The two soldiers from the castle whom I'd had cause to argue with the other day, Gilbertson and Brooks, came up at a run from the lower town. There was some hurried conferring.

I craned my neck to look at the group. I could smell mischief.

I ran at full tilt up the alley, turned right and sprinted at the back of the houses there. I quickly came out onto Kingsbury Hill, and then I sauntered down past the men on the other side of the road and into Johannes' alley, which led to the church. Luckily, I was screened by the bulk of the high cross as it reared up in three tiers.

Once out of sight in the darkness of the covered alley, I pelted for the gate, ducked into the doctor's yard and ran to the kitchen door.

"Johannes! Lock and bar the front door!" I yelled through the opening.

Johannes always left the front door of his house open during working hours so that folk could come and consult him.

"What?"

"I think we shall have trouble with the townsmen and some castle soldiers. Best, I think, to get Agnes and Lydia to safety in the church."

I ran back to the alley and watched as Johannes quickly ushered Agnes and Lydia out of the house. I heard him lock the front door, then the back door. He opened the gate and then locked it behind them, hurrying the women up the few yards to the church. The west door opened and closed.

I looked behind me up the alleyway towards the church. Several men were coming this way. They were chatting animatedly and laughing openly. I recognised one of them as a man from the tanning yards. They seemed uninterested in the goings on in the alley. They were not part of the plan then.

I sauntered into the midst of the few men by the cross and nonchalantly put my thumbs through my belt.

"Well, well, Gilbertson, good day. What do you do here?"

They'd now crossed the road, and one man had tried the doctor's front door. Gilbertson spun round and I saw his eyes flare. He made a perfunctory bow.

"Good day, my Lord Belvoir."

"You are not on guard duty at the castle mint now?"

"Not now, sir. No."

I moved into the mouth of the alleyway. Out of the gloom, Johannes came up behind me.

"Ah, Gilbertson, how are you today?"

I saw the man flinch.

"Well, thank you, doctor."

"Did you wish to consult me?"

"I...I..."

The men from the tanning yards came up behind and made to squeeze past us. They realised that one of their betters was blocking the way and drew back from me, tugging their forelocks.

It was not going to be possible for them to exit onto the road, so they loitered behind us with a sudden interest in the goings-on.

"You must be careful. Wounds like that can so very easily go bad," added Johannes.

"Wounds, Gilbertson? Have you damaged yourself?" I asked, smiling.

"'Tis nothing, m'lord," said the man with an embarrassed grin.

"Nothing? Why, the man had the biggest boil I have ever lanced, Sir Aumary. A positive mountain…"

I saw Gilbertson squirm inside his clothes.

"I hope you are taking care of it as I advised you."

"I am, doctor, thank you," answered Gilbertson, rather abashed.

"A boil? Where was it then?" shouted one of the tanners from behind me.

"On 'is arse!" gave out one of the others who was obviously in the know.

Ah, yes, this was Gilbertson's brother.

There was a burst of laughter.

"What have you done with the witch, Doctor Johannes?" asked Jonson into that laughter.

"There's no witch here, Jonson," answered Johannes, his face losing its smile.

One of the townsmen thrust his hand to his knife hilt. "I reckon I saw her just now, going into the church."

I stepped forward out of the mouth of the alleyway. The tanners came forward with me.

"You'll not pass to the church, Brown," said one of them. "We saw no witches going in, and we have just come from the alley."

"Nothing but two young women going in to say their prayers, wasn't it, lads?" said another, looking around.

The townsmen moved forward as a group and met the tanners. There was much pushing and shoving, though no weapons were drawn.

"Disperse all of you and go to your homes!" I shouted.

"Let us get the witch!"

"There's no such thing, Will Dyer, and you know it!" said a tanner.

"She's just a little girl," said another.

Two townsmen managed to get past us with a deal of shoving and pushing and made a dash for the church door.

We turned tail and followed.

I made a grab for the nearest man as he fell into the church porch.

The west door opened abruptly, and Father Torold stood there.

His stentorian voice boomed out into the confines of the small area behind Johannes' yard. It bounced from the stonework and the cob walls with a lingering echo.

"What's this? Who is disturbing God's peace in this Holy place!"

The tanners and townsmen ranged behind me clattered to a halt.

The men who had burst through slid to an abrupt stop. One slipped and fell to his knees before his priest.

"Perriot Baudler, what are you up to?" Father Torold steadied himself against his door as the man bowled into him.

The man got up and rubbed his barked shin and his bruised knees.

Another man from the back of the crowd shouted, "We have come for the witch, Father Torold."

"Yeah!" said Baudler, standing upright and grimacing. "We know she's in your church. Fetch her out!"

"There is no witch in my church, young man," said Father Torold sternly.

Johannes and I had now come up to the porch.

"I have said it before. Go to your homes NOW, or I will

have you thrown into the town lockup!" I yelled.

A few of the men shuffled their feet.

Some at the back of the crowd thought better of their bravery and disappeared. A hard core remained. The tanners held their ground. Father Torold lifted his black-garbed arms. His sleeves fell back like wings. His arms rose slowly.

"Do you think that God would allow a witch...a real witch to foul the Holy ground of St Mary?"

There was a sullen muttering.

"Nooooo! A witch could not set foot past the Holy water stoup. You all know this for a fact!"

More muttering. Torold's voice died away.

"And we must all pass the Holy water to enter into this House of God, to travel to the core of this building. Anyone coming to do harm to any person who has entered into this holy place to pray will be in great peril."

The two soldiers looked at each other.

"God would be most displeased."

I saw Gilbertson shrug his over-tunic onto his shoulder more firmly. A nervous habit with him.

Brooks looked round at the men behind him. Now, only three remained, and they were looking confused.

Father Torold raised his voice a notch. "Our king of blessed memory, Henry, second of that number, did penance for the sin he committed against the blessed martyr Becket in asking for his murder, that death doled out in his very own church of Canterbury." The final words were delivered in a loud whisper. "Would you risk your souls? God looks down on you now. Would you deal out violence in God's domain? This place of sanctuary?"

Some of the tanners crossed themselves.

Gilbertson watched them and followed suit.

"No man can do harm here and not pay with his soul.

Would you risk your immortal souls? Doing harm in God's abode carries with it the terrible punishment of ex-commu-ni-cation!" Torold drew out the syllables of the word like the strikes of a hammer, and the sound bounced around the small space, his voice rising in strength and pitch.

I turned and watched as Brooks backed off and walked down the alley. I saw the remaining townsmen turn with him.

Gilbertson blinked.

"Ex-commu-ni-cation!" repeated Torold, smiling secretly after the fleeing bodies. He leaned forward into Gilbertson's face. "Your soul will be forever in torment..."

It was enough for Gilbertson. He turned and ran.

Father Torold let out a huge breath and laughed on it.

"Thank you, Father," I said, smiling up at him standing on the step.

I wiped my hand over my brow.

His booming bass rang out down the alleyway, following the townsmen and soldiers. "Forever burning in the fiery pit!"

The remaining tanners crossed themselves again and, with a nod to me and Johannes, made their way to the road.

Agnes and Lydia came meekly to stand behind Father Torold.

"My flock shall be told, Sir Aumary," he said quietly. "I will not have such behaviour in my people."

"And I will ask Father Columba at the castle to warn the garrison," I said.

Johannes came out of the porch with Agnes under one arm and Lydia the other. "Thank you, Aumary, for your quick thinking," he said.

Father Torold winked at me.

At last, I passed under the arch made by two adjacent properties with flying rooms above and into Coombes Yard, less than halfway down the High Street. I pushed open the door of the cutler's workshop.

Here was everything to be found which required a sharp edge, or which was made of metal. Here, too, were bits and buckles, spurs, and other small metal objects, for this was Master Lorimer's shop, where he made and sold many things made of different base metals. I hallooed, and he came bustling from the back of the shop.

"My lord, I am honoured." He bowed.

"I'm not here to buy, Lorimer, sadly," I said. I saw his face drop.

He turned away and busied himself at his counter. He lit a candle, for it was dark in the little shop.

I put the little knife on the counter with a click. He twisted to look.

"I am not buying."

"Neither am I selling."

I waited for his curiosity to get the better of him.

Eventually, he sighed and turned.

He picked up the ivory-handled knife, and his eyes narrowed.

"What are you doing, m'lord, with such a piece? 'Tis a lady's knife. Does it need mending?" He tested the edge with his finger. "Quite new."

He brought it nearer to his eyes and squinted. He brought the candle burning on the countertop closer to him and rolled up his hand so that there was a tiny hole in his fist. He peered through it at the little knife.

"Gets more detail this way...for me tired eyes."

"Too much to hope, I suppose," I said, "That this is one you have made, or one of your men?"

"No...no call for such things in Marlborough."

He pulled a piece of birch bark paper towards him and began sketching the little piece. He worked very quickly. No call…no - but you will copy it anyway, I thought.

"I'll tell you this, though. When we had the fair a month back, there was a man there. Said he came from somewhere called Cirencaister or something like that. He had little things like this. Fancy, expensive, decorative. I figured he wouldn't be selling much there, so I doubt he'll be back next year."

"You mean you are afraid of competition, Master Lorimer?" I was feeling peeved at the little cutler's attitude and had decided to bait him a trifle.

"Not at all. There's some of us know what it is our customers want, and some as doesn't. We know what Marlborough people will buy. That's why we are so successful and don't feel the need to go traipsing around the countryside looking for business at fairs, m'lord."

He sniffed.

"You don't happen to know the man's name?"

"Why should I ask him his name, for goodness sake?"

"Oh, I just thought, seeing he was taking the business of Marlborough people at the fair from Marlborough tradesmen, you might want to know who he was."

"Like I told you, sir, he didn't do well. No one was going to pay his prices."

"I saw him," I said, "from afar…he seemed to be doing all right to me."

Lorimer sniffed again. "Well, you saw wrong, m'lord."

I picked up my little knife and threw it in the air, catching it again nonchalantly, smiling into my beard.

"Thank you for your help, Master Lorimer. Good day."

I turned to exit.

He blew out the candle and as I opened the door, he said, "Fulbert, Fulbert Cuttelar."

I turned and nodded.

Later that day, I picked up my daughter and her little friend Petronilla from the Snap household at the side of the lane running down to the Meadow by the river.

Hawise sat before me on Bayard and Petronilla sat with a groom, who would leave us at Durley and be back in Marlborough at sundown.

We jogged nicely up the hill and, in no time at all, were approaching the manor from the Salisbury road end, past John Brenthall's house, turning right, skirting the orchard and taking the lane which bent around the priest's house and onto the church path.

A loud yelling was coming from the front of Swithun's house.

I sent Hawise and her friend on to the manor. She scowled at me, for she so wanted to know what our priest was doing now.

I dismounted and walked Bayard around the house.

Swithun was yelling at the top of his voice and pointing to the sky.

Edmund Brooker was standing with feet wide-planted, looking at him in hatred.

"I was not, I tell you. Why should I? God is my witness. I am a celibate priest!"

I looked on. There was no doubt they both knew I was there.

Edmund Brooker scowled. "Father or not, celibate or not, Edith caught you, you filthy spy!"

Swithun was apoplectic. "She was mistaken in my intentions. I merely called out to ask..."

"Swithun, what is the matter here?" I asked, coming closer.

"As soon as I saw that she was...nak... that she was as

God had made Eve, I averted my eyes."

"Well, Edith says you did not and that she had to grab a blanket to cover herself. What were you doing peeping through the window if not spying on a young maid?"

"Swithun," I said, "answer the man."

He turned to me, his face as red as a summer sunset. "I was passing the house. I looked through the window. The shutters were open. There was no intention to give offence."

"Passing the house?" I quizzed. "Going where?"

Edmund shouted at that. "The path goes nowhere but into the forest."

I had noticed, when I arrived, that he was carrying an axe. I now took it from him, and he made no demur.

"Can one not freely walk where one wishes into the forest or out of it without censure?" said Swithun.

"I have spoken to you before about wandering the forest."

Swithun shrugged.

"What were you doing with this, Edmund?"

"Splitting kindling, m'lord. Out the back of our cottage. I heard Edith screech. She told me the priest had looked in at the window when she was washing and dressing. She had been up last night, looking after the woman who keeps the poultry, who is ill, and so slept late this morning."

"And you followed him with an axe?"

"It was in my hand...I...I...did not mean to use it."

"Were you, Father, spying on a comely maid through the windows of her house?"

"Most certainly not."

"Then let us say no more about it. Swithun, if I were you, I would stay away from the Brookers' cottage. You cannot be accused of spying if you are not anywhere near."

Swithun's eyes bored into mine. Then he was gone into his house.

Edmund sighed, "He is an odd one, m'lord," he said. "Edith is a good-looking woman. Priest or no priest, he is first and foremost a man."

"And a young one at that," I said.

"I think we shall keep going to the Bedwyn church of a Sunday with some of the others," Edmund said cheekily. "We can steer clear of him then, m'lord."

As their lord, I should have told him that their duty was to be in their local church of a Sunday, but somehow, I thought he and his sister were probably right to avoid the man. If I had my way, he would soon be gone. I handed him back his axe.

Chapter Nine

I sat in my little office at Durley Manor the next morning with the ivory-handled knife in my hand.

Should I go to Cirencester, a little town some twenty-six miles due north on the Gloucester road, or should I send someone to talk to this man Fulbert Cuttelar for me?

I knew nothing but his name and the place from which he came. It might be that he did not have a trading place there but went from fair to fair. If this was the case, I might never catch up with him, for he could be in any of the places where John had sold fair charters.

> *Yes, Paul, you are right. I could have waited until the following year and checked to see if the man had returned to the fair, but I wanted answers then and there. I couldn't wait a whole year.*

Truthfully, I did not know for sure if the man was the cutler who made and sold the little knife. Perhaps it was best to leave it for a while.

I was passing the little room I'd given to the master glazier as his office and workplace. This was situated at the end of the row of small lean-to chambers I'd had built in stone a few years ago onto the southern wall of the courtyard.

The door was open, and I heard a rustling of parchment from within. I scratched at the door and entered.

Perkin Glazer was a small, compact man of some forty-five years with a shock of blond wavy hair curling onto his collar. He wore a small, pale moustache but no beard, and his eyes were a startling ice blue. His hair showed no trace of grey and his face was surprisingly soft and unlined. His hands and forearms, however, were peppered with old scars of the burns and cuts he had received from plying his trade as a master glazier.

He turned at my entrance and bowed, a drawing in his hands.

"My lord" He took up another parchment. "The solar will be complete in a day or so."

"I will go and have a look, Master Glazier. And thank you for taking on young Piers. He's a fine lad. You won't be disappointed."

The man smiled. "He's a willing lad with a good brain. I am sure we can make something of him."

I smiled in my turn. "And if you are able, I have another commission for you. The windows in the church. Have you the time to make those too in glass?"

"Glass in all the windows, my lord? That is quite a task."

"You cannot do it?"

Perkin chuckled. "It can be done certainly. I will set to and work out a price for you."

As we chatted, I heard a pony clopping into the manor yard under the gate arch. Feet hit the ground as the man dismounted, and I heard Henry, my steward, direct the rider to the little room in which I stood.

The door opened further, and a young man, tall

and blond, raked the space with his gaze. His eyes met that of Perkin Glazier. I felt a frisson of menace dart through the room.

Aha!' I thought, there is a tale here.'

Glazer turned and dropped the parchments to the table. He planted his feet wide, stuck his thumbs into his belt and stared up at the wall.

"Harry."

"Da."

Harry Glazer bowed low to me. "Sir, my master, Gilbert Cordwainer, sends his greetings. He failed to catch you yesterday before you left for Durley and he bid me come to bring the pair of soft shoes you asked for. He was unsure when you would next be in the town, and so..." Harry, Gilbert's apprentice, held out a cloth bag to me, "I have brought them to you as requested."

"That's kind, Harry," I said, leaning over and taking the string of the bag from him. "Thank you."

I wore boots for riding and working but had ordered some soft, thick, felt ankle boots with a leather sole to pad about the solar when at my leisure.

"My old ones have holes in the soles. Perhaps you could take them back with you and mend them?"

"Certainly, sir." His eyes slid sideways to his father.

Perkin turned to face him. "So, you are enjoying playing with leather and fiddling about with felt, eh, Harry?"

"It's a good trade. I am content."

"This good-for-nothing son of mine, my lord, didn't want to be a glazier like his father. Oh no. He'd rather go off to be a cordwainer. A shoemaker. Enjoy working with people's smelly feet, do you, lad?"

"No worse than the smell of molten glass."

"It's a trade, as you say, lad... Glassmaking is...an art."

"I am four years into this trade. I'd not change it for all

the grains of sand in your kilns."

"Pah!" said Perkin Glazier. "You'll never be a wealthy man, Harry, poking about with sweaty feet."

"Perhaps I do not have the desire for wealth which makes you the grasping man you are, sir."

"I live in a fine new house whilst your cordwainer…"

"Is an honourable man and has no need of finery. I have never known a more contented and humble man," said Harry.

"Ah well…when you are out on your ear and begging in the street…"

"Why should that be?"

"Well, we both know you're a lazy sod, and your temper gets the better of you, and one day…one day…"

"And we all know, sir, that you are a liar and a…"

"Liar, am I? So what have I done to you that you should call me thus?"

"You know full well what I think of you. And why."

"Your Ma well and truly poisoned you against me, didn't she?"

"She would probably be alive today if it weren't for you, you lecher."

"Ah, we're back to that, are we?"

"You killed her as surely as if you stuck a knife into her heart."

"Pah! She shouldn't listen to gossip, lad."

"She saw with her own eyes…"

"Peace, peace," I said, my hands on my hips. "You are like a couple of children."

Glazier turned his back and scratched his chin.

"Sorry, m'lord," said Harry. "It's just that my father and I…"

"Have a quarrel which has nothing to do with me. A quarrel which can be kept off my manor."

I turned to the glass-maker. "Thank you, Glazer, I will return to speak to you about the church windows. Come, Harry, let's go and find…" Turning as I spoke, I noticed that Father Swithun was surreptitiously looking in the doorway, observing the altercation.

"Eavesdropping again, Swithun?"

"Certainly not, my lord."

"Then what do you want?"

Swithun blustered a little at that."I wanted to speak to you…but it can wait."

Perkin Glazer sneered at his son. "Off you go to your smelly shoemaking, then," he laughed pointedly and took up his parchments again.

"You are a vile lecher and an abomination," said Harry. "I never want to see you again. You could drop off the edge of the world this hour and it would not be too soon for me!"

Swithun drew himself up and stepped into the room. "That is no way to speak to your sire, young man, the man who gave you life. Honour thy father and thy mother: that thy days may be long upon the land which the Lord thy God giveth thee," he intoned.

"Honour my mother, sir, I will, to the end of my days, but this putrid…"

"This man is your father," spluttered Swithun. "He is deserving of…"

"Nothing from me. He is an adulterer, sir, and a…"

"Harry…" I said sternly.

Harry turned to me, tears in his eyes. "That man is responsible for my mother's death. His philandering killed her, sir. His twisted nature made sure that…"

"Thou shalt not bear false witness…" said Swithun. "That is the ninth commandment of our Lord God…"

"Swithun," I turned to him. "Go back to your church."

"…Offences against the truth express by word or deed

a refusal to commit oneself to moral uprightness: they are fundamental infidelities to God and they undermine the foundations of the covenant with God." His voice rose in volume.

"Swithun!"

"Such foulness should not..."

Harry stared open-mouthed at the priest. "What is this to you, sir priest, that you should interfere with...?"

Swithun noisily drew in breath through his nose."It is a grave sin to falsely accuse a man of adultery. Injustice to one's father must be..."

"Oh, go to Hell!" shouted Harry pink in the face. "You know nothing."

"Swithun!" I shouted, "Go!"

He looked up at me with venom, breathed in heavily once or twice, swished his black cloak and was gone.

"Come, Harry." I took his shoulder and hurried him out of the room, shutting the door. We strode over the yard to the hall steps. I almost dragged him by the arm.

"I had no idea that you and your father were at such loggerheads..."

"Aye, sir. I'm very sorry. I boil over when I think what that man has done."

"Aye, well. We'll say no more. No more arguing, do you hear? No more. Though it was unfortunate that Swithun chose now to lecture you. Now, run up to the hall and ask Agnes Brenthall to find my holed shoes. I will collect them when I am in town sometime. Get a drink and something to eat."

Harry bowed low and was gone up the steps.

I watched him go, shaking my head. What was Swithun doing? The man was really becoming a nuisance here in the village.

A little while later, I went up to look at my new windows. They had indeed done well with them. Each space had been filled with an opaque greenish glass which let in a watery light not too dissimilar to that available from an open and unshuttered window. Now, though, the solar would be snug and warm. No more gales blowing through, no more driven rain. No more putting in the frames of waxed paper or slivers of horn.

I was proud of my manor. I had completed more work on it than any of my previous ancestors, apart from the one who built the first house in about 1089. I had rebuilt parts of the wall and had caused the gatehouse to be rebuilt in stone. I had added some new buildings to the courtyard structures. I had put flagstones and cobbles in the courtyard, and all the upper floors were now of good solid oakwood. There were no longer beaten earth floors in my undercroft or other ground-floor rooms. They were all finished in good cobbles or stone. I'd installed new chimneys, the sort which funnel away the fumes from the fire, and had rebuilt the kitchen stove with a fine chimney and new ovens. And now, I had put glass in the windows of my private rooms.

The next thing was to glaze the church windows.

Why would I do it if Swithun was not staying and would not be objecting to the birds in the church? No, I would still do it. It was an offering, if you like, to God and to Cecily, my deceased wife.

I realised that I was thinking of Mistress Wolvercote again. I smiled. I would, as Hawise had suggested, get her to come to see Durley and my new windows.

I hailed my master glazier and told him how pleased I was with the results.

I discussed the apprenticing of Piers to the glazier and

negotiated a cost, and he was quite willing, for he had gauged the mettle of the lad and was losing one of his journeymen soon, as the man graduated after making his masterpiece.

He accepted a price for the church windows and agreed that they would begin the next day.

That next day dawned fair but chilly. We were now a few days nearer to the autumn feast, our Autumn Equinox celebration, which this year was on September 22nd.

I needed to consult with John and with the reeve, Walter and also with young Henry. This would be the first time he was to be totally in charge of the manor festivities. He seemed quite happy to take the whole thing under his wing.

"Shall we have the service in the church as usual this year, sir?" asked Henry when I passed the office later in the day.

"Ah...yes..." I ruffled my hair.

"I had better go and see Father Swithun and gauge the lie of the land there. I know that Benedict used to bless the animals and the orchard, but somehow, I think Father Swithun does not believe it is his duty to do such a thing."

"He accused us all of being pagan and godless," said Henry, "when you weren't here, on May Day, when we were setting up the pole and decorating everything with hawthorn blossoms, as we always do. He told Walter Reeve, and me too, that this tree was associated with a wicked goddess who led men astray, much as Adam was tempted by Eve and that the devil would enter us all, for our bodies would be prey to lasciviousness and lust, should we leave ourselves open."

"Really?"

"Music, too, apparently, is the devil's weapon. It inflames the blood and fills our minds with erotic thoughts," Henry laughed. "It's difficult to see Old Tom, who plays the bagpipes for the dancing, filled with erotic thoughts, isn't it, sir? He's ninety, if he's a day."

"It is indeed," I agreed, chuckling.

"And he said that the smell of the hawthorn flower was the smell of woman the temptress and should not be allowed anywhere near the holy places, lest it defile the sanctity of God's House. But we have always decorated the church with hawthorn. And holly and ivy at Christ's mass."

"I thought the hawthorn blossom was a reflection of Mary, Mother of Jesus, and a symbol of chastity," I said. "I am obviously wrong." I pursed my lips. "I'll see what I can do, Henry," I said.

I could not at first find Swithun but ran him to ground in his own church, where he was watching the glass-fitters.

"Are you pleased, sir priest, with your windows? You will have no further incursions by swallows now."

"Indeed, thank you, m'lord. I am."

"It will be warmer, too, now that the winter winds cannot whistle through the spaces."

"Cold is good for the soul. It focuses the mind. No church should be too warm, for it encourages daydreaming and turns one's thoughts from God. Hell is warm, m'lord, and none of us wish to go there."

"No, indeed." I coughed.

"Swithun, have you had any more thoughts about the celebrations we have in the village for the change in season from summer to autumn and the blessings which the church may bestow on...?"

"My thoughts have not changed on the matter. It is pagan and, as such, has no place in the church calendar. There will be no more dancing and junketing whilst I am priest of this place."

"Can you not find it in you to...?"

"That is my final word." He rudely turned from me to

watch the glass fitters.

"Then I will have no choice but to overrule you and ask the priest of Bedwyn to help us."

"If he wishes to imperil his immortal soul, he may do so. I shall not."

I shook my head. "You are a stubborn man, Swithun."

"Principled, my lord," he answered. "I stand by what I believe in."

We watched uncomfortably side by side for a short while, the glass fitters cutting the glass and measuring so exactly the space to be filled.

Young Piers was there. He was sitting with his back to the wall, and he had a board on his knee on which he was rolling some substance that resembled dough.

"They have given you a job, I see, Piers."

The young man tried to rise, but I put a hand on his shoulder to indicate he should carry on with his task.

"Aye, m'Lord Belvoir. I have the job of kneading the putty. 'Tis none so difficult, as it's just like kneading the bread for mother." He smiled up at me.

"It has to be just right, though, does it not, Piers?"

"Well, yes, but I do not make the putty, I just mix it. The quantities of whiting and oil are already worked out. They pour them into a bowl, and I mix them, and then, when it begins to set, I knead it like bread dough...see...sir?"

And he showed me again how it was done.

"Then the fitters take it and seal the window glass around the frames with it. It goes hard after a while, like stone."

"We shall see you as a master glazier in seven years' time, Piers. And then you will have a boy to mix the putty for you."

"Yessir, thank you, sir."

A glass man came over and took the putty from Piers

with a nod. The lad stood and wiped his hands along his flanks, leaving white marks on the dark fustian of his leggings.

I walked back down the nave.

I did not see it happen, but as I reached the church door, I heard the crash and the cursing. Oh dear, I thought, one of the workers has dropped a pane of glass and I walked on. I wish I had turned back.

The glass men had a large wooden board on two trestles. Here, the glass was prepared for fitting. Flattened pieces of about two to three-foot square were laid here so they could be cut to fit. Smaller pieces lay on the surface, too, off-cuts from the window pieces.

They told me later what they knew they had seen and what they thought had happened.

Swithun, I imagine, had turned to leave too quickly, and his habit of swirling his cloak behind him had allowed a free edge to catch a smaller, jagged piece of the glass. It crashed to the flagstone floor with an almighty noise.

One of the younger glassmen, being surprised, jumped and cursed, I am told.

It was not a bad curse, but they were in church, and it was not the place for any cursing, even in shock, especially within the hearing of its priest.

Father Swithun had drawn himself up to his full height, turned and glared at Piers.

"Such words rend the very body of Christ!"

Piers had defended himself. "It was not me...I didn't say..."

"Do not add prevarication to the sins of blasphemy and clumsiness," Swithun had boomed.

Piers was not taking this lightly. "I did not sweep the glass from the table, you did, Father."

The glassmen told me later how Swithun had made a

grab for young Piers, and there'd been a tussle.

More glass had slipped from the table as they bumped into it. Swithun's robe was torn. The priest took hold of Piers and dragged him roughly, to the priest's robing room, which lay to the side of the nave. There, he locked him in.

The young man who had cursed felt bad. After a while, he went to the priest's house and confessed his sin. Swithun did not relent. Perhaps he did not believe the man. Piers stayed in the little room.

Piers' mother came looking for him a few hours later. The church was in semi-darkness. The glass-men had gone to their bivouacs and tents. Margaret walked to the village green and asked if they had seen her son. Was he eating with them this night?

At last, she found the group who had been working on the church windows, and they told her Piers had been locked in the priest's room by Swithun.

She came for me.

I banged on the priest's door with the flat of my hand. He took his time to come.

"The key to the robing room, if you please, Swithun. NOW!"

"It is my church and…"

I put out my hand. "No, it is MY church."

Swithun reached into his scrip and gave me the key.

I hollered Piers' name as we ran up the nave, his mother pattering behind me. I fiddled with the key in the lock.

"Piers…Piers…answer me."

There was silence.

It was so dark now we could see very little.

I managed to turn the key at last and pushed the door. It caught on something snagged behind it. I pushed and pushed, and eventually, I made enough room to squeeze through.

I stumbled.

Piers had been lying just behind the door

I picked him up, and his mother gave a little yelp as she opened the door more fully and as she saw the state of her younger son. Her elder one was now running up the nave with a lantern, having been alerted by the comings and goings and the gossip from the glass-makers' camp. Walter was limping up behind him.

I laid Piers carefully on the bench at the side of the nave and turned his silver gilt head up. Henry stood behind me and lifted the lantern.

"I'll kill him for this," he said quietly. "I'll kill Father Swithun."

His mother fell to her knees and stretched out her hand.

Piers' sightless blue eyes stared up at me.

His asthma had indeed been the death of him—that, and Swithun the priest.

Margaret was stretched over the body of her younger son, weeping

Henry was dry-eyed and seething.

More candles had been lit. We were all in a state of shock.

I recovered first and said, "Can anyone tell me what happened?"

"The glass-men said that Piers was blamed for some misdemeanour and that the priest locked him in the robing room as a punishment," said Walter.

"But why should that prove the death of him? He has been in there about three hours, I suppose, since after I left the church?"

Henry looked up at me, his mouth a tight line, "Piers would have been anxious and upset. Feelings like that used to bring on his attacks. He was not yet fully recovered from the beating his lungs took from being amongst the straw thatch with Master Giles, sir."

"And something like this might bring on an attack?"

"Yes, that and the cold in the priest's room as the sun went down. It's an airless place" A tear trickled from his eye.

I patted him on the arm.

A few more people had now come into the church, and there were gasps of horror as they took in the scene. Walter turned on his heel and shooed them out. After a little while, he brought the priest back into the church.

The man would come no further than the doorway. Walter stayed behind him in the dark.

His face was white, and for the first time, I saw him as a flawed human being, not as an arrogant, pig-headed, zealous churchman.

He blinked, "No, no, this was not meant to happen. When I left him there to think about the heaviness of his sin, he was whole and hearty."

"You do not know what has happened here?"

"No, no, I do not," his voice trembled, but there was still that arrogance.

"We cannot have you officiate for Piers, even though you are the priest here. Walter, can you have someone ride to Bedwyn for Father Godfrey? Bring him as quickly as you can."

"Aye, sir."

"And find someone to look after Margaret."

Out he went.

I lifted my chin and glared at the priest, though it was hardly necessary, for he seemed shrunken and withered already.

"Perhaps, Swithun, if you had paid more attention to the people of this village, to their needs and wants, to their lives, you would understand them better. If you had not thought them beneath you, if you had taken the time and made an effort to know the folk around you, you would have known that Piers was vulnerable and weakened, and you might have thought twice about pushing him into that tiny airless space."

"I...I...I do not understand, my Lord Belvoir."

"No, Swithun, that is the trouble. You don't."

I rubbed my forehead. I had a headache coming.

"Piers, like his father before him, suffered from a weakness of the lungs. Dust from the threshing, from haymaking, from many of our daily activities, and flying pollen from the orchard would make him fight for breath. The weather, too, dry cold, humidity, too much heat. It was an illness he could not control. You sent him into that tiny room to die alone, suffocate, Swithun, to fight for breath and suffocate as surely as if you had slipped a noose around his neck and strangled him."

"No, it is not so."

"It is so."

His chin jutted, "I do not believe you."

"Why would I lie? Come here and look. Look on the result of your folly."

He took two steps towards me. He saw Piers' white face.

"No, he is not dead. You can revive him!"

"I am not God that I can bring him back from the dead, Swithun," I growled.

He took two more steps forward and crossed himself.

"Ask forgiveness from God, Swithun. I doubt any of us here can extend a forgiving hand towards you."

Swithun fell to his knees. "God forgive me, I did not know."

Margaret rose and launched herself at him, beating him about the head with her fists and screaming inarticulate sounds, the sounds of a mother's grief. Henry simply watched, tears streaming down his face. Swithun took the beating and did not defend himself. I let her beat him.

John Brenthall came into the church, looked around quickly, and in two strides was at Margaret's side. He took both her hands gently in his and held her close, and she subsided. At that moment, a couple of the goodwives of the village arrived and Margaret collapsed into their arms, and they left.

Swithun was repeating, "I did not know...how could I know...?"

"It cannot be undone, Swithun," I said. I motioned him to stand and to follow me. I went back into the tiny priest's room.

He stood in the doorway.

"This room is a disgrace."

I looked around. No cleaning had been done here for some time.

Dust was everywhere. The parish books were haphazardly thrown on a small table. These were the books kept by the church, which recorded the history of the village: who was born here and when; who married and when; and who died and where they were buried. The relationships of all the villagers and the wider forest were documented in these little books. We could consult this tome and others like them when we wished to know if people were related from generations gone by. Some of the books went back to the founding of the village under the Conqueror. We were unusual here in Durley to have such books. I knew of no other place which recorded such things, not even the larger churches in the town. In these books, too, were recorded events like extreme weather and national events like the coronation of a king.

I picked one up, blew off the dust and realised that some of this was not dust, but little particles of mould, like that found on the trees of the forest sometimes. I coughed.

No wonder Piers could not catch his breath.

"Why have you not allowed the women in to clean and tidy? You allow them in the church itself."

"They have no business in here. Here is where the priest's vestments are kept. The holy oils are stored here, as are the holy vessels for Mass."

"You do not do any housekeeping, Swithun? Is your cottage as untidy and filthy as this?"

He said nothing.

"I order that you let Old Joan back in here to tidy and clean. She did it for Benedict. She will do it for you. And let her into your house, too. I will have it orderly. After all, my grandfather built it."

I left the little room. John was still standing in the nave staring down at Piers, and Walter had returned to the doorway.

"Poor lad, he was such a happy creature. Even though he was set on a difficult pathway. First, his father was murdered, then his illness and now..." said John.

I knew that he was thinking about his own young son, Peter, a little younger than Piers.

"Can we fetch the parish coffin, John, and lay him in it for decency's sake for a while?"

"Yes, we can do that. I can organise that."

Most people went into the earth merely in their shroud, but they were taken to the graveside in the parish coffin. Only the wealthy could afford a coffin in which to be buried.

"Swithun, I think it is time you prayed for poor Piers. Pray hard. Pray for forgiveness for yourself, too, for you are certainly in need of it."

Swithun bowed his head. "I am truly sorry that this thing has happened. It was not my intention to punish the lad unto death. I will pray for him as you request."

"You did not intend that he die, Swithun, that I know. It

was an accident, one which could have been avoided with the exercise of a little more human kindness from you. But die, he has, and whatever we might say, you are responsible. You will have to live with that for the rest of your life."

"Think on that, priest!" spat Henry, "Such a stain on your oh-so-superior soul." He wiped his hand across his eyes. "If I were not a Christian man, I would tear you limb from limb for what you have done to my little brother."

Swithun's eyes grew large. "I did not know he was your..."

"Something else you might have learned, Swithun, had you been a little more friendly," I said.

There was a small silence, and I heard Henry take in breath. "I cannot kill you, Swithun, the priest, but I can curse you," he said. "I hope you go blind and mad. I hope your heart swells and bursts within you. I curse you twenty times with twenty knife blows."

I, too, drew in breath to speak, but decided to stay silent. Let poor Henry have his say.

I sent my steward home to his mother with his lantern and waited until the coffin arrived, whilst Swithun prayed in front of the altar. Then, I accompanied him home.

His house was as untidy and dirty as the robing room.

"Why did you let it get like this, Swithun?" I said, looking around and removing a pile of rubbish from a stool before I could sit.

"I have never had to look after myself. At the abbey, all was done for us: the cooking, the cleaning, the laundry..."

"Then why did you send Old Joan away? She looked after Benedict well for twenty years."

"I wanted no one in the house with me."

"She has her own house by the manor wall. She needs no place to dwell."

He shrugged, "I am not used to women. I have had little to do with the secular world."

"That much is obvious."

He made himself comfortable on the stool opposite me. "I have been at the abbey of Sarum since I was young."

"You were a child oblate then?" I reached for a jug of ale on the table and found it empty and full of dead flies.

He nodded, "My father gave me to the abbey when I was ten. He had fallen ill and was like to die. I was a younger son and expendable. My brother, Ralph, the Attwood heir, was there, ready to inherit the manor in Hampshire."

"I know all about the position of the younger son, Swithun, and the resentments which bubble up under the surface." I think this explained Swithun's attitude toward me, for in his eyes, we were of the same class, nobility. "Go on."

He looked at me under his brows. "You are not the younger son?"

"No, I had a brother once…a half-brother, to be exact, but that is for another day." I stretched out my long legs. "So what happened? I thought that when one reached puberty, there was a possibility of leaving the abbey and making one's own way in the world?"

"My father recovered. He pledged me to Sarum as a bribe to God. For me, there was no escape. I was there to pray for his soul and to give thanks for the throwing off of the illness which so consumed him."

"He made a vow, then?"

"He did. 'If I recover from this terrible malady, my younger son will become a monk and pray for me every day, and I will pay the abbey a great sum to have him.'" The bitterness was apparent in his voice. "Besides, my whole adult life had been spent in the cloister. The world outside was an awesome place. What could I do except be a clerk, a lowly scribbler? At least in the abbey, I had a chance to rise, perhaps to abbot."

"Aye. I thought the practice of giving children to the church had been stopped?"

"Some years ago, it was still a custom practised in some places. Money is a very persuasive tool, my lord."

"Ah, but there is a gulf between becoming a monk and taking holy orders and becoming one of the priesthood. Why did you do that if you…?"

"The bishop—not the present one, the last one—wanted men to take the word of the Lord to the people. It is hard to refuse when your whole life has been spent in obedience to your superior."

"Yes, I suppose it is." I thought 'he has no obedience to me though.' I looked him straight in the eye. "You have no calling at all, do you?"

He looked down at his hands. "I have tried. I am the son of a titled lord. I have never lost sight of that fact. I have kept that fact in my heart these 15 years. It is who I am. That knowledge helps me to come to terms with my life as it is now."

"Hence your disdain for my people. You believe them far beneath you, as your serfs and villeins were on your father's manor."

"Do you not, my lord?"

"No, Swithun, I do not."

He stared at me and quoted, "Let every soul be subject to the authority of the great, for there is no authority that is not from the same God, and those authorities who are from God are under orders."

"By the same token, you must then accept what has happened to you, for it is God's will. God ordained it."

"It was the will of an unfeeling father."

I shrugged. "I do not feel myself superior to my folk on the manor, for we all pull together to make it work. I have a responsibility to them. They look up to me, and I do what I can to make their lives bearable. They provide their labour for me, and the fruits of those labours, we share."

"But God made you a lord."

"Perhaps he did. He also then made Hurbert Alder a blacksmith. He cannot do my job, though he try, and I... well, I might make a fist of it, but I don't think I could do his job. No. Not well at all."

Swithun stared at me, trying to understand my reasoning.

"You did not wish to be a priest. So why such zealous pursuance of the word of God as you see it?"

"It is the only way I can make sense of what I have been sent here to do. I must teach right from wrong. I must bring the people back to the true way. How else am I to validate my life?"

"Well, for a start, by getting the folk on your side, and you will not do that by bullying, by being distant and making everyone hate you."

Too late, I thought...far too late.

"Listen, Swithun, I do understand what it is you have told me. I do not, however, think you can stay here now. There is too much bad feeling. I must tell you that I have written to the bishop to ask that you be removed elsewhere. He may see fit to take you into the abbey again. I hope that he will. The daily round of prayer and contemplation may suit you better than the irksome tasks you must perform in my church."

He hung his head, though I wondered at the suddenness of the contrition.

"It should be a penance that I perform for my part in the

death of the young Piers, but I see, m'lord, that it would do no good. I do repent, most sincerely, the ill I caused here today, but I cannot find it in my heart to be a good priest to your people. I am too hard because I must be hard on myself. The bishop sent me out into the world to learn its ways. Its ways are evil."

"Aye, I see that you scourge yourself...no, no...do not deny it. I know you do. No amount of self-loathing will be driven out by that exercise."

He shrugged again. "It was good enough for our forefathers. Becket, they tell me, wore a hair shirt under his clothes till the day he died."

"He is a saint, Swithun, you are not."

He stood and stared up at the rafters. "No, I am Swithun Attwood, younger, unwanted son of Phillip Atwood, Lord of the Manor of Stockbridge. I should be living there, still, in the fine house with my horses and my hounds, my hawks, and my fine wines. Instead, I am thrown out here on this dungheap."

There was an agonised catch to his voice. I almost pitied him.

Chapter Ten

*F*ather Godfrey from Bedwyn came a little while later and performed the rites for young Piers. The women of the village cleansed and washed him and laid him in the coffin again.

We buried him the next day in our little churchyard. We did not see Swithun, but I knew he was there; I saw him slip into the church when we were all leaving. One of my woodwards, doubling as the gravedigger, was left behind us to fill in the hole.

I asked John—for I could not trouble Henry—to let me know when a missive came from the bishop, for I was going back to Marlborough and my task there.

I clattered into Johannes' courtyard some time later that day in a little shower of rain. A young lad was there mucking out the stable. Had Johannes taken on a servant, I wondered?

I found him in his workplace looking into the ear of a small lad who wriggled and squealed in his mother's arms.

"Hold him very still."

I stayed at the door and held my breath.

Johannes reached for a long pair of tweezers. The little lad screamed.

I strode into the scene and took off one of my riding gloves, on which was a fringe of leather. I danced it before the eyes of the little child. He was immediately pacified and reached for the glove. I dandled it some more. Johannes retrieved a tiny acorn from the ear of the child, and I gave the glove over. The child immediately put it in his mouth.

Ah, well, I thought. It will dry.

"It always worked to take Geoffrey's attention from things being done to him," I said.

"There," said Johannes to the mother. "He will not be deaf now. Try not to let him do it again, for often a child will do over what he has done once."

The mother bobbed. "And you say I owe you nothing?"

"None but the service your other son is performing for me."

The woman grasped Johannes' hand and kissed it.

"You are a good man…a good man," and she was gone.

"A bit of barter then…?"

"All I can do for those who have no money but are in need," he answered.

I noticed then that Agnes was sitting on a stool at the back of the room, behind the table.

The concentration on her face was comical; her tongue was wiggling from the side of her mouth, and she was cutting with shears the linen squares which I had seen Johannes trimming what seemed like months ago.

He turned. "Aye, I have another assistant."

I smiled. He was overcoming his first doubts about the girl and was beginning to like her. "No further trouble with the folk of the town?"

"None yet."

"Hmm."

"Come into the parlour."

"I have a tale to tell you, and I need to know something

about asthma…or lung disease."

Johannes led the way, frowning.

Over a cup of wine, I told him what had happened at Durley.

"Tell me, in your experience, can such attacks be brought on by the person being upset or under an anxiety of some nature?"

"It does not help, no. Their airways are narrowed, and as they panic, they begin to try to breathe quickly. This does not fill the lungs with air but makes one dizzy and light-headed. If one passes out, the breathing might return to normal, but if the airways are still lessened, phlegm can accumulate, and coughing and gasping can begin. Breathing in the noxious specks of dust, which you say were abounding in that little airless room, could cause him to pass out and die in a short time."

"So it is like one being strangled, except it's the lungs which are constricted and not the throat?"

"And the little passageways which lead to the lungs, yes."

I nodded. "Thank you. I thought it was so." I brooded over my wine cup.

Johannes brought me from my reverie. "Have we any news of the little knife?"

Aye, we have," and I told him of my visit to the cutler.

"I doubt the man will know the name of the person to whom he sold the knife, but he may be able to describe the purchaser," he said.

"That was my hope."

"Oh yes, and I met with Master Gallipot in the road the other day," said Johannes. "We fell, as we medical men do, to discussing the remedies we prescribe. He remembered the man for whom I prescribed the laxative, and so we know who took away the little twist of paper. When he told me, I recalled him too. Gallipot remembered him because he is a near neighbour up on Kingsbury Street. Naturally, he would not tell you, but me…well I am a fellow medical man."

"But you will not tell me?"

"No."

I tutted.

"But I can tell you that it was a tradesman. I have had cause to get him to sole my boots. And he could once be found working with your friend the cordwainer."

"Bertold…Bertold Taske?"

"But you did not hear it from me" he laughed.

"You mean that you would not like it to be known that you had inferred that the man has consti…"

"What are you two laughing about?"

"Oh, nothing," said Johannes, fingering his right ear.

"You are always telling an untruth when you fiddle with your ear like that…" said Lydia.

"I am not…"

Her tinkling laugh rang out in the parlour. "I know you too well, Uncle."

This, I think, was the first time she had given him his title and referred, in my hearing, to the relationship between them.

"I was hoping to find you here, mistress. We are at present, at Durley, mourning one of our own, a young lad by the name of Piers Pierson, but when the time for grief is over, will you do me the honour of travelling with me to Durley to see my manor and meet again with my daughter?"

Lydia's eyes twinkled and her whole face lit up. "Oh, I should like that very much, sir," and she bobbed a curtsey.

Johannes and I trudged up Kingsbury Street. It was very steep and the recent rain had made patches of it quite muddy.

Just a little under a third of the way up, we entered a

small yard where the premises of Bertold Taske, cobbler, were to be found.

Gilbert had been right, for the man was long-faced and sour. No smile cracked his face as we entered.

He did not know me well and ignored me, but he nodded to the doctor and turned back to the work on his last.

"Bertold, my fine man," said Johannes, looking at me, tongue in cheek. "How is your 'old trouble'? Have we managed to sort it for you?"

Taske turned back to the doctor. "You have, and you have my thanks for it, doctor. Nothing like a good shi…"

"Taske," I interrupted.

"Aye, my lord. You are not here to talk about my tardy bowels are you?"

"No, indeed. Your bowels are your own concern. What concerns us is the twist of parchment in which the apothecary put the powder. I assume," I said, looking at Johannes, "that it was a powder."

"Aye, it is."

"It was."

Both spoke at once.

"What did you do with the paper, Taske?"

"Do with it?" He frowned. "Well, I opened it, poured half the measure into me ale, and drank it up as the doctor said."

"And the other half?"

"Drank it the next day. In me ale."

"Where were you when you did this? Here? How did you dispose of the parchment?"

"No, in the Green Man, with the rest of my racing pals and I didn't…"

"Ah."

"And…who was there when you drank the draughts, Taske?"

"Why…?"

"Just answer the doctor, please, Taske."

"Well..." He scratched his thinning, lank hair. "Christian Shoveller, the midden man. Stephen Chasier. Your man Stephen were there, too, sir."

I nodded.

"Rolfe Taylor, Gregory Hughes, um... Gregory Lyeman and that lord what owns... owned the horses and was killed at the castle, and his man..."

"Guy de Saye...?"

"Aye, and his man, Gerald of Broughton."

"Any others?"

"Folks what I didn't know. You know, folks from out o' town."

"Were they drinking at the Green Man, Taske?"

"What else do one do at a drinking place, sir? That and betting. I remember it well 'cause, see, when I had me ale with the powder and I set it down, that Guy de Saye picked up the paper and laughed at me. He could read it, you see. The paper. He read it out."

"He read the direction?" asked Johannes. "In Latin?"

"He did...in a silly voice, and it were right embarrassing, in front of all my mates an all. A 'corse he didn't speak the Latin, just the English."

"So all your friends now know you suffer from constip..."

"Aye...but I got my own back."

"You did?"

"Aye...as he was stowing the paper away in the front of his jerkin, I gave the most almighty fart, so I did! Cleared the room I did...Pah ha ha."

We walked back down the road, minding the holes and the traffic coming down the hill, splashing in the puddles. It had begun to rain again. The road ran with little muddy rivulets. I looked up to the grey sky. Not a chink of blue could I find.

"Guy...Guy had the parchment?"

"Not Gerald."

"No."

"This doesn't make sense at all."

But by the time we reached the house, it began to make eminent sense to me.

We washed our boots off in the yard. Johannes was adamant about not bringing foulness into the house.

Then Johannes and I repaired once more to the parlour and the flagon of good ale, kept topped up on the table.

We sat in silence, each with our own thoughts for a moment. In came the little maid Agnes, bringing the cups and I gestured for her to sit with us and take a cup of ale.

She looked to the doctor, and he nodded to her. "Aye, Agnes, you are welcome."

I had taken out the little knife and was toying with it as I cogitated. I spun it on the table top. I stopped it, took it up and tapped it a couple of times. I took the hilt and turned the little ivory lady round and round to look at her.

Agnes gave a quick intake of breath. I looked up.

"Agnes?"

She closed her eyes and put up her hand in a gesture that meant, I think, 'I am all right.'

"What is it, maid?" asked Johannes, leaning forward.

Agnes was shaking and shaking her head. She pointed to the little knife and put out her two hands in a gesture of puzzlement.

"Do you know it? Have you seen it before?"

She nodded.

"Where?"

She gestured down the street, out of the front door, to the castle end of town.

"The castle?"

No.

"The High Street?" I asked.

No.

"Oh, we need parchment, Johannes, for Agnes to write her answer."

Parchment and pen were fetched.

"I know it. I saw it." She wrote. "How do you come to have it?"

"It's the murder weapon, Agnes, the knife which killed de Saye."

"No, it cannot be."

"Well, we think it is," said Johannes. "It was found in the moat and fits the type of wound in de Sayes' throat."

Agnes went white.

In a quavery hand, she wrote, almost reluctantly, "My mistress bought it from a cutler at the fair. Before she died."

We all sat in silence. I put down my cup.

"Johannes," I said." I know what happened. I think I have solved the murders of that locked room."

Agnes crossed herself.

I needed to think it out some more but I did think I had almost solved it.

I jogged Bayard back to the castle and ran up to my office. There, for several moments, I put my thoughts down on parchment, all coming out in a rush and not always in the right order. I scribbled and crossed out. I moved the facts about on the parchment's surface. Eventually, I was satisfied.

Now to write to the Lords de Neville and de Saye.

I would not commit to parchment what I had learnt and the conclusion to which the facts had pointed me, for it was far too sensitive. If they wished to know who killed their children, they must come to Marlborough Castle and hear me explain it face to face.

I ran up the steps to the little murder room. The door had now been mended and the key was in the lock. I opened it and walked in.

I wanted to re-enact the scene as I thought it had happened. I shut the door and locked it.

I moved the jug of wine, now an empty one, and two of the several cups lying on the side table to the main table in the centre.

I took the chair and placed it where I had found Matilda's body slumped over the table. I looked at it all for a few heartbeats. Then I dragged the chair to the north-facing window and then back again to the table.

I picked up the chair again and placed it where the body of de Saye had lain. The boards of the floor were still stained with his blood. I sat on it for a heartbeat before moving back to the table.

Then, taking the chair once more in my hands, I walked to the window, set it down and mimed the action of dropping the knife from the opening.

I moved the chair back to the table where Matilda de Saye had died.

I picked up one of the cups and dropped it on the floor. It rolled and rolled and was stilled, just as it had on that day.

I stayed there for a few moments. Then I put it all back, left and locked the door, taking the key with me in my purse.

On the table, I left the little ivory knife.

The rain was steady that night. I heard it dripping and gushing from the castle roof as I sat long, thinking about what I had to do.

It was a good job, I considered, that I had, in deference to Henry and in memory of Piers, cancelled the celebrations of the 22nd. We would still have the showing of the Belvoir regalia in October, but the junketings, as Swithun had called them, of the night of the Equinox would now not happen. Anyway, it was pouring down.

De Saye came in on the 30th of the month with a small retinue.

De Neville jogged in from his manor in Lincolnshire through pouring rain and sodden roads two days later, and he was not in a good mood.

"What's this, Belvoir, that I must come at your insistence to the castle I have just left? Why can't you just tell me what you need to say and then we'll get the malefactor and hang the bugg…"

"My lord," I bowed, "It is a matter of some delicacy, and I am sure when you hear of it, you will be glad that you came."

I bowed to the other lord, "And you, too, sir."

They looked at each other quizzically.

"Shall we do the thing now, or do you wish to refresh yourselves and take your ease before we climb up to the tower room?"

"Climb up to…? Now, my lad, I am sure you are a very …" This was de Saye.

"Climbing's not something I like doing, Belvoir, with my bad foot," said de Neville.

"No, sir, but it is very important we be there."

After a short consultation, they both nodded at each

other and gestured for servants to accompany them, but I motioned for them to be still.

"Sirs, we must go alone."

"Alone?" said de Neville. "Why?"

"It is most sensitive, sir."

De Neville sat down heavily on a stool in his office. "I knew it. I did. The damn girl killed herself, after all. Sensitive, you say. Yes, well, it would be. Just us need to know, eh?"

"Something like that, sir," I said.

Johannes met us at the door of the tower room.

"Ready?"

I unlocked the door and we passed into the sad little room, all four of us.

I turned and locked it again, leaving the key in the door.

De Saye asked me why we needed to be locked in. Was one of us here a murderer?

"No. It is because I want to show exactly how it was done, and when the murders were committed, the door was locked from the inside."

I indicated the space behind the door where there was a good view of the whole room. "Please, will you stand here?"

They moved.

"Your daughter, sir, and your son, my lord, were affianced, but they did not, either of them, wish to be married to each other."

"That's old news," said de Neville, "but I would like to think my daughter knew her duty after all. Now you tell me that rather than be married, she'd risk the Almighty's wrath and kill herself."

I ignored him and ploughed on. "It seems there was a great enmity between them, I fear."

"Who says so? Belvoir, you had better have evidence for this, or..."

"My Lord de Neville, neither of them wished to be married to the other."

"Aye, we know that," said de Saye, "and Guy's mother and I hated each other on sight, but we manage all right. 'Corse...I have had my little dalliances, who hasn't?"

I smiled. "Your son, sir, did not wish to marry Matilda, even though he could, as you say, carry on dalliances with other women, should he wish, out of wedlock once they were married. Except this was not his—please excuse me, sir—desire."

De Saye narrowed his eyes. I wondered if he knew.

'I wonder if he knows?' I asked myself.

I took from my cotte the little book with the drawing of de Saye and his palfreyman and laid it on the table.

Johannes cleared his throat and leaned against the wall, his arms folded. What would happen now? Both men stared at the drawing.

De Saye blinked.

"This drawing was made by the limner who was painting in the church of St Peter. He recorded this and one other event, which I will show you when we get to the relevant part. His body was found in Savernake some time after he was murdered, but he was not killed there."

Both men were gaping like landed fish.

"Please, sir, sit." I was concerned for de Saye, who had gone very white. He did indeed sit on the chair.

"The limner recorded the relationship between the palfreyman, Gerald of Broughton, and your son, sir. They were lovers and used to meet in the church where the limner was working. He was not seen, for it was dark, and most of the time, he was dead drunk, for he was a toper, we are told."

"No! This is a complete lie!" shouted de Saye. "How dare you, Belvoir!"

"I fear it is the truth, sir. I do know that Broughton and young Sir Guy were lovers, and I have the testimony of two people who say that they believe the bond between them was an unnatural one."

De Saye put his head in his hands.

"One thing I could not understand was this—and now we come to the second picture." I took the second book from my cotte. "If the limner had recorded this correctly, Guy and Gerald were overheard plotting his death. 'Will have to die. Has heard us. We must kill him' is what is written above the drawing. I pointed to the words on the page.

Both men craned their necks and took in the second book. Neither of them could read.

"This could be anyone, Belvoir!" growled de Neville.

"And you believe this, sir? You, who know what the two young men looked like. Does this not seem to you, this drawing, a good likeness of the two of them?"

De Neville screwed up his eyes and peered at the drawing again.

"It is most certainly the same two men from the first picture embracing. Alan of Didcot, for this was the limner's name, then fled to Hungerford. He thought himself safe. But for some reason, he returned. If the limner knew that his life was in danger, why did he return? We are unsure why. But Master Johannes of Salerno," I gestured to Johannes, "and myself believe that the limner was going to try to blackmail the lovers. The wedding had been postponed; perhaps he felt himself safe because he didn't know this. Maybe he came home believing that everyone had gone. Perhaps we shall never know that...but one thing is sure: those words were not the words uttered by two men who simply wanted to keep their clandestine trysts secret. Yes, of course they did not wish to trumpet it from the rooftops. However, perhaps there is another reading." I let that statement sink in.

De Saye ran his hands over a perspiring upper lip.

"In full, the words should perhaps read, 'The painter will have to die; he has heard us plotting murder. We must kill him, too.'"

Two surprised heads looked up at that.

"So the limner is killed in the church, we have evidence to suggest this, and the body is dragged to a borrowed cart—I have evidence for this, too, and this fact can be corroborated under oath, should we need to do it—and trundled out into the forest, where one of my lads found it some time later. It was much decayed but it was identified by one of his fellow masons.

"The painting gear and the first little book were found stuffed behind the altar in the church of St Peter, where the limner hurriedly stashed it before he went to Hungerford. I myself found it.

The second book and more painting equipment were found in the pack of Gerald of Broughton after he drowned in the mill leat. I, too, was the one to find this.

"He drowned because he ran from me. He was wearing the dead painter's boots, which he had stolen from the body, and as such, this proved his guilt. The fact that he ran also showed me he was guilty of something."

De Saye was shaking his head over and over.

"What the limner had actually overheard was the lovers plotting to murder another."

De Neville looked shocked at that as the words sunk in.

"Now we come to the murders in this room. One person murdered by poison, the other by a wound to the neck. Odd, don't you think, that we have two methods employed in one room at the same time?" I picked up the little knife. "This tiny object was found in the moat when the water receded a little in the dry spell. Again, I found it. Johannes of Salerno and I believe this is the weapon which was plunged into the neck of Guy de Saye, causing the wound from which he bled to death."

The two fathers watched me as I held up the knife, but neither of them reached for a closer look. They stared at me in shock.

I went to the door and turned the key. Agnes was sitting there as she had been on that day.

"Agnes, step in for a moment." I held up the knife. "Have you seen this before?"

She nodded.

"Was it bought from the cutler at the Marlborough fair?"

Another nod.

"Were you with your mistress when she bought it?"

She chewed her lip and nodded reluctantly.

"Thank you."

I closed the door on her once more and relocked it.

"Agnes was sitting outside the door when her mistress was murdered. She heard, as did I, one floor down, what was said. We have compared our memories, and we agree that no one entered this room before the deed was done or left after the murders were accomplished."

Johannes stood up and placed the little scrap of parchment in which the poison had been contained on the table.

"This twist of parchment is a receipt, written by me, for a remedy collected at Master Gallipot's apothecary in the town. The scrap was reused to house a laxative powder."

"It was then acquired by your son, sir." I bowed to de Saye. "Some poison was taken from the priory, either from the rat traps or directly from the cellarer's stores, for he was ill, and in his latter days was less than scrupulous, God rest him, in looking to his poisons, which he used to control rats at the priory. Both your son and his palfreyman had access to the poison, for they both stayed in the priory."

"NO!" shouted de Saye.

"The twist of parchment was found under the body of your son when removed for burial."

"Nooo!" De Saye's voice was agonised.

"I have a witness who can testify that he saw your son put the parchment into the breast of his cotte a few days before he died."

"I tested the poison left in the twist. Aconite. The same as killed the Lord de Neville's daughter," said Johannes.

Hugh de Neville looked as if he would explode.

I took up the tale again. "This is what we think happened. Remember, I was in the room below and heard much of what went on, sirs. The rest, the little maid-servant who sat outside the door, supplied."

De Neville looked up sharply. "How can she tell you? She is mute?"

"She can write, sir. At the abbey of Amesbury, she was taught to write."

His mouth fell open and he shut it with a snap.

"Matilda asked Guy to step up here to the room, for he wished to discuss their situation. I think that she had almost set up the meeting, for everyone knew she could be found here during some part of the day, and the room is private and cannot be overlooked. De Saye knew this too and was more than happy to go there, for it was a private space just right for his plan.

"His plan?"

"Oh yes, sir. This was all very carefully planned."

De Neville's eyes narrowed again but he didn't reply.

"She asked her maid to stay outside the room. Why? If she were truly worried for her reputation she would make sure the maid was with her inside. No, she did not want any witnesses. She knew that there would be no stain on her, for de Saye would soon be dead. What she would say to

Agnes, her maid, after the deed was done, we cannot guess. I suspect that Agnes would have been cowed into silence."

"She is silent, Belvoir!" yelled de Neville, "And better stay that way."

"I have no doubt that Agnes will keep to herself anything she may have worked out, sir."

Hugh de Neville harrumphed.

I carried on. "De Saye then locked the door. Why did he do that? To prevent anyone from entering and to forestall discovery. He did not know that he was also sealing himself in. Both bride and bridegroom thought that they would be leaving the room alive that day. Guy passed to the table and poured two cups of wine. I think he probably took a sip from his own. Perhaps Matilda's back was turned. He poured the powder from the twist of parchment into her cup. Perhaps he stowed the parchment in his cotte, but as he did not fully push it in, it fell to the floor. Or perhaps, as he fell injured, it fell from his cotte.

"A chair was dragged from the window to the table—I heard it—probably by de Saye, and Matilda was asked to sit. I think she remained standing. There was then some conversation, quite amicable. Then Matilda said loudly, 'I do not wish to marry.' Guy answered her with, 'I do not wish to marry either, do I? I do not wish to marry you. Why would I?' When I heard this, I thought that Guy was merely, forgive me, my lord, commenting on the plainness of his bride. But, no, for Matilda, in those few quiet words, had accused the man of sodomy and he was trying to justify himself." I continued, "I think then perhaps that Matilda took some of the drink. Booted feet paced about as de Saye began to be agitated at what he had just done—I heard him—Then there was a little about the king willing the marriage and not being divorced. Now Matilda was becoming irate. The chair leg screeched again, and I think Matilda pulled at it and sat down heavily. She was feeling upset.

She began to cry. She needed to get de Saye close so she could carry out her plan.

"You are a foul creature. I hate you. I cannot bear to be in the same room with you, let alone the same bed. Oh my God!' she shouted, the words of a woman who was about to be tied in matrimony to a sodomite.

"More conversation—we know not what—and then it sounded as if Matilda began to be unwell. De Saye, by now, knew she was dying and wished to—forgive me, sir—push her further towards death. Calm yourself, try this', he said, putting more poison to her lips. The voices were soft now as if they had drawn together and were embracing. Indeed, I think they almost were, for I think Guy was holding the girl up. Then, I believe Matilda realised she had been poisoned. 'I feel ill,' she cried. She suddenly, I believe, then had a surge of energy. I heard boots clip the floor as if Guy had stepped back quickly. There was a cry—your son, sir."

I nodded to de Saye.

"He fell to one knee, this little knife embedded in his neck. It was in his neck, but he did not remove it. He yelled at her, 'What are you doing?' I do not think that he felt himself in too much danger at that point, for I do not think he realised that the damage inflicted upon him was so great. He fell onto his side just here. I think she probably said something like 'die, for you have killed me.' Though I think it was always her intention to kill him here in this room and she had bought the knife to do so. I think Matilda knew that she did not have long to live then.

"Guy asked again, "What?". Why would he ask that again? He knew she had stabbed him. He repeated it because she was now doing something else with the last of her strength. She dragged the chair over to him and placed it over him, pinning him down so that he could not move.

He was on his side, one arm beneath him and the other trapped tightly against his body. She may even have sat upon the chair to give it more weight. I heard the dragging of it to and fro from my room below.

"Oh, my God, no!' said Guy. It was then, I think, she pulled out the knife, and he began to bleed to death. She waited, and all the while, the poison was working on her."

De Neville's face softened. His expression was one of total shock. This hard man, who cared not for his daughter, I felt sure, was crying inside for himself. He soon pulled himself round.

"She waited for some time sobbing. He passed out, we think," said Johannes, "and began his descent into death."

"Matilda staggered to the window, dipping her dainty shoes in some of de Saye's blood lightly as she passed, dragging the chair with her and then standing on it. Then she threw the knife out of the space. A little of his blood was on her hand," I said. "She then dragged the chair again, sat, and, in anger, dropped or pushed the little cup of poisoned wine over the edge and onto the floor. I heard it roll. I heard it cease rolling. She fell over the table and she passed into a semi-sleep shortly after.

"I woke her when I arrived ten minutes later, and she said, 'Killed him.' That should have been, 'I have killed him.' Then, as Sir Andrew Merriman, a soldier from this castle, and I watched, she died."

There was total silence in the room.

"And that is how we think the murders were accomplished," I said. "Forgive me, my lords. It is, I know, not what you wish to hear, but it is, we think, the truth. Matilda de Neville had planned to kill Guy de Saye. Guy de Saye had planned to kill Matilda. Sadly, they chose to do it on the same day, in the same place. And so we have two bodies in a locked room."

There was complete silence as the two men digested this information.

Hugh de Neville wiped his shaking hand across his sweating brow. His face grew hard again. "So what do you propose to do with this information, Belvoir?"

"Nothing, sir."

"Nothing?"

"There is no wrong to be righted, for that has already been accomplished. The murderers have paid the ultimate price."

"Sir Aumary and I are the only people who know what happened here in this little room," said Johannes, "and we shall keep silent, sir. There is nothing to be gained by publishing this abroad."

"Aye, let my poor tortured daughter rest. Nothing good can come of making public the knowledge that she … that she…"

"Was a murderess…?" supplied de Saye.

"Aye, and your son too… a murderer."

"No," said de Saye, weakly.

"If you will, I ask you, gentlemen, that you write to the king and tell him of our conclusions. I feel duty-bound that John knows what has been done here. You, sir," I turned to de Neville, "asked the king to give permission for me to investigate. I feel he ought to know the outcome. I feel sure he will have no more to say on the matter, and he, too, will keep his own counsel."

There was a terrible silence.

"Aye, it shall be done. De Saye?"

De Saye screwed up his forehead. "Aye, we shall do it together."

I, too, would write to the king. How could I be sure that the two fathers would be fair and would tell the absolute truth? John would know the facts from my pen, too.

SHE MOVED THROUGH THE FAIR

De Neville stood, pulled down his jerkin and adjusted his belt. "What can I tell her mother? Oh, Christ!"

"That she died of natural causes," I said. "Perhaps we should put it about that Guy died accidentally and Matilda, in her grief, died beside him of a broken heart. No one but the four of us knows the truth. There's none can gainsay us."

De Saye took a deep breath. "Aye, perhaps that's best. It cannot do anything but harm to..." He stopped, jutted his chin and sniffed. He nodded to me, then to Johannes, strode to the door, turned the key in the lock, pushed past the little maid and was gone down the steps.

De Neville stuck out his hand. "Thank you, Aumary. Absolute silence?"

"Yessir."

I shook it. It was our bargain. He didn't even look at Johannes. And then he, too, was gone.

Within the day, there were numerous stories flying about the town. The favourite, naturally, was witchcraft.

It was, sadly, much more exciting than the truth.

Chapter Eleven

*M*y task was done.

I could now return to Durley and begin the autumn round of manor duties.

There was much to be done. The winter stocks of meat must be laid in and we had to decide which beasts to keep and which to slaughter and salt down.

The sixty-day pannage season, where the pigs would be turned out to graze the forest floor for beech mast and acorns, was upon us.

The forest must be made safe for the winter storms. Dead and dying trees must be assessed and felled, if necessary, to protect others. The deer fences that kept the beasts in certain parts of the forest must be maintained and strengthened.

We should also have the ceremony of the showing of the Belvoir regalia. This time last year, I recollected, I had been ill, and immediately after the showing, the regalia had gone missing, precipitating my dash for the continent and my prolonged visit to Normandy.

No, that would not happen again.

Things would be much more settled this year.

I decided to ask Lydia to be our guest of honour at the showing, and she willingly assented. She would stay with us for a short while, and Agnes Brenthall would act as her chaperone for the duration. Hawise was beside herself with excitement and began plotting all sorts of amusements for poor Lydia. Hal of Potterne was her willing accomplice, and soon, there were all sorts of plans afoot for the day itself.

The day dawned cold and clear. Johannes had brought Lydia to Durley on a borrowed horse the afternoon before. She sat well on it and allowed me to lift her down.

I slept in my little office at the end of the hall on my trusty daybed whilst Hawise and Lydia took over the solar. I could hear them now laughing and chattering as they chose the dresses they would wear for the day. Agnes came down the solar steps with a pile of bedding in her arms.

"Like two children, they are," she smiled. "It's good to hear so much laughter. It's been too quiet and sad these past few years."

I looked up from my work, "Lydia, Mistress Wolvercote, is a very good influence on Hawise, Agnes. They laugh much together."

"They do. Mistress Wolvercote loves the child, you can tell."

"And Hawise is much in love with her, too."

"Aye, as is someone else we know!" She threw over her shoulder as she passed my door and was away.

I mused over what Agnes had said.

Was I in love with Lydia? Was it not just an affection, or was it a friendship gone beyond being mere friends?

Could I find a place for her in my heart, next to the place where I kept Cecily, my dead wife?

Had it become apparent to others and not to me?

The girls came tripping down the solar stairs in their holiday finery.

Hawise first, in a gown of deep warm olive green, known as Lincoln green, for the dyes—woad and weld—which coloured the cloth were special to that town.

Lydia stepped daintily from the solar in a gown of Coventry blue, which beautifully set off the blue-black of her hair.

My heart lurched.

She could see me through the open door of my office, and she smiled demurely as she descended.

She walked down the hall. I could not take my eyes off her.

She reached the door and twirled around in a circle, lifting the long sleeves of her gown from her side. "Might this be the sort of gown, my Lord Aumary, which would please your folk to see on such a day, or am I overdressed for the occasion? I have never been to such a celebration before. Hawise tells me that the village dress in their best on this special day."

"Hawise is right. Each dons their finest clothes if they have them," I said. "It is one of our little traditions, and you will be just perfect."

"Doesn't she look beautiful, Dada?" said Hawise, taking Lydia's hand. "I think Lydia looks like a princess."

So now, Hawise was content to call Mistress Wolvercote by her first name.

"You have never seen a princess, Hawise." I laughed.

"No, but I have heard stories about them, and Lydia looks just like them."

"She does," I said.

"Come on, Lydia, let us see if they have dug the pit for the roast yet." She dragged the poor woman away.

At the door, Lydia turned and smiled apologetically. I gestured for her to go,

Enjoy yourself," I said. "I shall follow soon."

The day passed in dancing, singing, eating, drinking and playing games. I walked about the manor. Folk gathered on what passed for our village green in my best cotte and the Belvoir regalia: the sword and scabbard, the belt and the horn hanging from it.

I was pleased to see Margaret Manton sitting with her goodwives, chatting amicably. Life for her was returning to normal. I knew what grief did to a person, for I had had my fair share of it.

Henry, too, had been busy, though I had said that if he did not feel the merriment of the day was for him, he need not take part. However, he threw himself into the organising of the day as if it were a beast that needed taming.

He was standing smiling now at Edith Brooker, and she was staring up at him, rapt in what he was telling her.

My two villeins, Edwina and Ralf, were sitting on the grass quietly with Ralf's parents. I spoke to them gently. I understood their grief, for I, too, had buried children—Geoffrey, five, and a still born girl, whom we had called Evisa for her maternal grandmother.

Stephen and Peter, my two men-at-arms from the castle, were talking to Hawise. She was trying to get them to turn a skipping rope for her.

At last, Johannes and Lydia were pulled together and coerced to stand and do it. Lydia stepped up and gently took the rope from Stephen's hand. His red face, at having to perform such a task, soon returned to a normal colour. Johannes laughed. He did not care. They turned, and Hawise jumped.

They all laughed.

The feasting and singing, as was the tradition, went on long into the night. Gradually, though, folk wandered off to their homes in the village and the wider forest. The flames from the bonfire sank low and glimmered under a harvest moon.

Lydia and I stood on the top step of the manor house stairs, watching the stars peeping out in an inky blue sky.

I took her hand; she was beginning to be a little chilled.

"Shall I fetch you a cloak?"

She looked up at me, her long, dark lashes framing her violet-blue eyes perfectly. "No, but you can hold me to keep me warm."

I put my arms around her.

After a short while, I said, "Do you think that Johannes might be able to do without you at home?"

"I am not his chattel that I must ask my uncle's permission to leave, Aumary."

"I know, but…if I ask you to marry me and come and be mistress of Durley, he will have no housekeeper again."

"He has, I am sure you have noticed, quite taken to Agnes. She is able to fetch and carry for him and help him in the workroom. She cannot cook yet, though, but she is a good help-mate."

"Then will you consent to be my wife and come to be a mother to Hawise and mistress of Durley?"

She kissed me quickly on the lips. "I will, Aumary Belvoir, for I love you as I have never loved any before."

I was about to tell Lydia that I loved her with all my heart but was overtaken by a yelp behind us.

We turned.

There was Hawise in her shift, jumping up and down and grinning for all she was worth.

"Oh, Dada," she said, "I thought you were never going to ask her. I have prayed aloud five times…five times…to ask God to put it into your head to ask Lydia to come and live here with us. And he did. He did."

"Ah, so it was nothing to do with me then?"

She dived between us and hugged us both about the thighs, for that was as far as she could reach.

"We shall be so happy, all of us together."

"Yes, I think we shall," I said, at last, smiling.

We agreed, the next day, after much consultation between the three of us, that we would wait to marry until a successor to Swithun might be in place at the manor.

No letter had come from the bishop yet, but I felt that it would not be long before we had an answer to our problem.

I did not think it would take the form it did.

I escorted Lydia back to Marlborough on October 3rd, and we both caught Johannes in his parlour and told him our good news.

"I have expected it," he said, "almost from the first day." He grinned, "And I am heartily happy about it."

"You and I are to be relations now," I joked. "I shall have to call you 'Uncle', you realise."

He laughed. "God forbid!"

I reached the castle and was hailed by Andrew Merriman as he crossed the outer bailey.

"Ah, Aumary, wait. I have a note for you from de Neville. He left it before he was off back to Lincolnshire. He was much quietened and seemed somehow to have shrunk into himself. I suppose it is his gout bothering him again."

"Aye, most likely," I lied.

The note merely thanked me for the service I had rendered him. He had written to the king—as had I—and would I please use his office should I feel the need of somewhere to work when he was not at the castle? At other times, a larger room by the castle gatehouse, with two windows—I was rising in the world—was to be made available to me.

This was as much thanks as I would get from him. There was nothing from de Saye; neither did I expect it.

I trudged up the castle keep stairs one more time to retrieve my goods and possessions from the little airless, windowless room where I had worked for the past year.

I would miss it, in a way, but I was glad of the change, for somehow, the atmosphere in the building was different, and it had become a sad place.

I sat at my scarred table.

A magpie called somewhere out over the moat, and its rattling call reached me through the open lancet window in the passageway.

Children called, running past on the road beyond the moat. I sighed and began to pack up my possessions in a canvas pack.

I heard a door close above me. I took no notice.

Then faintly, oh so faintly, I heard voices. A chair scraped across the floor. The voices became louder, but I could not hear what was said. I held my breath.

The chair scraped again. Then there was sobbing. Oh yes, I could tell it was sobbing.

The hairs on the backs of my arms and neck stood out.

Suddenly, there was a thud. Far away, but a thud nonetheless, and I thought I heard someone say, 'Oh my God, no,' as if muffled and from a distance.

I raced round the passage and up the stairs. The door to the tower room was closed. I tried to open it. It would not budge.

I heard the chair screech on the wooden floor again and a tiny sound like something being dropped into water. I wetted my lips.

I was cold, but the sweat stood out on my forehead. The wine cup fell and rolled.

Then…silence.

I tried the door again. It opened. The key was in the lock on the inside.

With my heart pounding in my ears, I entered the little room. Naturally, there was no one there.

I had left the little ivory knife on the table when I had quit the room with Johannes on the day we had told de Saye and de Neville about their children's murders. We had locked the door.

It was gone.

I turned quickly for the door, and I swear, close to my ear, a soft voice whispered, "It will not be long, till our wedding day."

I have never packed anything so quickly. I threw everything into my pannier, and I fled down the keep steps.

I vowed never to set foot in that room again.

Yes, Paul, I swear to you, that is what happened. You, I suppose, have never been in the castle keep. No, I thought not. You have, you say, just looked at it from the road. Let it stay that way, my lad. I was there, a few feet away, when Matilda and Guy murdered each other. I think they are still there...somehow.

I promised you a ghost, did I not, when we began to write?

Well, now you have two. Ask anyone who has had to spend some time in that little room at the top of the tower what they think. They do not, of course, know the truth, for that has been a secret kept by myself and Johannes of Salerno until now.

You can make up your own mind.

We are coming to the end of our tale. But there is one more thing of which we must write.

*Something so unexpected which will lead us onto
the tale I shall tell next.
Take up your pen again, Paul, and write.*

That evening saw me back in Johannes' house and the
safety of his parlour and the company of beloved friends.

We did not talk of the murders, for as we had promised,
we stayed silent in front of others. I stayed there that night.
The castle was not somewhere I wanted or needed to be.
For the moment, I had little to do there. The masons were
extending the walls, building towers at the corners; the
water engineers were re-routing the moat, and the keep
was to be roofed with a conical dome, much as some of
the castles in France now had, they told me. It was not the
simple place it had been when I was a boy. It was now a
grand royal residence, a palace fit to entertain kings and
princes of the church, a royal mint and treasure house. It
dominated the small town and loomed over it like some
Olympian god of old. I no longer felt at home there.

On October 7th, I escorted my lady love and her
possessions, piled in a cart, to Durley, for she would come
to live with us until we were officially married. I had sought
permission from the king, permission to marry Lady Lydia,
once of Wolvercote, widow, and the answer had come back:

'Do what you wish, Aumary, you have earned it.'

There was, of course, a fee. There was always a fee with
John. I chuckled. If he had not been a monarch, I am sure
he would have made his way as a usurer.

Lydia was ensconced in the solar, and I stayed in
my little office at the other end of the hall. All propriety
was observed.

I was there one evening, talking to Hal of Potterne and
watching a game of shovelboard between my daughter and
Lydia through the open door when a terrible screeching

began somewhere in the vicinity of the church. A chattering gathered pace as whoever was making it neared the manor gates. Everyone turned to the door, a puzzled expression on their faces.

I leapt up and threw open the outer door. Several voices were mingled, speaking and shouting, one or two crying.

"Open the door, Wyot!" I cried, for it was past curfew, and we had closed the main gates.

The night watchman opened the wicket gate, and Walter Reeve and a few others, accompanied by Old Joan, stumbled over the threshold.

"Sir," cried Walter, catching sight of me on the top step in the light of the flares, "You had better come and look at this."

I threw on my cloak, for it was a little chilly now of an evening and ran out.

The people parted for me to walk through. I turned to Lydia. "You two stay here. Joan, what has happened?"

She was wringing her hands, this dependable old dame, who had been a quiet presence for order about the manor for as long as I could remember. Indeed, I could not remember her as anything but old and wizened.

"Sir, I was taking the priest his pottage from the kitchen as you instructed..."

I nodded.

"And, well, sir, come see for yourself."

The village was in darkness, save for those nearer houses whose occupants had been disturbed from their early slumbers. Most of my folk slept with the going down of the sun and rose with its rising.

Flares and lamps were lit, and we were escorted around the manor path to the church gate and past it to the priest's house.

Here, folk waited. Joan and Walter entered, and I

followed, Hal of Potterne keeping close behind me.

We climbed the wooden stair, in truth little more than a gently inclined ladder, and I remembered to duck my head at the top, for I was tall enough to hit my forehead on the beam at the entrance to the spacious loft room.

The last time I had been in here, it was with my brother Robert, a year ago, and Father Benedict had been alive, although he had died soon afterwards.

Walter lifted the lantern.

Hal swore.

Father Swithun lay on his back, one arm flung out beside him. He was dressed in his black robe, and the front of it was covered in blood. His arms, visible where the sleeves had fallen back, were lacerated as if he had tried to defend himself from blows which had rained down on him from above. The wounds which he bore were many—a frenzied attack. Some had pierced his throat, and others had gone down as far as his belly. There were so many I could not tell one from another. Blood lay everywhere, splattered up the wall next to him, spreading out on the mattress beneath him, and sprayed onto the floor beside him.

Joan came forward. "I found him like this, sir. I went for Walter straightways. His wife Alice came to look too, sir. She started up the keening as soon as she saw all the blood."

"That was the noise I heard."

"Then, we came for you."

I looked around. "You touched nothing?"

"No, sir."

"Good. Walter, can you send a rider to Marlborough to Dr Johannes and one to the coroner, too, please?"

I looked at Swithun's face. One expected there to be anger and torment, pain and horror in his expression, but he looked at peace, his eyes closed, his jaw slack.

"We need a priest too. Father Godfrey will come."

I took Hal by the arm and moved him to the wall. "Hal, what do you think?"

He sucked his teeth. "Someone very angry and upset, if you ask me. There's a lot of 'ate in those wounds. Stabbin' over and over. Almost as if the killer wanted to make sure he suffered. Revenge, I'd say, though I don't like to say it."

"Aye, my thought too. Can you look in on Henry and Margaret as you pass back to the hall...make sure they are all right?"

Hal winked. "Right you are, sir," and he swung himself onto the first step and was away. Hal knew exactly what I meant.

Whoever had done this deed would be covered in blood.

The next morning, the priest from Bedwyn came again to the manor and performed those rites he was able for the soul of Swithun of Stockbridge.

Johannes followed him shortly afterwards.

"We shall wait until the coroner gets here to see what we need to see. He must be uncovered and the wounds examined. Little point in doing it twice."

"Swithun was a very private man, Johannes. I will see if the coroner will make his judgement here in this room and not outside with the naked body on a bier in the courtyard."

My friend nodded.

"There is room for his twelve men if they squeeze up."

A while later, a messenger came through the manor arch. He was dressed in the livery of the Bishop of Salisbury, blue and gold with a white and gold bishop's mitre on the right breast of his tunic. He held a letter from the bishop in his gloved hand.

I stared at it. 'Too late. Too late,' I said to myself. It asked me to send Swithun back to Salisbury. Another man would take his place. I would send him back. Indeed, I would, in sorrow. In his winding sheet.

So, there we have the sad murder of Swithun, the priest.

I suppose that you think that you know who the murderer was, Paul.

Haha. Yes. That is what many believed. Sad? Yes, it was sad, I think, for Swithun was a disappointed man, a man who could not come to terms with the loss of his former life and the new path which had been laid before him.

Ho, Paul, that is a little unkind. No, he was not an amiable man. Yes, he was a hard man and unfeeling. He was a troubled soul. He had created a shell around himself, like the soft-bodied shadfly we see trundling in the gravel at the bottom of our trout streams. It protected him from people he despised and loathed, those he must go amongst every day. His shell, however, could not protect him from a knife thrust.

I must rest now, Paul. I will tell you the story of how Johannes and I solved the murder of our unloved priest another time.

I will tell you how I married Lydia, my beautiful Lydia, and how my manor was turned upside down by the events of that winter and spring.

Leave Lydia and I now, on the night of Swithun's murder, once again standing at the top of the manor steps, staring at the stars in the firmament, arm in arm, one cloak wrapped around the two of us. This time—for my daughter was tucked up, fast asleep, in the cot in her room at the top of the solar stairs—I was able to kiss Lydia long and lovingly, as I had wished to do for oh so long.

"Oh," I sighed. "If only Swithun had been a different animal, if his unpleasantness had not proved the death of him, we might have been man and wife by now. Instead, we must wait for the new priest to arrive and settle in before he can marry us, and goodness knows how long that might take."

"Can we not ask dear Father Godfrey?" said Lydia. "He has been coming and going to Durley all autumn for this and that." She stopped, suddenly aware that the Bedwyn priest had been called too often for the most unpleasant tasks. "We know him well...he is a good man."

"He married me for the first time around," I said, "at Bedwyn, in the private chapel there, to Cecily."

Lydia crossed herself with a little gesture. "God rest her."

We were silent for a while.

"If we ask Father Godfrey," said Lydia, smiling into the dark. "...and he agrees, then...it will not be long till our wedding day."

I shuddered involuntarily at her words.

Glossary

Aconite - A flower from which poison can be obtained.

Apothecary - A mediaeval dispensing chemist.

Barbette - A band of linen encircling the face and pinned into place.At first, it was only worn by royal ladies with a circlet or coronet, but was eventually adopted by all classes. It was usually worn with a small gathered linen hat above.

Becket, Sir Thomas - Sainted Archbishop of Canterbury, murdered in his cathedral on December 29th 1170

Bliaut - Voluminous over garment worn by both sexes (but mostly women) and pleated to the waist or under the bust.

Bothy – A small, simple building often of daub and wattle, roofed with thatch and with a beaten earth floor.

Chausses - Stocking-like leggings attached to the shirt at the top and covered with a tunic.

Common - A piece of land shared by all.

Cordovan - The best leather from Spain.

Cordwainer - A shoemaker

Corrodian - A well-to-do elderly layperson who paid or was sponsored for accommodation and food for the rest of their lives. This payment might be in cash, but would more usually be by donating land/property to the religious house in question.

Cotte - A long-sleeved shift or tunic; a coat

Crowner/Coroner - The man appointed by the Crown to deal with unexpected deaths. The Coroner was the man who drew up the jury of twelve men to decide the cause of death and, if need be, impose fines.

Curfew – From the French *couvre feu*, to cover the fire. The time when all should be within doors.

Dagged - A series of decorative scallops or foliations along the edge of a garment,

Darioles - Little pastry tubes.

Dock Fever - diphtheria

Downland - Chalk hills with steep coombes and valleys, thin soils and few trees.

Forest Exchequer - The place where all monies from a royal forest were gathered and accounted for.

Frumenty - A pudding made primarily from boiled, cracked wheat - hence its name, which derives from the Latin word *frumentum*, grain

Gambeson – Padded, usually defensive, jacket, but can be worn as a normal piece of clothing.

Garderobe - Primitive toilet in a building

Gascon - French white wine.

Hosteller - Brother in an abbey responsible for the guests in an abbey or priory.

Hue and Cry - A loud clamour or public outcry. The pursuance of a felon.

Infirmarer - Brother responsible for the sick in an abbey or priory.

Journeyman - An individual who has completed an apprenticeship and is fully educated in a trade or craft, but not yet a master.

Keep - The large defensible building built on a rise (motte) in a castle.

Kitchener - Brother who oversees the work of the kitchens in an abbey or priory.

Lauds - The divine office which takes place in the early hours of the morning.

Leat – An artificial watercourse dug into the ground to supply water to a mill.

Limner - A painter

Lych gate - Small gate at the entrance of a churchyard, often for the resting of the coffin.

Manchet loaf - White wheat bread of good quality.

Murrey - A cloth in a cherry maroon colour.

Oblate - The gift of a person, often a child, to a religious house, to pray for the well-being or soul of a parent or guardian.

Palfreyman - Man who looks after horses.

Pannage - Practice of releasing domestic pigs in a forest, in order that they may feed on fallen acorns, beechmast, chestnuts or other nuts. Historically, it was a right or privilege granted to local people on common land or in royal forests.

Pavage - Medieval toll for the maintenance or improvement of a road or street in England.

Pillycock - The original of Pillock. An idiot.

Pontage - Medieval toll levied for the building or repair of bridges.

Quittances - A legal term, to pay no tax.

Receipt - Prescription.

Reeve - An official elected annually by the serfs to supervise lands for a lord.

Rhenish - German wine

Salley Gardens - Collection of willow trees.

Sarum - Old name for Salisbury

Shadfly - Caddisfly

Skep - Old term for hive.

Slickstone - Primitive iron made of metal or glass.

Solar - Generally on an upper storey, a room designed as the family's private living and sleeping quarters. The room was usually situated so that sunlight would be caught for the maximum amount of time in the day.

Supertunic - One garment worn over another to show off the hem of the dress underneath.

Tally stick - an ancient memory aid device used to record and document numbers, quantities, or even messages.

Tinker - A person who makes a living by travelling from place to place, mending pans and other metal utensils.

Tithe - One-tenth. The clergy's entitlement of a manor's income and produce.

Toper - A drunkard

Town Reeve - Forerunner of the town mayor

Wicket gate - Small gate in a larger one designed for just one person to enter or leave when the main gate is closed.

Woodward - Man responsible for the trees of a forest. A woodsman

Author's Note

Marlborough was an established settlement by 1204 but began to expand with the rebuilding of the castle, at both ends of the wide, long High Street. The charter was indeed granted to Marlborough in 1204 by King John. The fair continues to this day but it has moved to October and is now a Mop Fair - once a hiring fair. There are still two markets a week - much shrunken, but still operating, as John intended.

Savernake Forest lies at the southern edge of Marlborough town in Wiltshire and can still be visited today. Access is along the A4 to Newbury or the A346 to Salisbury. It is much smaller now than in the 13th century when it was at its most extensive, covering some 150 square miles. Today the Forestry Commission manages it but there is still an hereditary warden, the Marquess of Ailesbury and it's Britain's only privately owned forest.

Now, it's a forest of mixed woodland but in the days of the 13th century, it had for example, few of the large beech trees we see today planted, in the 17th century, and which sadly are coming to the end of their lives. The oaks are of considerable age though. Big Bellied Oak, is one of the oldest, already being about two hundred years old when King John rode past it!

In the days of John, the L'Estourmi family were the wardens of the forest. It's true that Geoffrey L'Estourmi fell foul of King Richard, having to pay a huge fine for supporting Prince John in his uprising against the King. In my tale, I have changed the name of the family. Unless we know who they really were and what they actually did, I'm loath to make them do anything, so I'd rather make it up and have fictional characters, though the names of some of the minor players are to be found in the annals, if you look. The name Belvoir (IS pronounced Bell voir and not 'Beaver' as it is nowadays. The English pronunciation 'Beaver' was built up over many centuries through the inability of the Anglo-Saxons to master the Norman French tongue. It's the name of a small town of eastern France and there is still a castle there owned once by a noble family of the same name.

Now to Aumary, (pronounced Aymery.) He is a minor lord, not terribly wealthy and more a business man than pure aristocracy. As warden of the forest he has quite a practical job and needs to know about the forest and its trades. He is a knight - yes, but first and foremost, a forester. I have made him a sympathetic character as so many folk of his class in novels, are portrayed as proud, haughty and nasty. I fail to see how many of them could be so. They were dependent upon their peasants for their livelihood. If the peasant didn't prosper, neither did they, at this level of society. Grander folk perhaps could be less amenable. Aumary takes every man as he finds him and isn't averse to rolling up his sleeves and getting on with it.

Durley is now a small hamlet on the edge of the forest. It was once well hidden in the trees. The manor can no longer be seen but there is a farm and a house called Durley

Manor though this Manor wasn't founded till the 1400's. The manor which most people know about of course, is the one in Hilary Mantel's Book, Wolfhall, probably a timbered building very near Burbage, which belonged to the Seymour family (who were hereditary wardens of the forest too, in the 16th century) and was the childhood home of Jane Seymour. I didn't want to go anywhere near there.

The Regalia existed. It was extant until the 17th century when it disappeared. It was very likely broken up and melted down in the Civil War. However the ivory and silver horn is in The British Museum and can be seen to this day but is not on display.

The manor I have invented is a walled courtyard house with a stone hall of two storeys and a mezzanine floor, accessed by a staircase of stone and an undercroft below, very much like Boothby Pagnell Hall in Lincolnshire, the finest surviving mediaeval house of its type in the country. The village around it owes much to Sheila Sancha's portrayal of Gerneham (Irnham, near Grantham) village, again in Lincolnshire, in her wonderful children's book The Luttrell Village - Country Life in the Early 14th Century. This is a depiction of the home of Sir Geoffrey Luttrell in the 1300's, so beautifully documented in the Luttrell Psalter, (now in the British Library,) considered to be one of the richest sources for visual depictions of everyday rural life in Medieval England.

Salerno in Sicily was one of the finest medical schools in the known world from the 10th to the 13th century. It was the most important source of medical knowledge in Western Europe, both of the Arab and Ancient world and people flocked from all over to enrol there. Books were the mainstay of the school, hundreds being translated from Arabic, Greek and other languages. As a result, the medical practitioners of Salerno, both men and women, were unrivalled in knowledge and practicality.

Sadly the school declined in favour of Montpellier later in the 13th century and then as the church tightened its grip, medical research came to a grinding halt, not to be resurrected until the 17th century.

Many manors chose their own priests. Those who did not have the luxury of a pool of educated boys whom they could send to a larger town for ordination, relied on the Bishop of the diocese to help out.

Peasants were tied to their manor and must have the permission of the Lord to travel, marry and extend property. Freemen could do as they pleased within reason. Aumary is a good Lord. There are too many books written where the Lord is a tyrant. I'm sure some were but generally it was not in his interest to be so, for he relies on his workers for his own living, prosperity and safety.

If you have enjoyed
SHE MOVED
THROUGH THE FAIR
(book 2 in the
Savernake series)…
read on for a snippet of

DOWN BY THE
SALLEY GARDENS!

Down By the Salley Gardens

Down by the Salley Gardens My love and I did meet;
She passed the Salley Gardens on a flutter of snow-white
        feet.
She bade me take life easy, as the grass grows on the lea;
But I was young and foolish and with her did not agree.

In a field down by the river My love and I did stand,
And on my leaning shoulder she placed her snow-white
        hand.
She bade me take life easy, as grass grows on the weirs;
But I was young and foolish, and now I am full of tears.

William Butler Yeats reconstructed
from a fragment of Old Irish Folk song

Chapter One

I looked down at the body again; the body of Swithun of Attwood, priest of my manor of Durley. I sighed.

The coroner had come and gone. He had packed his little jury—for so they were becoming known—of twelve men over fourteen into the little attic room of the priest's house on my manor and had asked for their verdict on his death.

Some shuffled their feet, I noted whom; some looked aghast, shocked at the ferocity of the attack on a priest, a man of God. Others stared as if they had never seen a naked body before or perhaps so much blood spill from a human being.

The verdict was delivered quickly. Folk wanted to get back to their dinner and to their homes, or was it that they wanted to go and find their womenfolk and pass on what they had seen? Gossip. Oh yes, they loved to gossip. No one seemed surprised that the body they had viewed and had been called to identify was the village priest, the most despised man in Durley. Murder by persons unknown. Let me explain.

Do you think I should explain, Paul? You are here to write all this down for me because I can no longer hold a pen, so I wonder what you think.

Do you think it important that my reader knows the history of this unfortunate man? How he had been appointed by the Bishop of Salisbury, to our little forest village after the death from liver disease of our long-serving priest Benedict of Cadley and had turned it upside down with his harsh treatment of the folk living here, free man and unfree villein alike. How he had accidentally caused the death of one young man, turning the village against him. How he had refused burials of the young and the old, had issued penances far in excess of the sins committed, and had terrorised the villagers with his nastiness. You do? That's good. Write it down, then.

What? What do you mean you can't remember it all? Goodness me, boy. I can give you fifty years or more and I can remember it. I'm an old man and you are a young thing. Who is supposed to be the one failing in memory, eh?

Oh well...yes, I suppose so. It did happen to me, Aumary Belvoir, lord of the manor of Durley and hereditary warden of the king's forest of Savernake. I was there and you are just here to write it down for me and be my scribe.

Well then, write this.

Swithun had been the priest of Durley for just about a year. In that time, he had managed to alienate the whole community, including me. I had recently written to the

Bishop of Salisbury, who also happened to be my godfather, to ask if Swithun might be removed from Durley.

Swithun had confessed to me that he never had a wish to become a religious nor a priest and that he had been happy in his previous life - that of a second son on a prosperous manor in Hampshire until he was ten. I well remembered the last conversation I'd had with him.

"You were a child oblate then?" I reached for a jug of ale on the table and found it empty and full of dead flies.

He nodded. "My father gave me to the abbey when I was ten. He had fallen ill and was like to die. I was a younger son and expendable. My brother Ralph, the Attwood heir, was there, ready to inherit the manor in Hampshire."

"I know all about the position of the younger son, Swithun. And the resentments which bubble up under the surface." I think this explained Swithun's attitude towards me, for in his eyes, we were of the same class— nobility. "Go on."

He looked at me under his brows. "You are not the younger son?"

"No, but I had a brother once....a half-brother, to be exact, but that is for another day." I stretched out my long legs. "So what happened? I thought that when one reached puberty, there was a possibility of leaving the abbey and making one's own way in the world?"

"My father recovered. He pledged me to Salisbury as a bribe to God, to aid his recovery. For me, there was no escape. I was there to pray for his soul and to give thanks for the throwing off of the illness which so consumed him."

"He made a vow then?"

"He did. 'If I recover from this terrible malady, my younger son will become a monk and I will pay the abbey a great sum to have him.'" The bitterness was apparent in his voice. "Besides, my whole adult life had been spent in the cloister. The world outside was an awesome place. What could I do? Except be a clerk, a lowly scribbler. At least in the abbey, I had a chance to rise, perhaps to abbot."

"Yes, I suppose you might. I thought the practice of giving children to the church had been stopped." I said.

"Some years ago it was still a custom practised in some places. Money is a very persuasive tool, my lord."

"Ah, but there is a gulf between becoming a monk and taking holy orders and becoming one of the priesthood. Why did you do that if you...."

"The bishop....not the present one...the last one...."

"Hubert Walter?"

"He wanted men to take the word of the Lord to the people. It is hard to refuse when your whole life has been spent in obedience to your superior."

"Yes, I suppose it is." I looked him straight in the eye. "You have no calling at all, do you?"

He looked down at his hands. "I have tried. I am the son of a titled lord. I have never lost sight of that fact. I have kept that fact in my heart these fifteen years. It is who I am. That knowledge helps me to come to terms with my life as it is now."

"Hence your disdain for my people. You believe them far beneath you. As your serfs and villeins were on your father's manor."

"Do you not, my lord?"

"No, Swithun, I do not."

He stared at me and quoted. "Let every soul be subject to the authority of the great, for there is no authority that is not from the same God, and those authorities who are from God are under orders."

"By the same token must you then accept what has happened to you, for it is God's will. God ordained it."

"It was the will of an unfeeling father."

DOWN BY THE SALLEY GARDENS

I shrugged. "I do not feel myself superior to my folk on the manor, for we all pull together to make it work. I have a responsibility to them; they look up to me, and I do what I can to make their lives bearable. They provide their labour for me and the fruits of those labours, we share."

"But God made you a lord."

"Perhaps he did. He also then made Hubert Alder a blacksmith. He cannot do my job, though he try, and I... well I might make a fist of it, but I don't think I could do his job. No. Not well at all."

Swithun stared at me, trying to understand my reasoning.

"You did not wish to be a priest. So why such zealous pursuance of the word of God as you see it?"

"It is the only way I can make sense of what I have been sent here to do. I must teach right from wrong. I must bring the people back to the true way. How else am I to validate my life?"

"Well, for a start, by getting the folk on your side, and you will not do that by bullying, by being distant and making everyone hate you."

Too late, I thought, far too late.

"Surely you must honour your father's wish."

He shrugged.

"I was there, remember, when you quoted the commandments at Harry Glazer, Swithun: 'Honour thy father and thy mother: that thy days may be long upon the land which the Lord thy God giveth thee.' One rule for Harry and another for Swithun? Hardly fair."

"He is a tradesman's son."

"He is. You do not see the similarity, do you?"

In his mind, he was still nobility, far above those around him. He must have found obedience to be the hardest of the rules by which he had had to live at the abbey in Salisbury. I can imagine he had been flogged often for the sin of pride.

And now he was dead.

When he was found by Old Joan, one of the village women, Swithun lay on his back in his bed, one arm flung out. He was dressed in his dark brown robe and the front of it was covered in blood. His arms, too, were lacerated as if he had tried to defend himself from blows which had rained down on him from above. The wounds which he bore were many; a frenzied attack. Some had pierced his throat, others had gone down as far as his belly.

When I first saw him, I could not tell one wound from another. Blood lay everywhere, splattered up the wall beside him, spreading out on the mattress beneath him, and sprayed onto the floor by him.

Now, he had been stripped of his clothes. His robe had had to be cut from him, for the blood had melded it to his body, and the blows, in some cases, had driven the material into the knife wounds.

He now lay under a thick hempen cloth supplied by my blacksmith.

The coroner had measured and counted the wounds: twenty.

Twenty major wounds and some little scratches.

Are you alright, lad? You do love the tale of a gruesome murder, but your stomach seems to rebel at the writing down of it. What? Something you ate last night? Oh, I see.

Shall we carry on Paul my scribe, or do you wish to avail yourself of the pot situated just over there, behind that screen? No? Good.

I lifted the hempen cloth. Yes, possibly twenty wounds. Some much deeper than others. Two to the throat.

"Johannes, come look at this."

My friend and the doctor-surgeon from Marlborough town, Johannes of Salerno, had been staring out of the small window at the back of the cottage.

He had come by my request from his duties in the town last evening when the body had been discovered and had stayed with us at Durley so that when the coroner had done his work, we might get to work also. We had a history of looking at dead bodies, Johannes and I. I did not know it then, but we would gain quite a reputation for the solving of mysterious deaths in time. It was now our turn to look at the body and see what we could fathom. Bodies do speak to you after death. They do - but not with the voice.

For example, the first thing we both noticed was that Swithun had been tied. There were rope marks around his wrists. As he had twisted in his agony, the ropes which had held him to the bed had scored deep red lines on his flesh.

"He was not tied at first. Asleep perhaps."

"He was lately relying on the flagon to rid him of his memories, Johannes. He may have been insensible with alcohol," I said.

"He woke with the first blow and defended himself. See his arms and hands."

"Then he was tied to the bed. Why would someone do that? Surely they would just keep knifing him till he was dead."

"I don't know," said my friend, "but we cannot tell which was the first blow. My guess is that it was one that missed its mark somehow. Then the murderer decided to overpower him—no mean feat, for he was a young man—and tie him so he could not evade the blows."

"That would be hard to do. Do you think he was

tortured?"

He shook his head. "I don't think so. The wounds are nearly all to the chest. One or two lower down." He peered carefully at the corpse. "The lower ones are not delivered with quite so much venom. See how they don't pierce as far as those in the upper body? Almost half-hearted."

Johannes reached for a straw from the floor, a sturdy piece of chaff, and inserted it into the wound.

"A few inches only," he threw it away, "even though the target is softer here and the ribs protect the upper body."

"Aye, I see it."

"He was not killed immediately, for he bled a great deal and you and I both know that, upon death, the heart stills and the bleeding stops."

"And the position of the sprayed blood upon the floor and wall indicates that he was still alive after many of the blows."

"Yes, indeed," said the doctor.

I cupped my hand around my chin, my elbow leaning on the heel of my hand and scrutinised the body of Swithun, the priest.

"Poor man. Shall we let the women have him, Johannes? Then, once he is cleaned, we shall look at the wounds once more and try to decide which killed him."

"Did the coroner look for the weapon?"

"Aye, he did."

We were crossing the courtyard of my little walled manor.

"It was a large knife of some two-inch blade and twelve inches long. The hilt was wound with silver wires. It was thrown in the rushes by the bed and bore Swithun's blood up to the hilt."

"Did you know it?"

"No, I had never seen it before." The coroner had it now. "I will make a drawing from memory when I get back to my office. We might need to remember it."

"A good thought," said Johannes.

In my office, a small room off the screens passage of the hall, we sat and fiddled with our wine cups. I got up and shut the door. No prying eyes, no flapping ears would look or listen to our conversation. Then I closed the shutter to one of the small windows and lit a lamp. We were one floor up, but I would have no eavesdropping.

I reached for parchment and a piece of charcoal and drew the knife as best I could from memory. I was no limner, but I could make a drawing of a knife.

Johannes watched me. "It looks a finely made knife to me, one such as a nobleman might own."

"Yes, it was." I finished my drawing with a flourish. "No gems. Serviceable but fine. Not a cheap one. And made for defence. For fighting. Not one that Swithun would own."

"A wide blade, pointed and sharp on two edges. Yes, just the type to have made those wounds," said Johannes. "We shall know better when we see the body once more.

Tell me again what you found when you reached the scene."

I sat back on my chair and folded my arms. "Swithun on his back. Blood everywhere. Knife on the floor. I did not touch it. Left that for the coroner. No light. All candles and lamps extinguished. All shutters closed. Door to the upper floor open. Downstairs door closed—so Old Joan tells me. She had to put the pottage she was carrying to Swithun for his dinner on the floor to open the outer door." I looked up at the ceiling and pictured the scene. "His right arm flung out. No sign of any rope with which he might have been restrained that I could see, but I did not search every corner then."

"Any other item nearby?"

"Nothing."

"No wine cup?

"Ah, yes. On the floor. Turned up and empty."

"We might find that."

"It was, I think, kicked under the bed by the jury crammed into the space."

"Good."

We sat in silence for a moment.

"Then I called for Hal of Potterne to go and see if Margaret and Henry were all right."

Johannes' eyes grew wide. "You suspected them above all?"

"I did. For Henry had cursed the man in my hearing and was the one in my mind who had the best motive—the death of his little brother Piers by the priest's hand—and the anger to carry out the murder."

"You told me of it. Piers had a lung disease, and Swithun locked him in the priest's robing room, an airless and dusty place..."

"To 'think about his sins'." I tutted. "For Heaven's sake, the boy was fourteen...just."

"And he died of asphyxiation?"

"You told me it was possible."

"It is. It is most possible. One can die of an asthmatic attack, yes."

"The boy was asthmatic. I wondered if Henry had taken the law into his own hands for, naturally, the priest would plead 'Benefit of Clergy' had we accused him of murder."

"He did not mean to do murder?"

"No. Swithun didn't know that Piers' asthma could kill him. He did not know the boy well at all. It was a surprise to him that he was Henry's brother." I took a sharp in-breath. "Henry cursed him...wait!" I held my breath as I remembered what Henry, my young manor steward, had said to Swithun.

"'I hope you go blind and mad. I hope your heart swells and bursts within you. I curse you twenty times with twenty knife blows.'"

Johannes leaned forward on the table. "I know the coroner has done it, but we must count those blows very carefully, Aumary."

Swithun had now been moved in the parish coffin to the altar in the church where he had officiated for twelve months. Count we did. There were exactly twenty blows. Each one was delivered with the wide-bladed knife now in the coroner's possession.

Two to the lower throat.

"Missing all major blood lines and the spine," said Johannes upon close investigation. "Amazing. Two to the belly, very weak. Almost as if they were an afterthought."

"The rest frenzied attacks on the major part of the torso," I said, replacing the shroud.

Johannes stepped back. "No....I think we are meant to see that."

"What?"

"Sixteen blows. All in the area of the chest. Only two are in the area of the heart. See...?" He lifted the shroud once more.

I held my lantern higher. "I do see."

"If you were going to kill a man, wouldn't you try to plunge the knife into his heart, his black wicked heart, as you see it? Here, we have blows all over. Some to the left, some to the right. Then there is this one." He pointed with one of his doctor's tools, a thin metal item about six inches long. "This is the blow which killed him, followed by another one close by. The first is driven up..." he inserted his probe. "See the angle. Into the heart. Under the ribs."

"And the next?"

"Following the pattern of the first but not so strong. Just a blow to make sure, I think. How was he lying when he was found? Which side was to the room-side of the bed, which to the wall?"

"He was lying with his head to the back window and his feet to the door. Left side to the wall. Why?"

"It might be significant. It means the wounds to the heart were inflicted by someone bending right over the body. The others were mostly to his right side. You could be more upright when dealing the blows." Johannes stared at me. "I did not dare ask you what Hal of Potterne found when he got to Henry and Margaret, his mother's house."

"Nothing. They were not splattered with blood. They had no clothes around the house which were bloodied. They were calm and unruffled. I do not think Margaret could be so if she had just committed murder, even if she did think it was justice for her younger and much-loved son."

"No, indeed."

When in the room, Johannes had looked under the bed. There, amongst the soiled rushes, was Swithun's wooden cup. He'd picked it up carefully and smelled it.

"Yes, you are right. Wine. Strong red wine. No water with it, I think."

The flagon in which the wine had been held was missing. I had looked around. It, too, had been kicked away from the bed. I stooped and lifted it by the string loop. The empty leather bottle wound around the handle, which was used to hang it from a peg on the wall by the bed. I undid the stopper.

"Empty."

"Now we know he was insensible when he was first attacked," Johannes said.

We replaced the shroud around Swithun and left him in front of the altar on his bier. We should have to look elsewhere, we thought, for our murderer.

Is that a good enough description of the murder, Paul, my scribe? By the way you are nodding, you think it's an adequate explanation. Then we shall continue.

We shall carry on, and you shall write, and you will be the first to know the story of how Doctor Johannes of Salerno and I, Aumary Belvoir, warden of the forest of Savernake in my thirtieth year, in the autumn of 1204, solved the murder of Swithun of Attwood, priest of Durley manor.

I was crossing the courtyard when I caught sight of my wheelwright, Phillip. His father, my senior wheelwright, was laid up with a bad back at that moment, and though Phil was only 18, he was more than capable of doing what I asked of him. Could he please, along with Alfred Woodsmith, make good the old cart that was lying in the threshing barn? I wanted it to carry the body of Swithun of Attwood to his spiritual home at the Abbey of Salisbury, and I wanted it quickly.

Phil knuckled his forehead in obeisance. "Right you are, sir. Just needs a little tickling—be as right as night."

I wrote to the manor of Stockbridge, asking one of the carters who trundled the road to the castle at Marlborough to entrust my letter to my friend Andrew Merriman, one of the senior men there. He would see that it went out in the royal post with other missives for Hampshire. I had hopes that my letter telling the lord of the manor of Stockbridge that his brother was dead by another's hand and that his body was being returned to Salisbury Abbey would be read by Swithun's sibling.

Now, I must tell you all what had been happening in my manor of Durley whilst Swithun was being murdered in his little house by the church.

On one of my trips into the town of Marlborough, some miles away, nestling in the downs and at the foot of the forest where I had been born and raised, I had met Johannes' niece, Lydia of Wolvercote. She had come to look after him when his housekeeper was killed in an accident.

Lydia was the widow of a nobleman of Oxford, an arranged but good marriage. We had, we have to say, fallen instantly in love, and I had asked her to be my wife the same day we had discovered Swithun's body.

No, not really very romantic was it, Paul?
You're quite right. But Lydia was not a shallow
girl falling into a faint at the very mention of
murder. So we were not so put out.

Lydia had come to Durley to stay until we could be married. Do not worry, we were housed apart and had many chaperones to keep us chaste, not least my little five-year-old daughter, Hawise, a child by my first and much beloved wife Cecily, murdered in 1200.

We had that very day decided to ask the priest of Bedwyn to perform the marriage ceremony for us. The joy of it all had been rather eclipsed by the death of Swithun.

Joy it was. There was much to plan and I left it all to the women, for they excel at such things and would brook no interference. Henry, my steward, would oversee it all.

Coming up to the hall steps, twelve stone blocks rising steeply up to a sturdy door of seasoned oak studded with hard nails, I met my daughter Hawise hovering at the top, the edge of the outer door in her hands.

"Oh, Dada! Is it true...? Is he d-d-dead?"

I turned her round and marched her back into the screens passage and the hall again.

"Yes, the gossip you have heard is correct."

She ran on a few steps and then gave a little dance. "Oh....I am happy about that."

A sharp voice rang out in the rafters. "Hawise Belvoir... that is not a nice thing to say."

I had never heard Lydia speak so to my daughter, but she was quite correct to do so and I supported her, saying, "The priest was not a good man, Hawise, but he was a human being and one of God's creatures. He was flawed and foolish but did not deserve to die in the manner he did."

Lydia came down the solar steps from the second storey of the mezzanine, where the private quarters were situated. "Your father is quite right. Murder is wrong, Hawise, however and to whomsoever it is done, despite the circumstances."

"But I did not like him, madam."

"You may not have liked him, but that does not mean you may murder him, Hawise."

I decided to play with her a little. "Did you murder him, daughter?"

Hawise's face flushed, and her eyes grew large.

Hal of Potterne, my senior man-at-arms sitting at the long table in the hall at a pot of ale, got up and came up to Hawise. He put his hand on her shoulder. To him, my daughter could do no wrong. I was surprised when he said, "Oh, m'lord, shall I go for the irons? We shall need to keep 'er confined if she is a murderess…" He winked at me behind Hawise's back.

"Noooo! Nooo!" cried Hawise. "I did not kill him…why would I kill him?"

"Because you just said you disliked him."

"Well, there are a lot of people on the manor who did not like him. Some people even hated him," she said, her chin jutting. "You, Dada, you did not like him at all."

My daughter was, if nothing else, a feisty Belvoir girl.

"Like you, Hawise, I disliked him, but not enough to murder him."

"There, then…" she said.

"Well, we shall say no more. Though I would like to know Hawise, who it is you think hated him so much, enough to kill him, and how you have learned this?"

She smiled then, knowing at last that we were all playing with her.

"Come and sit down and I will tell you," she said, moving to the big oak table.

Hal of Potterne chuckled.

"Firstly," said Hawise, "there was Meg, the poultry woman. Her mother had been poorly and Swithun had refused to come to her bothy to minister to her when it was thought she might die."

I remembered this in a vacant sort of way for had not Edmund Brooker, one of my villeins, told me that his sister Edith had been looking after Meg senior some while ago? Yes, it sounded like Swithun.

Hawise went on to talk of poor Ralf and Edwina who had lost their baby, and Swithun had refused to baptise the infant. I knew about this too, for I had had cause to speak to Swithun about his dereliction and was angry with him about his failure to do his job.

"Then," said Hawise, "there was Joan, the laundress. Swithun had been seen staring at her through the bushes when she was down at the stream doing the washing. Some of the other women had challenged him. It was not simply the fact that he was watching them working. He also watched them if they went to relieve themselves in the bushes and that was not very nice, thought Hawise.

I could see Hal of Potterne trying desperately not to laugh, and Lydia turned away too at this information, so Hawise would not see her smile.

Swithun had fallen foul of Mat Fisher, too. Mat was one of my villeins who owed me his labour in my fields. He worked for me for three days and for the rest of the week for himself on his small plot of land. He also fished the local rivers and pools and was a useful chap to know, when fish Friday came along. Swithun had stupidly disturbed the fish by stomping up and down the bank when Mat was trying to catch trout and a fierce argument had ensued, which boiled over when Swithun accused Mat of not being married to his wife with whom he lived in a bothy close by the reeve's house.

"He called Mat's wife awful names," said Hawise.

Naturally, their children were called bastards by Swithun. My daughter delivered this information with a natural tale-telling flair, and again, we had to smile.

"And then, Sir Swithun," Hawise always gave the priest this title, "he went to town and started to argue with Harry, the cordwainer's man. You know him, Dada, he's the one with...."

"Yes, I know him. What did they argue about?"

"I don't know, but Harry was pretty angry. My friend Petronilla was in the shop at the time, and she said...."

"Thank you, Hawise, I shall ask him."

More of my manor folk, it seemed, hated Swithun.

Hawise wriggled in her seat. "Peter Brenthall hated Swithun."

Peter was the son of my head woodward, the man responsible for the work which went on in the forest itself and my right-hand man. One day, Peter would take over from his father. I knew all about the hatred between Swithun and Peter, for Swithun had tried to unfairly discipline the thirteen-year old for some transgression, and I had been called in to arbitrate.

Swithun had claimed Peter's bees. They had been the property of the previous priest and had been willed to Peter, a capable apiarist. In anger, Swithun had kicked over a bee skep, causing damage to the hive and difficulty to Peter, and the priest had been stung in the process.

Hawise liked this part of the story and made much of Swithun's leaping about and slapping himself, for the bees had taken their own revenge.

I remembered well the priest's attempt to flog Peter in the church and Hal of Potterne's intervention.

He spoke up now.

"You remember that, m'lord, Peter was proper angry, but I don't think the anger went so deep as to stab the priest time and again and with such venom...as we saw on that corpse. No, I don't."

"And neither do I, Hal."

Peter's father was a quiet man, with his temper very much under control. I did not think that John was responsible either.

"How do you know all these things, Hawise?" I asked, perplexed.

She sat up straight and put her hands in between her knees. "Well, when I go for a walk around the village with Felice sometimes, people talk to her and I talk to them too.

And they tell us things."

Felice was Hawise's nurse, and I could just imagine the gossiping between the women of the village and one who was privy to the goings-on in the manor house itself.

Next, Hawise spoke of Matthew. He was my cook. He, too, had argued with Swithun, apparently. Hawise was unsure of the exact nature of the falling out, but it had resulted in Matthew chasing Swithun from the kitchen with a meat cleaver and standing in the courtyard shouting that he would kill him. Well, if every man who uttered those words put his threat into practice, the village would be denuded of every second man and a few women to boot.

Hawise did not mention the people I had first thought were the culprits, namely Henry Steward and Margaret of Manton. Even though I was loath to think it, they were still, despite the lack of evidence, the most likely to have killed Swithun. Their hatred ran the deepest.

"So you see....lots of people hated him, so lots of people could have killed him."

I shook my head. "No, Hawise, I don't think it was any of them. Whoever did this was very, very angry. None of these people of the manor could be angry enough to kill Swithun in such a way."

Hawise tutted. "Dada...you have never seen Matthew when he is in a bad mood. He is really scary with his meat axe!"

Hal of Potterne guffawed.

I decided that I would go and have a look at Swithun's domain once more. I started with his church. He was still there, of course, before the altar in the parish coffin.

The church was an oblong of stone, flag-floored, with a Bath stone altar at the eastern end and one long bench against the northern side of the nave for elderly or infirm worshippers to rest upon. Ours was a simple little church. There was no fancy stone work, no carved re-redos, but we did have a colourful painting over the west door. I remembered it being done when I was a small lad. Many-hued devils were prodding sinners into the flames with sharp pitchforks. Above, standing on clouds, were pale silvery angels receiving the virtuous into heaven. I now know that it wasn't very well painted. I have seen much finer work elsewhere. As a child, though, it had terrified me.

The place was swept and clean. Nothing here.

I took the key to the priest's room from my scrip and fiddled to open the door to the small storeroom where Swithun and all the priests before him had stored the holy vessels and the vestments. It was already open.

Along the back wall, a large oak chest, iron-bound, housed the community's rolls, sometimes called descent books. These were records on rolled and stitched parchment of all the marriages, births and deaths of the people of the village and wider forest. Who was related to whom, and where they came from if they were not local. Here, too, were records of the weather and events in the village and forest.

These were begun by my Belvoir ancestor two hundred years ago and were unique as far as I knew it, for I had never heard of any other place recording such things.

The rolls were still piled haphazardly, some open, on the small table in the middle of the tiny room. The last time I had been in this room, I had discovered the body of Piers Pierson lying behind the door. The young man, son to Margaret and brother to Henry, who had died of asphyxiation after being locked in this small space by Swithun.

This room, however, had not yet been swept and dusted; the dust motes flew around with every movement.

It smelled shut up, and the air was stale, but it was better than when I had opened it to find Piers lying on the floor. Old Joan, no doubt, as I had instructed her, would soon pay a visit to clean.

She came now, down the nave, bustling up after me, in her black gown and blinding white headdress. I now realised, of course, that Joan must have another key to the priest's room.

"Oh sir, I saw you comin' in 'ere and I wondered if I might ask you to 'elp."

"Help you, mother...?" I asked.

"As you know, m'lord, I canna read, an' the rolls, well he's gotta go back ' ow he was. Could you jus' see your way to puttin' he's in order for me, on the table like, so I can store he's away right?"

I smiled. "Could you not have asked John or Peter, perhaps Henry...?" No, maybe not Henry, "or one of the others who can read, Joan?"

"John and Peter are out in the forest, sir, and Henry... well, sir...I don't want him to have to come in here for quite a while, if you see what I mean. The reeve has gone close to Bedwyn and won't be back till sunset. Young Giffard and Gervase are working out at West Baily, and Hamon is...well I don't know, sir."

I realised how few people on my manor could read or write. Some could sign their name, others might be able to make a mark that was their own, but few could read. I must try to remedy that by setting up a school and getting my new priest to teach what he might be able to those who had the opportunity to learn.

My eyes raked the table. I picked up one roll.

"You dust them of mould and I will stack them in order, then together we shall put them in the chest."

So we began our task.

We coughed and spluttered, wiped our eyes on our sleeves and went in and out of the small room as the need took us when we were unable to breathe freely any longer. We left the door open and I opened the shutters of the tiny window in the north wall. No wonder poor Piers had found this room deadly.

The rolls began in 1086 when my great-grandfather had built the church and the manor, and had extended the village. Naturally, then, the church and manor house had been built in wood, and as time passed, each generation had added to it and rebuilt much of it in stone.

I had completed more work on Durley Manor than any of my previous ancestors; I had rebuilt parts of the wall and had caused the gatehouse to be rebuilt in stone. I had added some new buildings to the courtyard structures. I had laid flagstones and cobbles in the courtyard, and all upper floors of the hall were now of good solid oakwood.There was no longer a beaten earth floor in my ground floor rooms. They were all finished in good stone. I'd installed those newly invented things, the chimney-piece, the sort which funnels away the fumes from the fire, and had rebuilt the kitchen fire with a fine chimney and new ovens and joined the stone building to the hall. Recently, I had put glass in the windows of my private rooms.

The early rolls were stacked together and had not been separated. The dates, ten years at a time—not much happened in a small place like Durley that we needed a roll for every year—still ran consecutively.

Then we reached the rolls for the end of the reign of old King Henry, our present king's father.

As we handled the rolls, I realised that some of them had markers attached at various places; flattened stalks of dried straw had been split and inserted over the edge. The nearer we came to the present date, the more markers there were. What had Swithun been doing with our descent rolls?

"There are only a few to put back now, Joan. Go and rest your old back. I'll do the rest."

She curtsied, thanked me profusely for the help, and waddled back down the nave, her white wimple not quite as white as it had been when she arrived.

I sat at the small table and pulled the rolls with the straw stalks towards me.

I unrolled the first, the roller to the top, and scanned the first part of each page.

Here were five markers.

I looked at the first marked page.

The first date on the page was 1173, a year before I was born.

I scrutinised the page carefully.

Nothing here seemed important. The priest before Benedict had kept the records meticulously. His handwriting was firm and strong, and his ink, good quality. He recorded famine and flood, storms and heat waves in the margins with little asides, and this had been kept up by Benedict when he took over in 1174. There were also small letters here and there, with which I was unfamiliar.

I could see the change in the handwriting style. Benedict's writing was smaller and more compact but still easy to read.

However, the light was not good in the priest's room and I wondered if it might be best to remove just these four last rolls to my office, to look at them in a better light and a less dusty atmosphere.

I gathered up the rolls, put them under my arm and locked the priest's room.

Lydia, my affianced, beautiful in a lavender-blue bliaut, caught me as I entered the manor courtyard.

"Ah, Aumary..., there you are." Looking round to make sure no one was looking, I kissed her forehead. Such intimacy in public was frowned upon.

My, what have you been doing? You are full of dust."

"Aye, I shall shake out my shirt and it will be fine again."

I balanced the books on top of a convenient cart and pulled the cotte and shirt over my head, ruffling my curly black hair as I went. Lydia watched me, smiling appreciatively. She caught sight of the scar on my shoulder, made by a crossbow bolt of the previous year.

"One day I will tell you the story," I said.

Her eyes raked my torso.

"Save those thoughts for our wedding night," I said cheekily as I shook out the shirt and donned it again. "We have work to do."

Back in the office, we sat side by side and scanned the rolls.

I read them and Lydia wrote a synopsis so that we might tease out whatever it was in these little rolls that Swithun had found so compelling. Did they have anything to do with his death?

February the twenty-fifth — Hamon Black died of the cold. Aged fifty-one. Buried seventh of March. 'Terrible snowstorm' was written in the margin.

"I suppose he could not be buried sooner because the ground was so frozen," I said.

March the first. Born of Godiva and Arnulf Brooker. A son - Benedict. "Oh, how kind to name the child after the new priest."

"But he did not last...look," said Lydia. There, under her

finger was a reference to his death four days later and his interment on the seventh of March 1187.

March sixth. Godiva Brooker died of a fever. Aged twenty-five. Buried seventh of March.

"Oh, how sad," said Lydia. "She followed her little son not long after."

"They were busy on March the seventh," I said.

There were more references to such events and I could see no reason why Swithun would mark them especially.

We looked through all the rolls.

All the children born on the manor were detailed here: Peter Brenthall, Henry and Piers Pierson, Phil Wheelwright, and the four children of Mat Fisher, who was a little older than myself, Gytha, David, Stephen and Alfred. Only three were alive now, for David had died in the winter of 1202. And here was his sad entry, too.

I leant back and scratched my unruly curls. "What can this mean, that he had a marker to every fifth page or so? I can see nothing unusual about the entries at all."

Lydia laid aside her pen. "It may become apparent at a later time, when perhaps we know a little more about the man Swithun of Attwood."

"Yes. Yes, I'm sure you are right." I closed the last roll. "Meanwhile the last set of rolls stays here with me, in the office." I stood. "I must speak with Henry."

Henry was in his own office, counting out the money paid by tenants who were freemen and who hired their labour to the manor in return for land and housing, for it was Michaelmas, when such things were due. Likewise, Henry paid those who worked for the manor. We did not have so many of them, but they had to be paid every week.

Before him, he had a chequered board rather like a

chess board and he had piled coins on several squares.

Men were coming in and out of his little room all afternoon. Some stayed to chat a little, others were in and out like a ferret down a rabbit hole.

The piles diminished and there were only two when I entered Henry's office.

He stood quickly, and in his haste, he knocked the table. The last two piles of coins teetered and fell.

"Sir," I saw his Adam's apple bob as he swallowed.

"Afternoon, Henry."

I looked around the little room. This was the place my half- brother Robert had lived in before his trip to Rouen and his demise there. I sat on the stool in front of my steward.

"Please,… carry on with the payment."

"The last two will be in later, sir, when they return from West Baily."

"Ah." I looked up at him. He was almost as tall as me. Fair of hair and skin. As fair as I was dark. He would grow thin on top, I thought, as had his father. His hair was worn at shoulder-length, and like Johannes, he took to catching it back in a queue sometimes. Today, it hung free and it shone like sunshine on silken fibres.

"Please, sit." I gestured to his hair. "You have washed your hair, I see.....it looks good. Mine is hopeless when I wash it....just goes curlier," I smiled, "and when the weather is damp...aw! It is a devil to keep tangle free."

He smiled but did not reply, and he did not sit. He began to pile up the coins again and stopped as I said,

"Henry, I would talk with you, for it will become open knowledge soon and I would that it be told to you now rather than later when things could be.....a little....difficult."

Henry took a deep breath through his nose. "Swithun?"

"Aye," I leaned forward. "I was there, you remember,

when Swithun came back into the church after we had found Piers, so I heard you curse him."

"I did," he said. "I did. I will not deny it. 'I cannot kill you, Swithun, the priest, but I can curse you,' I said. 'I hope you go blind and mad. I hope your heart swells and bursts within you. I curse you twenty times with twenty knife blows.'"

"You sounded then as if you meant it. Twenty knife blows. What made you say that, Henry? Twenty knife blows?"

He looked into my eyes. "I do not know. I was so angry and wanted him to suffer. Twenty knife blows seemed a small number for the hurt he had caused my brother and the grief he gave to mother and myself."

"You know that when we examined the body of Swithun, we found he had been pierced by twenty knife blows?"

"Yes. I have been told it was so."

"A coincidence, then?"

"A fulfilment of the curse." he said glibly.

"You know I don't believe that."

"If you are going to ask me if I caused the priest's death, then I will tell you under oath that I did not."

I blinked. "Alright."

From my scrip I took out the little drawing I had made from memory of the knife which killed Swithun. "Do you know who this belongs to, Henry?"

I felt him jolt and blink but the hesitation was gone in a heartbeat.

"No, I do not know who it belonged to."

I noticed the change in tense.

I nodded. "Very well then. I must tell you that of all the folk on the manor, it seems that you are the person with the most urgent need of revenge on Swithun."

He was going to deny it again, but I forestalled him with,

"There are others who would have liked to see him dead, it seems, and I am going to investigate and question them too. You, however, are the person most will suspect. I will get to the bottom of it, Henry, whether you are guilty or not."

"Does he deserve your efforts, sir?"

"Maybe not. But I am a man who likes to know the truth, Henry. What I do with that truth is up to me. But I do like to know it."

"The truth is many things to many people, m'lord. I hope you find your version of it."

He sat and began to rebuild the coins again. His hand shook a little.

"My truth is that I loved my little brother Piers with all my heart, and it is the truth that I am glad that the man who sent him to his grave is now awaiting burial in his own pit."

The Savernake Forest Series
Susanna M. Newstead

Belvoir's Promise
She Moved Through the Fair
Down By the Salley Gardens
I Will Give My Love an Apple
Black is the Colour of My True Love's Hair
Long Lankyn
One Misty Moisty Morning
The Unquiet Grave
The Lark in the Morning
A Parcel of Rogues
Bushes & Briars
Though I Live Not Where I Love
Wynter Wakeneth
Worldes Blis
Alysoun
Maiden in the Mor

Other Historical Fiction

I Am Henry - **Jan Hendrik Verstraten & Massimo Barbato**
The Sebastian Foxley Series - **Toni Mount**
The Falcon's Rise & The Falcon's Flight - **Natalia Richards**
The Reversible Mask - **Loretta Goldberg**
Beyond the Bukubuk Tree - **Loretta Goldberg**

History Colouring Books

The Mary, Queen of Scots Colouring Book - **Roland Hui**
The Life of Anne Boleyn Colouring Book - **Claire Ridgway**
The Wars of the Roses Colouring Book - **Debra Bayani**
The Tudor Colouring Book - **Ainhoa Modenes**

PLEASE LEAVE A REVIEW

If you enjoyed this book, *please* leave a review at the book seller where you purchased it. There is no better way to thank the author and it really does make a huge difference! *Thank you in advance.*